BULLETPROOF

JEFF LaFERNEY

TOWER
PUBLICATIONS

Jeff LaFerney

BULLETPROOF

Published by
Tower Publications

Dedication

It's about time that I dedicated a book to my awesome parents. Thank you, Mom and Dad, for your never-changing love, support, and devotion. Everything good that I am is because of your love and sacrifice and commitment, and everything bad I'll have to blame on me. I appreciate how proud you've been of me for writing three books—you two give me confidence. But what I want you to know is how proud I am to have you as my parents. Thank you so much. I love you.

Jeff LaFerney

Acknowledgements

I certainly didn't accomplish *Bulletproof* on my own, and for their help, many people need to be thanked. First, thank you to my family, especially my wife, Jennifer, for patiently letting me do all the things it takes to complete a novel. Thanks also for letting me bounce ideas off you, and for talking to me when the ideas weren't there. Additional thanks go to five awesome people who read my manuscript, noting errors, asking questions, and giving feedback. Thanks Aunt Linda (Smith). Special thanks to my wife and to Andrea McGlashen, who have both pre-read all three of my books for me. They're getting better at noticing my imperfections. Thank you, Renee LaRocque, for your valuable input and for your new friendship. An especially big thank you goes to Angie Edwards whose honest opinions, attention to detail, and literary analysis were just what I needed. I want to thank Officer Paul Clolinger for his detective tips and Attorney John Folts for helping me once again to understand law and procedures. Dan Brancheau gave me some much needed advice as I researched the brain and attempted to perform a fictional brain surgery as accurately as possible. Thanks Rhonda Groves Young for being willing to talk to me about ghosts. A special thank you goes to Nick Sorise, the owner of the actual Fenton Hotel Tavern & Grill. Nick shared stories and gave me a tour and access to his place of business. And finally, Dr. Brian Hunter has been an amazing help when I've had forensic questions. Once again, as with *Skeleton Key*, I could not have solved my murder without his help. I am incredibly grateful for his expert input.

Prologue

An orderly, accompanied by a nurse, wheeled the patient into the operating room. A blue-colored hue seemed to glow from the bright overhead lights. Several nurses, various technologists, an anesthesiologist, a resident, and a neurosurgeon participated in a swirl of activity in the cold room. There was moderate awareness of the surroundings, but the only vague memory the patient would have was being lifted from the rolling hospital bed and placed face down onto the operating table. There would be no memory of the somewhat anxious look in the surgeon's eyes.

The anesthesiologist made a final check of his charts and monitor. He leaned close to the groggy patient and said, "You'll be going to sleep now." As soon as the patient lost consciousness, a three-pin skull clamp was attached to keep the head absolutely still during the delicate surgery.

After all monitors were hooked up to the patient and all instrumentation was set in place, the surgeon stepped forward with his gloved hands held in the air. He spoke to the resident. "The patient has a medulloblastoma at the fourth ventricle which I'll be resecting." The resident's eyes focused on the patient's MRI and noted the tumor on the medulla oblongata at the opening into the fourth ventricle.

Jeff LaFerney

An operating microscope was put into place which would magnify the surgical procedure in three dimensions. Coagulation instrumentation, clotting agents, cottons, and clips of all shapes and sizes were at the ready to control bleeding. A three dimensional, computer-assisted guidance system would allow the hand of the surgeon to be monitored and even guided in mid-operation. The intern took in the intimidating surroundings but settled in beside the surgeon to observe the procedure.

"The tumor is in the fourth ventricle," the surgeon explained to his student. "I'll go through the back of the skull here." He pointed to the occipital bone at the bottom of the skull. Having an intern and other medical staff observing him was normal, but the doctor felt extraordinarily nervous as he was speaking. "I'll split the cerebellum, which overlaps the medulla, and go through the fourth ventricle to get to the tumor. I'll then cut away—resect—the tumor. "

"The cerebellum controls muscle coordination and body balance, correct?" the intern asked.

"That's right. And the medulla oblongata controls autonomic functions such as breathing, digestion, heart and blood vessel function, swallowing, sneezing, blinking..."

The intern spoke with uncertainty. "There's a bit of risk in this surgery, isn't there? Besides entering through a ventricle that's a communication cavity that connects information to the spinal cord, aren't you also risking the patient's coordination and balance?"

"All brain surgeries are dangerous, so yes, this one's no different. But all scans suggest an easily successful resection." The doctor was far less concerned about the successful removal of the tumor than he was with his additional surgical plans. He paused, taking a slow, deep, nervous breath before continuing. "Step one is to do a craniotomy. I'll cut a small opening into the skull. A section

8

of skull, called a bone flap, will be removed to access the brain underneath." The doctor made a skin incision. He then lifted the skin and muscles off the bone and folded them back. Next, he made two small burr holes in the skull with a drill just below the shaved hairline. Then he inserted a special saw through the burr holes and cut the outline of a bone flap. The bone flap was then lifted and removed to expose the protective covering of the brain called the dura. The intern observed the procedure while multiple sets of eyes watched the monitors closely.

Next, with surgical scissors, the doctor opened the dura, folded it back, and exposed the brain. Using retractors, he gently opened a corridor to the medulla oblongata. To remove the cancer, he first used a laser to carefully cut away the tumor. Then he used a fine jet of water to break up the tumor and suction up the pieces. While the technicians were observing the monitors closely, the doctor's pulse started racing. He was approaching the moment that he had been planning since the first time he had studied the patient's MRI results.

He took a deep breath, steadied his hand, and lied to the intern when he said, "The tumor has extended into the closed portion of the medulla." Using his laser, he cut another fistula, an opening, in the medulla oblongata, creating a connection in the closed part of that section of the brain. With a simple cut, he had manually created a second open part of the medulla oblongata.

The intern was unsure what the doctor was seeing or doing, but the technicians immediately became alarmed. One spoke out. "Do you realize what you just did? You've created a second opening in the medulla!"

As he sprayed another fine jet of water on the new opening, he went through the charade of suctioning up additional pieces of the make-believe tumor. "I had no choice. We went in to get the cancer, and I got it. I've seen cases like this. The patient'll be fine...quite possibly better off because the medulla will now be making two connections. It's possible that we opened up the patient's brain to function at a higher capacity."

The technicians eyed each other uncertainly while the nurses and the intern were not sure what to think. To near silence in the operating room, the doctor removed the retractors holding the brain and closed the dura with sutures. The bone flap was placed back in its original position and secured to the patient's skull with titanium plates and screws.

As the doctor left the operating room, he noticed that his hands were shaking. What he had done was unethical, but he did it for the good of science. His conscience chastised him for doing such a terrible thing, but his mind told him that what he had done was justified, and he planned to eventually prove to himself that it was orchestrated for the overall good.

Chapter 1

The majority of the 114,804 fans, the largest crowd in college football history, sat in stunned silence. "No!" said Tanner Thomas, his deep brown, hypnotic eyes hidden as he held his head in his hands. He had a Michigan ball cap over his short dark hair. His beloved Michigan Wolverines, his home university where he played college basketball, had finally taken the lead with two minutes to go in the fourth quarter, and then Notre Dame had stormed back and scored the go-ahead touchdown on a twenty-nine-yard pass with just thirty seconds to play. The score was Notre Dame 31, Michigan 28.

"There's still time, Tanner," Carlton Thomas, Tanner's grandfather, said optimistically. Like everyone else in the stadium, Tanner was experiencing quite a roller-coaster of a game as he sat with his father, Clay, and his grandfather in The Big House for the University's first night football game in its storied history.

It was just Coach Brady Hoke's second game as head coach of the Michigan Wolverines, and after three consecutive disappointing years, the Michigan faithful were hoping the new coach would begin to turn things around against one of their biggest rivals. Clay, who was Michigan's baseball coach, had spent time with Hoke on several occasions, and he really liked him. Tanner sat uncomfortably in the stands behind the Wolverine bench, willing his team to win. During the lengthy commercial break, he focused his mental energy on the Michigan bench. His lips began to move as he thought, "You can win. Be confident. You know you can do it."

Notre Dame kicked off, and Michigan's first play sputtered. It was second and ten when Michigan's quarterback, Denard Robinson, barked out the signals from the twenty-yard line. Only twenty-three seconds remained. Tanner focused on the quarterback who had become his friend on campus. "You can make a big play, Denard. You can win this game." Robinson took the snap and surveyed the field until finally he was forced to scramble out of the pocket. He stepped up between two Notre Dame linemen, and then to the amazement of everyone in the stadium, he lofted the ball to a completely wide open Jeremy Gallon. The receiver caught the ball just past the fifty-yard line, and a roar rose from the crowd as he ran all the way across the field before being forced out of bounds at the sixteen with just eight seconds remaining. It was a sixty-four-yard pass play bringing pandemonium to The Big House. Tanner jumped in the air and roared his approval. A thirty-three-yard field goal would tie the game, but Robinson moved to the line of scrimmage and started barking out signals. Was there time to get the play off and still kick the field goal if it failed?

Tanner Thomas stood with his father, his grandfather, and the rest of the Michigan fans, hoping for the big play that would send them home happy. The ball was snapped and immediately the crowd noise rose. Robinson quickly surveyed the field before lofting a pass to the right corner of the end zone. Roy Roundtree stepped back away from his defender and gathered the ball into his hands before being pushed out of bounds with just two seconds remaining. When the referee raised his hands to signal a touchdown, the stadium erupted into bedlam. Clay jumped into the air with his arms extended above his head. Tanner screamed, "Yesssss!!" He grabbed his grandfather around the waist and lifted him off the ground in a glorious, celebratory hug. Clay's smile got even bigger as he observed his ecstatic father and his son celebrating together. It was a game to never forget and a feeling that Clay wished would never go away. But as things often are in the world, the happiness would be short-lived.

***

The crowd at Mo Doggie's Bar and Grill erupted when Roy Roundtree caught the touchdown pass. Matt Royster raised his beer bottle in celebration. Old time rock and roll music played in the background. He held out his hand to his Catholic buddy who just lost his bet with Matt for the third year in a row. Notre Dame had lost for the third year running.

"It was luck, Matt. The Irish outplayed Michigan the whole game," the buddy said as he handed over fifty dollars.

"I never doubted. As they say, 'it's not over 'til the fat lady sings.' I knew they'd win."

"What? D'you see into the future or something? There's no way you should have won that bet."

"But I did," Matt said smugly as he took a look at his watch. He'd been a bit distracted the whole evening. Though he was a huge Michigan fan, he had other things on his mind, so he pocketed his cash and moved off to take a leak. Somewhat drunk, he approached the restroom with his regular scowl on his face. Another drunken patron arrived at the door at the same time but backed off after looking into Matt's bloodshot eyes. Something told him he was better off avoiding conflict with the man.

After Matt emerged from the restroom, he weaved his way back to his table, paid his bill, and stumbled off to his car. He had one more thing to do before heading home.

***

Zander Frauss slid into the booth at Joe and Lewie's Penalty Box opposite Becca Fonteneau. Zander had been waiting for a chance to speak to her for nearly two hours while he sat at the bar and took in the football game that his wife thought he was attending. The restaurant was a hockey-themed sports tavern and eatery owned by former Red Wing, Joey Kocur, and former Red Wing assistant coach, Dave Lewis. It had arena-like ceilings and lights and was decorated with hockey murals, banners, and jerseys. It was quite a place to hang out.

Becca's work associates from the pharmacy where she worked in town were dancing to the music that they had requested from the DJ. She rolled her eyes and took a deep breath to compose herself before she said, "Are you stalking me?"

"Of course not. We need to talk."

"It's over, Zander. It's time you moved on with your life, like I have."

"It's not that easy. There are consequences for what we've done."

"Not if no one finds out. But that's really much more of your concern than mine. I'm quite capable of dealing with any problems of my own."

"I want to see you again."

"Zander, what part of 'it's over' don't you understand? Our relationship has been terminated. Besides, the last time we were together, you spoke of practically nothing but the guilt you felt."

"I made a huge mistake. I was selfish and shortsighted."

"That sounds like your problem, not mine. I'm finished with you, Zander, so go back to your lab and your career and your wife, and leave me alone…and stop following me." She reached for her purse, knocking a glass of water over on the table. She pulled out a twenty dollar bill and placed it on the table to pay her bill. "You can clean up the mess yourself." Then she grabbed her coat and exited the restaurant.

***

"That may have been the greatest game I've ever seen," Carlton Thomas said to his grandson. "Thanks for inviting me."

"I'm glad you were here, Grandpa. I can get you tickets to my home basketball games too, you know." Since entering college, Tanner had grown an inch and would be the six foot, three inch starting sophomore point guard for the Michigan basketball team. He'd made the all-freshman team the year before as well as all-conference honorable mention. The whole Thomas clan was excited about the upcoming basketball season.

"I just might take you up on that offer. My old knees are feelin' a lot better this year, and I'm gettin' around better. Plus it's a good way to spend time with your dad and that beautiful girlfriend of his," he smiled. Clay and Erika Payne had been an item for nearly a year. They had made plans to spend a good part of Sunday with Clay's father back at Clay's home in Flint.

After they left the stadium, they started walking toward campus. "Coming to my games'd give you reason to wear all that new fancy Michigan gear again," Tanner laughed. "Do you have on U of M underwear too?"

"Very funny, young man," Carlton responded.

They all slowed at an intersection. "This is where I have to head back to my apartment," Tanner explained. "Enjoy the rest of your weekend, you two." Tanner gave his grandpa a hug. "Love you, Grandpa. Can you give me a minute with my dad?"

He and his dad moved several steps away. "What's up, Tanner?" Clay asked.

"I had a vision this morning, Dad. I was brushing my teeth when the medicine cabinet door swung open—not literally, but that's what I saw. I actually ducked, thinking it was gonna hit me in the head. Then I saw a man in Michigan gear lying on the ground, and then there were flashing ambulance lights. That was it, but I only have visions about important things. I just wanted to warn you."

"You don't know who it was? Were either you or I there?"

"No...could only see the guy's back and no one else."

"Well, I don't know what it means, but I'll keep an eye out for anything similar. Have you had other visions?"

"Only that one...and there's no telling who it was or where or when, but keep an eye on Grandpa, okay?"

Clay didn't understand what his son was implying until he glanced over at his father and realized what he was wearing. "I will. I'll call you tomorrow after Erika and I talk to him. Don't worry."

"Okay. Tell Erika hi." He gave his dad a hug too. "See ya, Grandpa," he said as he headed to his apartment.

"He's a great kid," Carlton said to his son.

It warmed Clay's heart to hear his father say that about Tanner. Tanner's mother had been murdered nearly two years before, in the middle of Tanner's senior season of high school basketball. Yet Tanner had managed to move on with his life, in some ways better than his father had, and he was continuing to mature and develop as a person while in college. Tanner had a great smile, a tremendous sense of humor, and a sharp mind. What set him apart from the majority of college athletes was his fierce competitiveness

16

and his Michael Jordan-like leadership qualities. Clay was proud of him and even prouder to hear his father express his admiration as well.

Clay was a very young-looking forty-two-year-old who had matured quite a bit himself over the past two years. The brown-haired, brown-eyed, intelligent man had spent the majority of his life with the knowledge that he had the unique ability to control people's minds. Being a logical thinker, he decided to keep his gift a secret, often thinking of it as more of a curse than a "gift." But when Clay began to notice Tanner displaying signs of the same powers, his secret life took a remarkable turn. The end result was the loss of his wife, but also an improved relationship with his son, a new close friend, and the desire to use his power for good. He even shared his secret with a couple of people, including his current girlfriend, but he had never shared it with his father. It was during the upcoming weekend that he and Erika had planned to sit down with his father and finally tell him the truth.

Clay led his dad to the staff parking lot where both men had parked their cars. Carlton was going to follow his son to Flint and spend the night before spending an additional day with Clay and Erika. "I'll get you to the expressway, Dad, and you'll know how to get to the house from there."

"I need to get some gas on the way, but you head on home, and I'll be there shortly."

Clay had an uneasy feeling about losing contact with his father on the trip home after his short conversation with Tanner, but what was he to do? Tell his dad that Tanner had a vision, and it might have something to do with him?

"Okay. Follow me out of here, and I'll see ya in about an hour," Clay responded. He climbed into his red Chevy Camaro, backed out of his private parking space, and led the way out into traffic, feeling uneasy about the drive home.

Over the past two years, both Clay's and Tanner's abilities had grown, and one thing Clay knew about Tanner was that when Tanner had a vision or received some sort of clairvoyant message, it was important, and it was real.

Chapter 2

Carlton Thomas pulled off North US-23 at the Owen Road exit in Fenton—about halfway to Clay's home in Flint. In his rear-view mirror, Clay saw his father turn off the highway, and then he adjusted his radio to a music station for the rest of his trip home. His clock said 12:03 AM. Carlton took a right onto Owen Road and almost immediately turned right into a Speedway Gas Station. He pulled up to pump number two and shut down his engine. There were only two other cars in the lot, one at pump number six and one at a side customer parking space.

Inside the station, one employee was back stocking the cooler. The other was manning the cash register at the checkout counter. A customer wearing a Michigan jacket entered the store, head tilted down and eyes mostly covered under a maize and blue U of M knit hat. The cashier— "Eddie" it said on his name tag—bitter because he had to quit watching the game to cover third shift, assumed the customer was a fan on the way home from The Big House. He closed the Cosmopolitan magazine that he was secretly reading, but left it on the chair in which he had been sitting. "Hi, can I help you?" he asked, disguising his embarrassment about being caught with the magazine.

There was no answer. The customer gave no eye contact but rather appeared to be looking at the magazine cover. "21 Naughty Sex Tips: Bold, Breathless Moves That Bring on That Crazy In-Lust Feeling" was displayed on the cover. The customer's lips never moved, but in his head, the cashier heard, *"Empty the money from your cash drawer in a bag, and give it to me."*

The cashier hesitated a moment. He hadn't emptied any of the contents of the drawer into the safe since he had arrived at 11:00. There was quite a lot of money to be taken. *"I have a gun,"* he heard in his head. Eddie felt an irresistible urge to do as the voice in his head had suggested, gun or no gun. He pushed the button to open the cash drawer, grabbed a plastic bag, and quietly placed all of the money from the register into it. He started to hand it over when he heard, *"I'll take the magazine too."* Eddie picked it up from his chair and put it into the bag. *"I'll be going now. You won't remember anything about what I look like. Just stay where you are, and don't call the police. Have a nice night."*

The thief, head still lowered to avoid any store cameras, walked very quickly to the exit door. Carlton Thomas had hung up his gas hose and was headed into the store to purchase some Tylenol for his aching knees. He reached into his back pocket and pulled out his wallet. He was sliding out his credit card, oblivious to his near vicinity to the store's entrance when the thief stumbled and blasted a shoulder into the door, sending it flying open. The door's edge struck Carlton directly on the right temple. He crumbled into a heap on the parking lot at the door's entrance, smashing his right temple a second time on a jagged rock. The thief stepped around his body and hurried to the car parked in the side customer parking space. The car eventually pulled around the back of the station and exited onto Owen Road while

Carlton lay unconscious, his head bleeding on the rock on the pavement in front of the store.

***

Tanner had reached his apartment and was changing his clothes to get into bed when his world starting tilting and spinning. He had become familiar with the feeling, but it was still disconcerting. Tanner, like his father, had a brain that didn't function exactly as the brains of other people. Because of a second open portion of the medulla oblongata, they were both able to receive and control impulses to their brains that other people could not. Clay Thomas could control and read minds but only when he made eye contact. He also had ESP and telekinetic abilities. Having a "sixth sense" and the ability to move things with his mind had come in handy on occasion. In Tanner's case, he could control minds without eye contact and could see into the future—precognition was the official term for that ability. He could also easily hypnotize other people and gain information clairvoyantly—information could be gained from an external source. When Tanner felt the dizzy feeling, he didn't know if it was going to be a call from some external object or a vision of the future. This particular time, however, it was a call. He saw a sign that said "Owen Road" and then he saw the "Speedway" sign that advertised the gas station. The vision wasn't complete because he next saw the entrance door to the service station with a reddish spatter on its edge above the sign that said "Enter." He quickly redressed, grabbed his car keys and his phone, and headed for his car. He needed to get to the exit in Fenton. He had a feeling his grandpa was in trouble.

***

Two more cars pulled into the gas station just as the man on pump number six, Lyle Riddick, replaced the nozzle onto its hook, but before he climbed into his car, he noticed

Carlton lying on the pavement and hurried over to him. Bending to see what was wrong, he noticed blood pooling on the pavement, so he rolled the man over. There was a rock under his head that was covered with blood. Lyle immediately took two full steps to the door, pulled it open, and yelled for someone to call 9-1-1. The employee behind the counter didn't move a muscle, but the other employee happened to be exiting the cooler when she heard the cry for help. She ran to the front door, and when she saw the bloodied man on the ground, dialed 9-1-1 on her cellphone. Gawkers from the other cars began to watch curiously.

For the next ten minutes, the man from pump number six knelt beside Carlton Thomas, who was lying unconscious on the ground. From the gawkers' point of view, it appeared the man was checking the body for other injuries—possibly checking for vital signs. Lyle appeared to feel inside his coat for something, and then he took a handkerchief from one of his pockets and held it against Carlton's head to stay the bleeding. Carlton had a pulse, but he wasn't showing signs of regaining consciousness. A police car arrived first, and third-year police officer Micky Kidder went right to the body. Lyle backed away as the officer slid in between him and the victim, blocking his view of the body. The ambulance arrived a minute or so later, and Lyle took a few more steps back.

"What happened here?" one paramedic asked as the other checked for vital signs.

Lyle Riddick stepped forward. "I just finished pumping gas when I noticed him lying there. I couldn't tell you what happened, but it looks like he fell and hit his head on that rock there." He pointed to the rock. "I don't know if he fainted, had a heart attack, or what, but he was breathing and he had a pulse. I was trying to slow the bleeding down while we waited for you."

Within a couple of minutes, the paramedics had Carlton loaded onto a stretcher and placed into the ambulance. "Are there any family or friends here?" the paramedic asked the crowd. There was no response.

Lyle stepped forward again. "Here. This is his wallet. It was lying on the ground next to him. His name's Carlton Thomas. His credit card was in his hand." When Lyle handed them over, he had a smear of blood on his leather coat sleeve. Though it was a frosty cold night, his hair was beaded with sweat. He had seen enough tragic death in his life as the son of a mortician and was genuinely concerned about the injured man's welfare.

The paramedic nodded his confirmation as he took the items and slid them into a bag. When the ambulance pulled away, the police officer began asking questions. Lyle hung around in case the officer had any questions for him in particular, but the gawkers went back to their business and eventually left.

For the next ten minutes or so, Officer Kidder observed the accident scene—asking questions, taking notes. When asked again, Lyle repeated his story to the policeman as he checked out the location where Carlton had fallen. The blood had coagulated around the rock. "Is there any chance that he was assaulted?" Micky Kidder asked Lyle.

"I didn't see how he fell. It's possible, I guess, but as far as I remember, there was only one other car in the parking lot, and I don't recall seeing any driver. I wasn't facing the store while I was pumping my gas, though. I found his wallet and credit card and gave them to the paramedics. I already told you all those things."

While Micky was jotting down some more notes in his notebook, Tanner arrived at the gas station and anxiously observed the spinning light on the police car. His grandpa's car was sitting unoccupied at a gas pump. A car pulled out of the parking lot and Tanner did a double-take because it was a red Camaro, and he thought it might be his dad. To his surprise, it wasn't his dad, but he recognized the driver. It was Zander Frauss, his dad's best friend, whose Camaro was a slightly different shade of red and a couple of years older. Zander was a neuroscientist at the University of Michigan, and he was the man who diagnosed and explained the scientific, medical reasons for the powers that Clay and Tanner possessed. He had become a close friend. It was disconcerting to see him pull away when Tanner was so sure that something bad had happened to his grandfather.

He turned into the lot, parked the car, and hurried to the policeman. "My grandpa, did something happen to him?"

"Hold on, guy. Who's your grandpa?" Officer Kidder asked.

"The owner of that car," Tanner said as he pointed to his grandpa's car at pump number two. "Carlton Thomas."

"He had a fall, I think," said Lyle. "My name's Lyle Riddick." He reached out and shook Tanner's hand.

"I'm Tanner Thomas. Where is he now?"

"I found him on the ground by that door," he pointed. "He was bleeding and unconscious. An ambulance took him to Genesys Hospital in Grand Blanc. You said that you're his grandson?"

Tanner ignored the question and went right to the door. It was the door from his vision, and he had a flashback of it swinging toward his head. Tanner, in the second year of his major at Michigan, was studying criminology, and his most recent test included blood spatter identification. He carefully stepped around the coagulated fluid and noticed some slight spattering—evidence that there was more blood than just what was pooled near the rock. He knelt and dabbed a finger on one of the droplets, assuring himself that it was truly blood.

Micky Kidder followed Tanner to the door. Though he was getting nowhere, he was still investigating. "Are you Tanner Thomas from the Michigan basketball team?" he asked.

"Yes...do you know what happened?"

"I'm a big U of M fan," he replied. "You're a good player."

"Thanks...do you know what happened?" Tanner noted that Kidder looked quite young.

"Apparently he fell...at least that's what the other guy said." Kidder hadn't learned too much while investigating.

"He was hit by this door," Tanner thought as he examined it. *"There's blood on the edge."* The red spatter he had seen in his vision was a small, sticky mark on the door's outside edge. He took out his cell phone and called his dad to tell him that his grandpa had been rushed to the hospital.

A concerned Lyle Riddick stepped forward again once Tanner had concluded his call. "Tanner...here's my business card. Would you call me and let me know how he is?" The card said he was the owner of the Fenton Hotel Tavern and Grille.

Just then the female Speedway employee stepped to the door and addressed the policeman. "Officer, we've been robbed!"

Jeff LaFerney

Chapter 3

Zander Frauss pulled into the driveway of his house in Hartland. It was 12:40 AM. The game had ended at about 11:30, and it was barely more than twenty minutes away, but Zander would tell his wife, Lydia, that he spent some extra time at a friend's tailgate. He would not tell her that he never even attended the game. Zander had an extraordinary mind, but he was a terrible liar. He was a unique individual, nothing like the nerdy scientist most people visualize. He was a fashionable dresser, his blond hair cut stylishly. His athletic frame, a result of a frenetic workout regimen, was a direct contrast to a stereotypical office practitioner. Zander was a forty-five-year-old neuroscientist but also the director of the Division of Perceptual Studies at U of M since 1998. His glasses were his only indication of academia. His attractive wife was a behavioral therapist who knew Zander like a book, so he hoped she was already asleep and he wouldn't have to talk to her.

He quietly snuck into the bathroom and closed the door before turning on the light. He removed his glasses and stared into the mirror. His eyes looked terrible, and he dreaded using them to face his wife. He'd rather hold off his lies until the morning. Then he'd spend the rest of his morning in church, asking for forgiveness. Zander knew enough about God to know that he had been forgiven for what he'd done, but there was a voice in his head that kept telling him that he really wasn't. Maybe he just needed to forgive himself, but he was having a hard time doing that, and the lies and deceit were adding to the guilt. It was a helpless feeling. What was bothering him just as much was that the one person who might be able to make things right was Clay Thomas, but Zander was too ashamed and maybe a bit too prideful to ask for help.

"Zander?"

"Yes, honey," he replied to his wife, immediately feeling regret.

"What took you so long getting home?"

"Did you see the game?" he responded, hoping to avoid the question.

"No, I caught up on some shows on the DVR. Did we win?"

"It was one of the best games ever. We won with two seconds remaining. Everyone was celebrating, so I spent some time with the tailgaters." He kicked himself. He'd lied when maybe he could have avoided it.

She peeked inside the bathroom and squinted to protect her eyes from the lights. Zander immediately turned on the water in the sink and began splashing some in his face in an attempt to avoid his wife's eyes. "Why didn't you call?"

"It was late. I didn't want to wake you."

"Well, hurry to bed. I've been waiting for you. We haven't made love in weeks."

"Lydia, I'm really tired. We have to get up early in the morning for church. Can I take a rain check tonight?" He felt too guilty to have sex with his wife.

"What's wrong, Zander? Don't you think I can tell when something's bothering you? What're you keeping from me?"

"It's nothing, honey. Really. I'm just tired and not feeling too well."

***

Lydia pulled the door shut, a little too forcefully, and stomped back into bed. She couldn't help but wonder what was going on. Was she no longer attractive to her husband? What kind of man wasn't interested in sex? But she knew it wasn't her. Something was bothering her husband, and since he wasn't confiding in her, she wondered if he'd told his best friend, Clay. She needed to give him a call.

***

Clay arrived at his house but never bothered to as much as remove his jacket. He had grabbed a snack and something to drink and was sitting on his couch, waiting for his father's arrival or for some bad news. He sent a text to Erika. His beautiful, bubbly girlfriend was nearly always on his mind.

"Are you up?" he texted.

"Sitting here waiting to hear from you," she replied.

Clay smiled and knew by the smiley face that Erika had included in her text that she was smiling too. Clay actually hated to text, so instead of responding, he simply called. Talking was the way God meant for people to communicate; at least that's what Clay thought most adults over forty felt. She was first on his speed dial, so her phone was ringing within seconds.

"Hello, Sweetie," she said.

"Hi. It's nice to hear your voice." After Clay's wife had been murdered, Erika was the single best thing that had happened in his life. He never tired of her. They had dated for a short time in high school and had renewed their relationship as a result of a caving expedition that they shared nearly a year earlier. Clay, with help from Tanner and the Durand police chief, had solved the mystery of the seven-year disappearance and death of Erika's husband.

Since then, Erika had come into a lot of money and had sold her home in Durand and moved into a comfortable neighborhood in Davison, only about ten minutes away from Clay. On a recent date, they stopped to look at rings for fun, but Clay was actually quite serious about proposing in the near future. She was perfect for him.

"What a game!" she exclaimed. "I can't believe Michigan won!"

She had ridiculous amounts of enthusiasm, even late at night, and she loved football. She was a gift from God, and Clay loved her completely and believed he would love her forever. "It was awesome, and even more awesome to share it with my dad. Thanks for giving up your ticket."

"My pleasure. I ran on the treadmill, took a bubble bath, filed my nails, polished my finger and toenails, and still watched the game."

The thought of Erika in a bubble bath upped his marriage proposal plans from imminent to emergency. But as pleasant a thought as it was, he was worried about his father, who still hadn't arrived at his house. "I'm waiting for my dad to get here, and I'm worried, Erika. Tanner had a vision of someone lying injured on the ground, and there were ambulance lights. He had the feeling that it might be my dad."

Erika was immediately concerned. "Have you called anyone?"

"Well, my dad stopped off for gas, and I pretty much had to let him do it. He should be here by now, though. Hold on. I'm getting a call." It was Tanner. He didn't bother with a greeting. "Did something happen?"

"Grandpa had a fall. He was unconscious when they rushed him to Genesys in an ambulance."

"I shouldn't've left 'im alone. I could've easily stopped and waited for him to get gas."

"Yeah, and I could've kidnapped him and taken him back to my room, but then he might've gotten injured in my apartment. Dad, there was no clue when or where the accident was going to happen. Or even who was in the vision. You aren't responsible for things that are out of your control. I'm headin' to the hospital. See ya there."

Clay switched back to Erika. "You there?"

"Yes."

"My dad had some sort of a fall. He wasn't conscious when he was rushed to Genesys."

"I'm so sorry. You'll pick me up on the way?"

"Of course. Be there in a few. I love you."

"I love you too, Clay."

Jeff LaFerney

Chapter 4

Sparrow June Nester owned Stir the Imagination, a metaphysical store in the Holly Hotel. It was Sunday morning, and she had a plumbing emergency. The bathroom in the store had a terrible leak under the sink, and try as she might, she was unable to stop it on her own. She turned the water off and made a series of phone calls for help, finally able to procure the services of one Sherman "Septic" Tankersley. When Sherman arrived, pipe wrenches and massive toolbox in hand, Sparrow was taken aback. There before her stood the largest man she had ever seen. Her entire, tiny, birdlike hand fit in his massive, greasy palm when she introduced herself and they shook hands.

"Call me Tank," he snarled.

"What an appropriate name," she thought. He was as big as a Sherman tank and smelled like a septic tank. He was the first plumber she had reached that was available on a Sunday, so she was stuck with him. "Okay, I will," Sparrow said as pleasantly as she could.

Sherman was the size of a mountain and stronger than an ox. As a slow-footed, six-foot nine and a half inch, three hundred and seventy-pound offensive lineman for Wayne State University in the mid-eighties, he spent much more time in the training room and the cafeteria than on the football field and, therefore, became quite a disappointment to the Wayne State coaching staff. His adult life picked right up where his football career left off, and he'd been mostly a disappointment to everyone else, as well. He was rough, crude, often vulgar, and possessed a hot temper, but managed to somehow have a very soft spot in his heart for his wife, who was the only one who seemed to care about him. Now much, much bigger than in his college days, he barely crammed his way through the doorway to Stir the Imagination. Sherman started out as a commercial plumber for a very large construction company but was phased out of work and eventually let go completely when it became obvious that there were many jobs that he was simply too big to do. His despicable personality didn't help. Once he was forced to start his own business, he found that he had a difficult time making ends meet. At his jobs, he nearly always had to pay a plumber's helper since he couldn't fit in a large percentage of the compact areas he was expected to work. And no plumber's helper put up with his grumpiness for long.

He squeezed through the aisle while following Sparrow to the bathroom. Soothing meditative sounds came from overhead speakers and pleasant aromatic candles perfumed the air. "I heard this place is haunted," Sherman said uneasily as he passed a table of crystal balls and what appeared to be magic wands.

"Oh, it most certainly is!" Sparrow chirped out enthusiastically. "It's wonderful."

"Well, I don't much like ghosts."

"There's nothing to be afraid of, Tank. The ghost here can be a bit mischievous, but she's harmless." The hotel's "harmless" ghost slipped through the doorway when Sparrow opened the bathroom door. The store owner flipped on the light to a room soaked in a puddle of water. "It's been

leaking from under the sink, so I shut off the water valve."
She hesitated and pointed. "When the valve gets reopened,
water leaks from that pipe."

"It won't leak anymore as long as the valve's off,"
Sherman groaned as he lowered himself to his knees. His
butt crack was generously exposed while he gazed under the
sink.

The sight was sufficiently disgusting that Sparrow made
a face before asking, "What do you think the problem is?"

"Could be corrosion in the pipe. Likely it kin be fixed
with a coat of epoxy inside the pipe or with some external
solder. Worst case scenario, I might haveta replace part of
the pipe."

"Well, yell if you need anything. I've got some work to
do,"

Sherman just grunted an acknowledgement. He reached
a telephone pole-sized arm toward the problem pipe just as
the Stir the Imagination ghost turned off the light in the
room. The monstrous plumber jerked his head around,
thinking Sparrow had flipped the light switch, and he banged
his eye on the cabinet. He cursed in anger and woozily stood,
a slight stream of blood dripping down his right cheek from
a small cut. Sparrow wasn't at the doorway, however, so he
flipped the light back on, wiped the blood off his face with
his shirt sleeve, and groaned again as he lowered himself
with difficulty back to his knees. He double-checked the
water-valve to be sure it was off, and then he grabbed a pipe
wrench and started loosening a large gasket.

He wedged both arms under the counter top while
turning the wrench. Once the connection was sufficiently
loose, the ghost turned the valve back to the on position, and
water immediately started spraying Sherman in the face.
Surprised, he jumped back, banging his head a second time.
A new stream of blood trickled down his forehead and the

left side of his face. Tankersley reached for the shut-off valve as the ghost turned the light back off. Water continued to spray unabated while Sherman stood once again and turned the light back on. A few seconds later, he had the water valve back off, ending the jetting spray from below the sink. He grabbed his pipe wrench again and then began his third, groaning squat back to his knees where he continued loosening the gasket even more. Out of the corner of his eye, he saw a flicker to his left and a nearly transparent image laughed as it turned the valve back on, causing water to spray out of the pipe once again. A scream escaped his throat, and Sherman jumped to his feet as the light turned off again. He leapt for the doorway, smashing his chin on the frame. A third trickle of blood flowed down his neck as the plumber discovered a mobility he'd never known before.

"There's a ghost in your bathroom!" he yelled. "And I ain't comin' back!" At that, he blasted out of the door and onto Battle Alley behind the store.

***

Lyle Riddick and his bartender, Maggie, had gotten together at the Fenton Hotel Tavern and Grille to go over their books and place food and drink orders. Lyle looked tired.

"What's wrong, Lyle?" Maggie asked. She had been working for Lyle since the day he opened his place of business in 1992. She had seen the place go from a poorly operated hotel and restaurant to an extremely successful tavern and grille under Lyle's management. He had closed the hotel part of his business in 1995. After Bosley Pemberton, the custodian/caretaker, passed away, he had invested loads of money into upgrading, remodeling, repairing, and advertising his business. He was very conscientious. His place of business meant everything to him.

"I'm just tired. Didn't get much sleep last night. A man was injured at the Speedway by the expressway, and I ended up being the number one witness. Got home really late."

"Is the guy all right?"

"I don't know. I really should call the hospital to see. How're you doin' this morning?"

"Like always, I went right to bed after closing the bar last night. Slept good. I'm doin' all right."

"You still not dating anyone, Maggie?"

"Not interested in anyone, Lyle. You know that."

"You can't go through your life alone, Maggie. It can't be good."

"Since when do you give relationship advice, Boss? You're married to your work. At least I loved once. Have you ever?"

"Yes, I have, and I could love again. You on the other hand have stubbornly given up. What's it been? Eleven years?"

"She broke my heart, Lyle. She's the only person I ever really loved."

"But she's gone, Maggie. Ever think you're wastin' your life away tendin' bar for me and pining your loss?"

"If I am, you're wasting your life too—running your business and waiting around for me. You know I'm not interested in anyone else."

"Ever think of trying a man? Some of us—me, for instance—aren't so bad."

Maggie had no interest in men, and Lyle knew it. Lyle had always been interested in Maggie, but instead of a romantic relationship, they had settled into a friendship, and Lyle trusted Maggie completely. No one knew Maggie better than Lyle, and no one knew Lyle better than Maggie. They were a winning team at the Fenton Hotel, at least, and even though he wanted more, Lyle had adjusted to their friendly relationship.

Maggie smiled. She loved Lyle, but not the way he wanted. "Why don't you call the hospital and ease your mind. You're always the concerned citizen, Lyle. You won't be able to keep your mind on our work this morning if you don't."

Lyle smiled back. "You know me too well. I'll go make the call." After looking up the number and talking to a phone receptionist, all he could learn was that Carlton Thomas was in critical condition. There was no other information that could be shared. Lyle headed off to his office to try to get some work done.

Chapter 5

After spending the entire night and all day Sunday at the hospital, Clay and Erika decided to get out for a while. They walked together to an outdoor shooting station at Williams Gun Sight and Outfitters in Davison. It was a sunny afternoon, and the range was busy. As happened at most places they visited, nearly everyone lost concentration on their activities as Erika walked up. It wasn't all that common to have women at the shooting site to begin with, but to have a woman that looked like Erika make an entrance was enough to quiet the entire range. Clay didn't mind usually, but his father was still in critical condition at the hospital after two days, so he was somewhat less tolerant. He was hoping that spending time with Erika away from the hospital, and releasing some of his pent-up aggression at the shooting range would ease his troubled mind.

"Brain trauma" and "possible brain herniation" were words that were repeating unmercifully in his head. For nearly two days, he'd had to witness his dad lying in a vegetative state with his arms bent inward on his chest, his hands clenched into fists, and his legs extended stiffly with his feet turned inward. "Abnormal posturing," it was called. It was heartbreaking to see. Brain surgery had been scheduled for later that Monday afternoon, so on this particular day at the range, Clay was a bit stressed, to say the least, and the gazes at Erika annoyed him.

"Hey, Shooter," Erika teased in reference to one of Clay's favorite movies. "Do you want a little friendly competition?"

After two incidents in the past two years where people attempted to kill him, Clay had finally decided to purchase his own gun. When he made the decision, Erika jumped on board, so they both purchased Ruger LCP 380 semi-automatic pistols. The lightweight, compact pistols were purchased with concealed license permits in mind. The guns were not much bigger than a large pocket knife and were small enough for Clay to carry in a back pocket of his pants. Erika fit hers easily into even the smallest of her purses. After three hours of pistol safety training and one hour of firing range time, the permits were purchased and both people felt safer.

Clay's thoughts were filled with concern for his father, but there was nothing better for him than competition. "You're on, Annie Oakley. Loser buys dinner."

Erika smiled, and so did every man who happened to be staring at her—which meant every man at the shooting range. Erika was 5'3" and no more than 110 pounds. She had the bluest eyes that Clay had ever seen and short, curly, nearly white blond hair. An ex-college cheerleader, Erika had a near-perfect body, amazing coordination, and ridiculous stamina that she used while expertly caving, a hobby she loved. Her bubbly, happy personality made her even more attractive.

"You're on!"

They had purchased their daily use passes which included two targets each. Erika happened to be a very good shot, so Clay knew he had to shoot well. He was hoping that by beating her, it would improve his sour disposition. They headed first to two of the six shooting stations from just fifteen yards. As they walked by, Sherman Tankersley, the gigantic, repulsive plumber, who happened to also be at the range, continued to stare at Erika from one of the dozen thirty-yard shooting stations. Clay glared at him before putting on his required ear and eye protection. Sherman had ridiculous-looking bandages on his chin, forehead, and eye, and he was in a worse mood than usual. He was hoping that some range shooting would make him feel better, but when he recognized Clay Thomas and saw him with the most beautiful-looking woman in the world, his mood worsened.

Clay's gun, weighing only about ten ounces fully loaded, was glass-filled with a nylon frame and steel slide. The cartridge capacity was six plus one in the chamber, so the competition would be just seven shots. The competition would be for the tightest grouping. Clay ran a target out to fifteen yards and looked Erika in the eyes. *"You can go first,"* she thought.

"Are you sure?" Clay asked.

Erika smiled, knowing he had read her mind. She rather liked to communicate with him that way.

"I'm hoping that by the time you scatter seven shots all over the target, that horrible fat man will have quit staring at my breasts. The creeper's distracting me."

Clay glared at him again, a headache developing, but then sat on a bench at his station and prepared to shoot. From fifteen yards, he expected a tight grouping all within three inches. Clay's hands were too big to hold the tiny grip with more than two fingers, so his little finger dangled off the bottom. When Erika outshot him, he would make excuses for himself by saying that her small hands allowed her to have all three fingers on the grip, giving her an advantage.

"Hey, Thomas!" the oversized Michelin man yelled.

Clay pulled the headgear from his head. "Do I know you?" he asked as politely as he could manage with his head beginning to pound.

"You played high school ball against my brother. I remember you. Mostly I 'member how my boy schooled yours a couple years ago. Holly verses Kearsley. Don't see what was so special 'bout your kid. We even won the game. Your boy wasn't nothin'."

"That game was the first game he played after we buried his mother. Congratulations on your win." He turned back toward his target and replaced his headgear, even more agitated than before.

"That hotty of yours must not know what kind of loser your boy is," he taunted. "Rumor is you took a job at U of M so they'd give the loser a scholarship."

"I'm sorry. I must not've heard you right." Clay was getting angry.

"No, you heard me right. Why don't you come over here to a real man, honey?"

Erika replied sarcastically so only Clay could hear. "Because he's disgusting?"

"What, you don't like a man that looks like a giant stuffed swine? Maybe some days he has a good personality, Erika."

"Maybe you should hold me back before I run into his blubbery arms. I could slide in under his fourth chin and we could snuggle."

"What you folks sayin' over there, Thomas?"

"We're admiring your pleasant personality and lean physique," said Clay.

"Why don't you drop that little baby gun you got there, wise guy, an' step out an' fight me like a man…if you are one, that is."

Clay set his pistol down and stepped away from his covered shooting station.

"Clay, no," Erika said. "He's not worth the trouble."

"Don't worry, honey. I don't think my bullets could penetrate the lard, and I wouldn't have much of a chance in a fight. The plan that I'm workin' over in my head is to not even touch him."

"He'd probably squish you," Erika giggled.

"I'll try to be light on my feet."

As Clay headed in his direction, Sherman took a step away from his shelter. Using his mental telekinesis, Clay moved the obese slob's shooting bench to a position directly behind him.

Clay looked him in the eyes and began to control his mind. *"You're afraid of me, fat man. You'll run from me the first chance you get."*

Fear showed in Sherman's eyes, but as uncomfortable as he was, he was actually more afraid of losing face with all the other shooters at the range. "I ain't afraid of you."

"Yes, you are. You're afraid I'll hurt you." Clay could tell by the look in his eyes that the man was terrified. He got to within about eight feet before he faked a lunge forward. The massive hulk let out a girly scream, covered his face and turned to run. His legs hit the bench and he tumbled over it, cracking it into several pieces and knocking the wind from his lungs.

As Clay towered over the cowering, gasping man, he leaned in and said, "I'm positive my girl wasn't into you even before the girly scream, but now you must realize it too. Have you considered starting a diet? Hope you get your breath back soon..." He turned to leave, then turned back. "She really is a hotty, isn't she?"

When he walked back to Erika, she had all four targets in her hand. "Let's return these and use our refund for

43

dinner." There was a twinkle in her eye. "What did you say to him?"

Clay smiled for the first time in two days. "I said 'She really is a hotty, isn't she?'"

"Yes, she is…And it's nice to see that the old sad-faced, sour-dispositioned Clay is no longer with us. Let's get some dinner before we head back to the hospital."

***

After meeting with Becca Fonteneau two days before, Zander was more distraught than ever. Out of curiosity, he had been scanning the internet for news. He read about the mysterious theft at the gas station—the fourth of its kind. Each time an employee apparently simply handed over a drawer full of cash. What was most interesting to Zander was that one article indicated that there was a suspect in one of the robberies. It was a man who sources said was injured during his escape from the Speedway Gas Station in Fenton. Another surge of guilt jolted the doctor because he knew that the man was innocent, but there was nothing he would do about it.

He was sitting at his desk in his office at the University of Michigan holding his face in his hands. "Excuse me," he heard. His secretary was standing in the doorway. "Are you okay, Dr. Frauss?"

"Yes, Janie. I'm fine. Can I help you with something?"

"You've had three messages today from the University's chancellor. He's asking that you call him back. Is this about the Division of Perceptual Studies?"

"I assume so. We're having a bit of a disagreement about the funding of the program. But it'll get worked out," he said with no conviction. "Is there anything else?" he asked when Janie continued to stand in the doorway.

"Just that your wife called and said that Clay Thomas called your home and wants to talk to you. Apparently you aren't answering your cell phone."

"Okay, Janie. I'll give him a call," he said with no intention of making such an effort.

"She says Clay's dad has been in critical condition in the hospital with brain trauma the last two days. He was injured at a gas station in Fenton after the game on Saturday."

Shocked, Zander looked away from Janie. Could Clay's father be the suspect in the robbery? What was he going to do now?

Jeff LaFerney

Chapter 6

Clay, Erika, and Tanner were standing in Carlton Thomas's recovery room. The surgeon had entered, looked at his chart, and then turned to the visitors. "We've run CT scans, MRI scans, and EEG tests to continue to check for hemorrhaging, swelling, and seizures. There's still severely high intracranial pressure."

"Swelling isn't reducing yet?" Clay asked.

"We've used diuretics to attempt to reduce swelling and ease the pressure, but his symptoms could prove to be fatal if the pressure continues. He has a low level of consciousness, both pupils are dilated and don't constrict in response to light, and he continues to have abnormal posturing. Those are all symptoms of brain herniation. During surgery, we opened a window in his skull to accommodate the brain swelling."

"The surgery'll relieve the pressure, and then my dad'll start getting better, right?"

"Brain herniation occurs when the brain shifts across structures within the skull. It puts extreme pressure on parts of the brain and causes blood supply to be cut off. There could be permanent brain damage, and it also could still be fatal."

"I'm still trying to reach my friend, Zander Frauss, to consult about this whole situation," Clay stated for no particular reason.

"Dr. Frauss? I've heard of him down at U of M. A well-known neuroscientist. But he has some crazy ideas about parapsychology, I've heard. You sure he's the person to talk to?"

"He never returned any of my calls, so I took your advice instead."

The doctor was making a note on his patient's chart when the door to Carlton Thomas's room opened and two policemen entered.

Tanner jumped to attention. He had an intuition that made him feel immediately uneasy. "Is there some way I can help you?" his father said.

"I'm Fenton Police Chief Butch Casserly. This is Officer Micky Kidder. I'm aware that Mr. Thomas here has been injured—but we have to ask him some questions."

Casserly was the stereotypical drill sergeant. He'd gained a few extra pounds over the years, but he was broad-shouldered and barrel-chested. He was clean-shaven with a butch cut hairstyle. Kidder, the young officer who responded to the 9-1-1 call, seemed a bit embarrassed that Casserly had brought him along. He had a despondent look on his face and a U of M logo tattooed on his neck. Unfortunately, he seemed somewhat intimidated by his boss and rather uncomfortable being in the same hospital room where Carlton Thomas lay unconscious. He managed a slight, friendly nod to Tanner. Tanner noted that Kidder was at the accident scene.

"Concerning what?" asked Clay.

"Concerning an armed robbery that was committed a little after midnight on September thirteenth, at the Speedway Gas Station in Fenton."

"You're hoping he was a witness?" asked Erika.

"No, ma'am. He's the prime suspect. We have video evidence placing him at the scene of the crime and accepting the stolen money from the cashier. We also have video of him stumbling and crashing into the exit door, where he obviously was injured and then discovered lying unconscious."

"So you recovered the money and found the gun?" Tanner asked sarcastically.

"Well, that is a bit of a problem currently because there was no money or gun found at the scene. We believe he either had an accomplice or someone at the scene of the crime stole the items from the suspect."

"Officer Casserly," the doctor interrupted. "Mr. Thomas has severe brain trauma, and he just returned from surgery. He's still completely unresponsive. He cannot possibly answer any questions."

"It's also impossible that he could have committed an armed robbery," Clay protested.

"I've brought Officer Kidder in case he'd be needed to stand guard outside the hospital room. As soon as he's able to be interviewed, we'll be reading Mr. Thomas his rights and booking him for armed robbery." Chief Casserly nodded and left the room, followed by his sidekick who took his position in the hallway just in case a man with brain herniation decided to make a hasty escape.

"This is so absurd," Clay remarked.

"Don't worry, Dad. Just ignore Butch Casserly and the Sundance Kidder. We'll figure out what happened while Grandpa recovers. It looks like we've got ourselves another mystery."

***

Matt Royster had another screaming argument with his wife. She wanted him to vacuum the carpeting because "you never do anything around here." Matt had been on the computer, looking at the league standings for his son's fall baseball league at the Genesee Fieldhouse. His son, Ace, was beginning to live up to his name, and the talented pitcher was starting to get lots of feelers in regard to scholarship offers. The arguments were practically a daily occurrence, and they always seemed to coincide with a migraine headache. "*Chicken or the egg?*" Matt thought. Was it the arguing that gave him the headaches or the headaches that led to the arguing? He was pretty sure it was the arguing that gave him the headaches because it seemed like whenever his wife raised her voice in anger, the sound penetrated right into his spinal cord and shot into the back of his skull. The only thing that seemed to dull the pain was alcohol, so once again he was sitting on a bar stool at the Fenton Hotel Tavern, drinking the pain away.

Lyle Riddick had just come from his second floor office where he took a phone call from Tanner Thomas. He saw Matt and tried to make an about-face without being spotted, but he was too late.

"Hey, Lyle!" Matt called out as he pounded his beer mug to the counter. "I been meanin' to talk to you again 'bout sponsoring Ace's team this winter in the indoor league. Whatcha say about that?"

"Same thing I always say, Matt. I'm not gonna sponsor the team—not with you hangin' around at the games. You're so abrasive you'd run business *away* from me rather than bringin' it in."

"You sayin' I have a bad attitude, Lyle?"

"Yep. That about sums up what I'm sayin', Matt. That boy of yours has a golden arm, and he's a great kid, but *you* can't keep your emotions under control."

"I'm gettin' peeved, Lyle. As much money as I spend in here, I've probably paid the sponsorship fee myself. Stop being so tightfisted."

"Listen, I've always tried to be an honest man who runs an honest business. I don't want your antics associated with my Tavern and Grille. And maybe if you stopped spending all your money on liquor, you'd quit beggin' me for money!" he snapped. Lyle was tired of Matt on several levels. He wouldn't have minded if the man found another drinking hole somewhere else, but Matt Royster would continue to show up as long as his sister Maggie continued to tend bar. Lyle was a hardworking businessman, but patience wasn't his best quality. He was entirely fed up with Matt.

"Oh, I got me lots of money. Money's not the issue. The issue's that you ain't willin' to support your community. I got lots of people willing to hand over money to me. I just thought maybe you'd change your thinkin' and jump on the Ace bandwagon."

"You'd have to have superpowers to get me to change my mind, Matthew. Have a good evening. And Maggie?" He looked at his bartender. "It's about time you cut him off. I don't want him hurtin' some innocent victim on the way home. I don't want anyone's death on my conscience."

"Home? I ain't headin' home. The old lady gives me a migraine." Royster chugged the rest of his beer and belched. "I got plans." He tossed another ten at Maggie. "Don't spend it all in one place, Sis," he said as he rose from his wooden bar stool.

Lyle pretended not to watch Matt as he staggered out of the tavern, but he was watching him in the mirrors behind the bar. When Matt exited the long, narrow bar, Lyle spoke to Maggie. "No matter what you think of him, he's bad news, you know." Then he changed his tone. "Listen, there's someone comin' here to see me in a few minutes. I told him to meet me at the bar. Name's Tanner Thomas. He'll be with a couple others. Just text me when they get here, okay?"

"Sure thing, Lyle."

***

Zander Frauss had returned to his office at the end of a long work day. Once again, he was staring at Clay and Tanner's MRI images, wondering about his future. He had been working as a neuroscientist for fifteen years before he lucked upon his friendship with Clay. Zander had long before convinced the University of Michigan to approve of his Division of Perceptual Studies when he'd come upon his first patient with parapsychological abilities. Since then he'd worked hard to get funding from the school and to write grants for additional money. Zander was a brilliant scientist who was convinced that parapsychological abilities manifested themselves because of certain unusual brain conditions. He launched the idea for his scientific studies from a single patient fifteen years earlier, and he'd had other patients that manifested legitimate minor or occasional mental abilities since. His studies had convinced him that each of those persons had abnormalities in the medulla oblongata of their brains.

Then Clay Thomas walked in with genuine concerns and questions. Clay had abilities that no other patient had ever exhibited. And when he agreed to an MRI, Zander found that Clay's medulla was open in both parts—normal people had a medulla closed in one part. The impulses that traveled through Clay's brain were working differently than normal people. And Clay was additionally able to control the impulses. He wasn't just getting extra sensory impulses, he could control them—mind-control, telepathy, and telekinesis. His son's differing abilities made the two of them quite a team. But Zander had wanted them to cooperate with his tests. He wanted to learn from them. He wanted to prove to those funding his research that he was making new discoveries, breaking new ground in the field of parapsychology. Clay and Tanner felt differently, though. They didn't want to be tested. They didn't want to become specimens in Zander's laboratory. They didn't want people to know that they possessed mind powers.

Zander had honored their wishes and even become friends with them. But he had been receiving pressure to produce research results or have his funding cut off. The pressure was getting to him, and in an absurd act of pride, he didn't share his burdens with the people closest to him. Instead he turned to Becca Fonteneau, and now he was in trouble. Clay and Tanner might be able to help him make things right again, but he was too ashamed to ask for their help, and he couldn't face Clay, who could read his mind—even though Clay's own father was in trouble and he was reaching out for help. Zander's relationship with his wife, Lydia, was deteriorating fast, his research plans were falling apart, his friendship was fast becoming non-existent, his guilt was tearing him apart, and he wasn't sure how to put his life back in order.

He listened again to Clay's latest voicemail message. "Zander, what's the problem? I've called you a half dozen times. I've called Lydia. Why won't you call me back? My dad's in critical condition, and they performed surgery to relieve pressure on his brain. I waited two days for advice from you. And now the police are saying that he robbed a store. They have him on video tape. It doesn't make sense. Why won't you call me? You need to call me back."

Zander stared at his phone, then punched the number seven to delete the message. He had his own problems.

Jeff LaFerney

Chapter 7

Originally called Fenton House, the Fenton Hotel Tavern & Grille was constructed in 1856 soon after the Detroit and Milwaukee Railroad reached town in 1855. It was a three-storied, gray brick and wood-sided building on the corner of Main and Leroy Streets across from an old railroad depot. The upstairs windows were tastefully but completely covered on the outside, and the two upper floors were no longer used as hotel rooms. Except for a couple of second floor offices, only the bottom floor was still in use.

There was nothing more they could do, so Clay, Erika, and Tanner had left the hospital and traveled back to Fenton to meet with the witness at the gas station. They entered through the front door and made their way to the receptionist who was standing behind what was the old check-in desk for the original hotel.

"Hello," she said. "Will it be just the three of you?" She was cute, and she directed her gaze and question to Tanner.

Tanner looked into his father's eyes. *"She's cute,"* he thought, and his father smiled and nodded in agreement. "We're here to see the owner—Mr. Riddick," Tanner explained.

"Oh," she said. She was obviously impressed by Tanner. "Are you meeting in his office?"

"No, he said to meet him in the tavern. The bartender'll let him know we're here."

"Okay, sure. My name's Corissa," she blurted out. She blushed and seemed to forget what she was supposed to do. "Um, would you like a menu or a table or...anything else at all?" She blushed some more and was having trouble thinking clearly. Just then, three menus slid from some slots above Corissa's head, tumbling right on top of her. Already a bit flustered by Tanner, she again blurted out. "Oooh, you dumb ghost! It's not funny!"

Tanner shot his father a look. Somehow his dad was able to hear ghosts—at least he could hear the ghost of Erika's deceased husband. "Did you hear anything?" he quietly asked his father.

"Yes," he whispered so Corissa couldn't hear. "A voice said, 'Here's three menus.'"

Erika turned to Corissa and said, "When I worked at the Depot in Durand, we heard lots of stories about the Fenton Hotel being haunted. Are the stories true?"

"I've been working here for about six months, and there's no doubt in my mind that there're ghosts here. Plural. At least several different ghosts. There's no way I'd be in this building alone at night. But when there's lots of people around, it's okay." Her interest in Tanner was obvious as she nervously kept chattering while leading the way into the bar. "This is Maggie, our bartender. She's been here for as long as Mr. Riddick has owned the place. She says there're ghosts too."

"*She says it, but she doesn't believe it,*" said the female voice of a ghost.

Clay glanced in the direction of the voice as Maggie raised her eyebrows in wonderment. Lyle hadn't forbidden the employees to talk about the ghosts. Talk of ghosts actually seemed good for business, but it still wasn't a common topic of conversation. Then she noticed Tanner and understood that Corissa was trying to impress him. "Yeah, there're ghosts all right. Can't work here without seeing plenty of evidence. Can I get any of you something to drink?" She was eyeing Erika, clearly impressed herself.

"No, thanks. We're here to see Mr. Riddick. He asked us to meet him here in the bar," Clay explained.

"Oh, sure." She pulled her gaze from Erika. "He told me to text him when you got here. Lemme do that. He's expecting you."

Clay looked to his left. The tavern was long and narrow—maybe a hundred feet or so long but only about twenty feet wide. There was a dining area at the far end and a couple of small booths and six tables alongside the bar. There were probably eighteen or twenty seats at the bar where dark wooden chairs and stools were used for seating. There were maybe seven windows occupying the outer wall and seven televisions displayed on the inner walls. Everything was dark—floor, ceiling, tables, and chairs. There were pictures of old historical buildings on the walls and old menus framed from days gone by. As he was taking in the atmosphere, Maggie appeared to be flirting with Erika while Corissa was flirting with Tanner. When Lyle walked into the bar, Corissa scurried back to her post.

"Hello, folks. I'm Lyle Riddick." He held out his hand to Clay, who shook it firmly and introduced himself as Tanner's father. He then smiled politely at Erika and shook her hand as well. He liked what he saw; Clay didn't have to be a mind-reader to know that. Everyone liked what they saw in Erika, including Maggie, obviously. "It's very nice to meet you," he said. "You look a lot like a former employee—a singer actually—who once worked here." Then he turned to Tanner. "Hi, Tanner. How's your grandpa?"

"He's not doing well. He had surgery this afternoon," Tanner replied as he shook the man's hand.

"I'm so sorry to hear that. Clay, my best wishes go out to your father. Let me show you around, and then we can talk." They walked together to the back of the bar where he showed them a picture of some men playing cards. He explained, "The town's name of Fenton, Michigan, was literally decided in a game of cards. In August of 1834, William Fenton played a high stakes poker game with Robert Leroy and Benjamin Rockwell. The winner would claim the right to name the village. Fenton won the hand with a full-house and got to name the city after himself. The main business street was then called Leroy Street, and the principal residential street was called Rockwell. My building was first called the Vermont House. It's gone through lots of name changes and lots of owners since. I took it over about nineteen years ago and did a lot of renovations starting about ten years ago. When I closed down the hotel for good—it was barely usable anyway—I renamed it the Fenton Hotel Tavern and Grille." He led them through the kitchen, the private banquet room, and into the restaurant. "My offices are upstairs, but it's a mess up there. We can just sit in a booth if you'd like."

As Erika slid into the booth ahead of Clay, Lyle took one more thoughtful gaze before settling in beside Tanner. "Now, how can I help you?"

Tanner answered. "You were at the Speedway Gas Station the night my grandpa was injured. We just want to know what you saw. This afternoon, Fenton's police chief showed up and let us know that they'll be arresting my grandpa for armed robbery as soon as he's able to leave the hospital."

"You're kidding! Casserly is known for jumping to conclusions. But this one is more absurd than usual. I was right there. Your grandpa was unconscious on the pavement with no one around. I held his head and put a handkerchief on the wound. A policeman arrived five or ten minutes later, and the ambulance arrived a couple of minutes after that. There was no gun or money. How could anyone think he'd robbed the place? I found his wallet beside him on the pavement. His credit card was actually in his right hand still, like he was getting ready to use it inside the store."

"The chief says they have him on video taking money from the cashier and then stumbling into the door, which presumably caused the injury," Clay explained.

"That just doesn't make sense to me. I saw him pumping gas two islands over. I admit that I didn't notice exactly when he finished because I was looking out toward Owen Road instead of toward the store. But he would have had to go in, rob the place, and get injured in just a minute or two."

"And don't forget, there was no money or weapon. The police say that someone else might've robbed my dad," Clay explained. "Or they're suggesting he might've had an accomplice."

"There was another car in the lot, Clay. I never saw a driver, but it was a sports car. Possibly red...maybe maroon...some color like that."

"Well, I know that my dad didn't rob the gas station," responded Clay, "and I know there was no accomplice—he was at the Michigan game with us, and I watched him pull off the expressway while he was following me home. He stopped for gas, not cash. And he doesn't have a gun. What I'm thinking is that it was the person from that other car who committed the crime, so we need to find him."

"Is there anything else you remember about the other car?" Tanner asked.

"No, honestly, I'm not too knowledgeable about cars, and it was just a passing glance that I barely remember."

"Mr. Riddick, do you believe that people can be hypnotized?" asked Tanner politely.

"I'm willing to consider the possibility of ghosts—can't work in this restaurant long without wondering about that—so I guess I could consider that a person could be hypnotized."

Erika took her cue and finally spoke up. They had all agreed that he was much more likely to agree to hypnosis if it was Erika making the suggestion. It was time to crank up the charm. "Lyle? You don't mind if I call you Lyle, do you?"

"No, I prefer it, actually."

She smiled her perfect smile and held his gaze. Tanner was thinking he *already* was hypnotized. Who wouldn't be? "Would you be willing to give it a try? We might discover some details that your conscious memory is missing. I could hypnotize you if you're willing. I'll be gentle." She gave him a slight wink and then tilted her head, raising her eyebrows to better display her flirty eyes.

"Okay," he said hesitantly. "I guess so." He never took his eyes off from Erika's.

Erika took her necklace from her neck and started swinging it in front of his eyes. "Just focus on the necklace. You're getting sleepy. Very, very sleepy." Tanner and Clay were having a difficult time not laughing.

Eventually, after Erika had continued with the ruse far longer than she thought was necessary, Tanner said, "You're hypnotized." Lyle immediately fell into complete hypnosis and everyone laughed. "Great job, Erika. I was falling into your trance myself," Tanner quipped.

"You guys are like little boys sometimes," Erika giggled.

Clay leaned forward and began speaking. "Lyle, I want you to think back to the night that my father was injured. There was another car in the parking lot, parked in the customer parking section. I want you to tell me anything you can remember."

Lyle remained silent a few seconds as if he was carefully searching the scene for details. "I first noticed it when I started pumping my gas. The car was backed into its parking space, so there was no license plate visible. No one was in it, but it was running. The car was red. A sports car of some sort. Camaro, Mustang...something like that. I don't know cars. When I finished filling my tank, I hung up the hose, and then I saw the injured man. I hurried over to him. I rolled him over and saw the blood. Then out of the corner of my eye, I noticed the red car pulling away. I looked, but I could only see the side and back end as it drove behind the building."

Clay looked at Tanner. Tanner had a look of shock, then anger on his face. "What is it?" Clay asked.

Entranced, Lyle answered the question. "It's a red car that's pulling out of the station."

"No, Lyle. I'm talking to Tanner now." Lyle stopped talking.

"Dad, when I was pulling into the Speedway, I saw Zander pulling out."

"Zander?" both Erika and Clay said at the same time. "Our Zander?" Clay asked in confusion.

"Yes, Dad. He was in his red Camaro. He lives in Hartland and works in Ann Arbor. What was he doing in Fenton at 12:25 in the morning? It was twenty minutes or so after the robbery, but maybe after he robbed the store, he got concerned about Grandpa and came back to see if he was okay."

Lyle was sitting at hypnotized attention, his mind fully submitted to the next request of his new acquaintances.

"No way. He's a stand-up guy, Tanner." Lyle, obediently willing to fulfill orders, stood up. "You know that as well as I do. Just back up a minute." Lyle started walking backward. "Slow down and think this through logically." Lyle continued to back up, but more slowly, as if contemplating his next move.

"Stop and think a minute," Tanner responded. Lyle stopped and raised his hand to his face. With his thumb under his chin, he started tapping his lips with his index finger as if he was thinking deeply. "You've been trying to reach him, and he's avoiding you." Lyle starting ducking and bobbing as if he was avoiding a boxer's punches or maybe someone's reach.

Erika was watching Lyle, trying to let the guys talk while stifling a laugh at the same time.

"How could he ever steal something, Tanner? It's just an absurd thought." Lyle stepped forward to the table again and started grabbing silverware and jamming the utensils into his pockets. A slight giggle escaped Erika's throat. There was a pause as the two men considered the situation again. Finally, Clay spoke again. "You're jumping to conclusions with no real evidence." Lyle started jumping up and down, causing the silverware to start spilling out of his pockets and clinking on the floor.

Finally, Erika burst out laughing and the debaters noticed Lyle springing up and down like an excited child. Tanner realized, finally, what was going on. Lyle was still hypnotized and faithfully following orders. "Jeeze, Mr. Riddick. I'm sorry. You're no longer hypnotized." He snapped his fingers, and Lyle finally stopped jumping.

Several sets of eyes from customers at other tables were staring at him as he looked around. When he came to the realization that he was no longer sitting and that silverware was lying scattered all over the restaurant floor, he asked, "Did I just do something embarrassing?"

Erika burst out laughing again, but she was so genuinely cute and amused that Lyle just sat down, and all the men started laughing as well. They'd learned some information, but Clay was right. There was no use jumping to conclusions yet. However, he did need to have a talk with his best friend. Something was amiss; that was for sure.

Jeff LaFerney

Chapter 8

The door to the Mug and Brush swung open, and a customer tripped over the doorway, stumbling slightly into the shop. Dan Orton, the barber closest to the checkout counter looked up as the customer regained balance and walked, head down, to the counter. It was just before closing time and a couple of customers were waiting for a chair to become free while watching *Pardon the Interruption* on Sports Center. The new "customer" stood, back to the working barbers, ball cap pulled low. Dan set down his scissors and walked behind the counter.

"May I help you?" he asked.

Not a single audible word was spoken in return, but the customer handed the barber a leather bank bag. *"Empty the contents of the cash register into the bank bag,"* Dan heard in his head. He poked a register key with his index finger, and the drawer slid open. He grabbed the entire day's worth of cash from the drawer and stuffed it into the bag. When he was done, he zipped it shut and handed it back to the customer. *"You won't remember anything about me,"* he heard in his head. Dan nodded, walked back to his barber station, picked up his scissors, and resumed giving the haircut. The whole exchange lasted less than a minute.

The customer simply put the bag in a coat pocket and casually strolled out of the barber shop. After his haircut, Dan's paying customer handed over a twenty-dollar bill and waited, expecting some change. Dan opened his cash drawer to complete surprise. There was not a single dollar bill of any denomination inside the register. The Mug and Brush had been robbed, and he didn't remember a thing.

***

Clay, Erika, and Tanner decided to have dinner at the Fenton Hotel Grille, so after thanking Lyle for his time and waiting for clean silverware, they ordered from the menu and began a somewhat relaxing meal. The stress that had been showing on Clay's face was a little less obvious after the hypnotism, but his mind was still trying to process why Zander was ignoring him and what he might possibly have to do with the robbery and injury at the Speedway Gas Station.

One of the many, many fabulous things about Erika Payne was that she was loaded. Seven years after her husband's death, she finally received seven years' worth of withheld business income, fifty percent of the sale of a profitable business, and a load of life insurance money. She had tremendous wealth and enjoyed spending it. The 2010 Chevy Camaro SS that Clay drove was a gift. Clay's filet and Tanner's New York Strip were two more examples of her generosity. The petite Erika settled on a salad topped with grilled shrimp.

After the delicious meal, Tanner snuck away to chat again with Corissa. Clay's mind drifted back to his father, knowing that as soon as they left the restaurant, he and Erika would be heading back to the hospital. Eventually it occurred to him that a man was standing next to his table.

"Excuse me," Clay said awkwardly to the man. "Can I help you?"

"*I hope so.*"

There was an uncomfortable pause. Finally Clay spoke again. "How so?"

"Who are you talking to, Clay?" Erika asked.

Clay looked at Erika and pointed at the man. "Him," he said, wondering why Erika asked such a strange question.

When she looked to where he was pointing, there was no one there. "There's no one there, Clay. You must be seeing things," she said.

"*Like a ghost maybe?*" the ghost of Bosley Pemberton asked.

"I can't see him now either, but I can still hear him, Erika. He said, 'Like a ghost.' I can hear ghosts, but as far as I know, I've never seen one before."

"*Practically everyone's seen a ghost. They just don't know it. And people hear ghosts too, if we want them to. But you're different.*"

"Yes, I am, actually, but who are you, and how would you know?" he asked as he looked around.

"*Well, that's a fine question to ask. I don't know who I am—at least not much. I only know why I'm here.*"

"Clay? Are you really talking to another ghost?" Erika asked.

Clay nodded his head in the affirmative, but he continued to speak to the ghost. "I don't understand how you don't know who you are. You don't know your name?"

"*My name's Bosley Pemberton. And I belong here. That I know. And I know this is where I was killed. But I don't know who I really am or how I was murdered.*"

"How do you know you were murdered?"

"*Because all of us who are left behind are left behind for a purpose. I'm certain my purpose is to find my murderer, but I can't do it on my own. I think I need you.*"

"Murdered?" Erika said. "What's going on, Clay?"

"I don't know, Erika, but there's a ghost talking to me, and I'm sure that I saw him a minute ago. He says he was murdered and he needs my help to figure out who he is and how he was killed."

"*I was murdered*," Bosley said. "*I need your help.*"

"Show yourself to me," Clay said.

Clay caught a glimpse of movement in the doorway. He looked up, and the man that he saw near his table was motioning for him to follow. "I think he wants me to follow him, Erika. Do you mind?"

"Maybe I'll order dessert. You're something else, Clay Thomas. I'll wait here for you."

Clay excused himself and headed for the doorway. The ghost started up the stairway behind the check-in desk. Clay looked around, unsure if he should follow, but there were no signs saying he couldn't, so he quietly stepped up the stairs behind Bosley. When Bosley reached the top of the stairs, he headed down a short hallway, then took a left and headed down another short hallway. There were boards, buckets, empty bottles, and other debris along the way. At the end, on the left side was a door numbered 206. It was one of the old hotel rooms. He waited for Clay to open the door, then walked in and sat down on an old mattress in a dusty, cobwebbed room in disrepair.

"*This is where I died,*" he said. The room had light filtering in through the boarded-up window. The rest of the light came from a light bulb in the hallway. As he spoke, his ghost legs swung back and forth through the sides of a waste basket that was sitting on the floor. It was an odd, eerie sight in the dimly lit room. "*My first memory is of this room. It was dark. I didn't know where I was. I didn't know what I was. But I could see by the little bit of moonlight that there was a bed and someone was on it. I could see a door knob, so I walked as quietly as I could to the door to try to get out.*

68

I was scared. I didn't know why I was in the room or how I got there. I couldn't remember anything about who I was. I reached for the door knob and missed. I tried again and again, but I couldn't get a grip on the knob. I reached out and there was no wall or door—well, there was, but not one I could touch. That scared me even more. I don't know what I was thinking exactly, but I lowered my shoulder to crash through the door. I didn't hit anything at all, but all of a sudden I was in the hallway. I'd fallen through the door."

"Is that when you realized you were a ghost?"

"Actually, no, it wasn't. I felt alive. I touched my face and could feel it. I felt like a person. My arms, my legs, my chest and hips—I could feel them all. And I was sitting on the floor. Why didn't I just drop through? So I didn't know I was dead. I just knew something was terribly wrong. I was terrified and actually began to cry. I could feel emotion—sadness, fear, concern that I didn't know anything about myself. I sat there in the dark listening for any noises. It was dead quiet—pardon the pun—for several long minutes, maybe more. Finally, footsteps sounded in the hallway and someone carrying a flashlight walked by. I yelled for help, Clay, but the person behind the flashlight didn't hear or see me.

"Whoever it was just walked right by as if I wasn't there. And I wasn't, Clay. Not really; I was just a spirit. I didn't know it yet, but I was dead. The person with the flashlight entered my room—I learned later it was me on the bed. I heard what sounded like paper. You know...the crinkling, crackling sound that something like a paper sack makes? Then I heard a whispery voice say, 'Get out!' Almost immediately, the flashlight was shining in my eyes again, and the person—probably my murderer—rushed past me a second time, scrambled down the stairs, and was gone. I

don't have any idea who the person was or what he or she did to me."

There was a long pause before Clay finally said, "There's got to be more to your story."

Bosley continued: *"In the morning, when there was enough light, I went back into the room...Walked right through the door again. It wasn't so traumatic the second time. What was traumatic was what I saw in the early morning light. It was* me *lying there. I don't know how I knew because I didn't know anything else, but I was sure of it, and finally everything made sense.*

"Later in the day—in the afternoon—there was a knock on the door. I answered, but no one could hear me. I was afraid to leave, Clay, so I waited until someone came back. Lyle used his keys to open the door, and that's when it was discovered that I was dead. Before my body was taken away, I learned a few facts, and over the next few weeks, I heard things when people talked about me. Like I know my name...I know I worked here and lived here in room 206. I don't think I have any family, but I can't remember anything on my own."

"How did you discern that I was 'different'?" Clay asked.

"Most people don't believe in ghosts. Not really. Even Lyle and Maggie, who told you they believe in ghosts, don't really. If they did, and I wanted them to, they could see me or hear me. There are other ghosts in this hotel, but no one can see them or hear them without believing in them. We can tell who believes. You do. Your son does. Your girl does. Very nice looking lady, that one, by the way."

"Thank you."

"I might be dead, but I'm not blind. Anyway, a ghost has a sense about who believes, and if we're in the mood, we reveal ourselves to them. Angry ghosts sometimes scare

people. The more passive ghosts, like myself, reveal ourselves in simple, silly ways. Like little pranks, for instance. But my sense about you is that you're more than a believer, Clay; you're a whisperer. When the menus fell on the girl, your son asked you if you heard anything, and you heard the ghost of a boy that wasn't trying to reveal himself to you. It's obvious that you believe, but after that incident, I could tell you could communicate with ghosts too. Then you heard that sad, angry female ghost in the bar area. I saw you look in the direction of her voice. She wasn't trying to reveal herself to you either."

"I don't know if I'm a ghost whisperer or not, Bosley, but you're now the fourth ghost I've been able to hear. Erika's ex-husband was haunting the Durand Depot. I could hear him, but I couldn't see him like I can see you. You have any idea why?"

"He didn't want you to. Or maybe he didn't know that he could make himself seen. As time has passed, I've learned things. I mean, I was walking without falling through the floor, but I could walk through walls. I figured that meant that I had some physical control. In time, I learned to lift and move things. I learned to make myself visible and audible. But what I can't learn without help is who I am and how I died. I'll be stuck as a ghost until I fulfill my purpose, and my purpose is to find my murderer. I need you to help me."

"Let's say that I agree to help, Bosley. Do you have any idea where I should start?"

"I'd say a good place to start is to find out who I am. Then maybe it'll lead you to who would want me dead."

"My son and I have a unique set of skills. If anyone can find out the answers to mysteries, we're definitely better equipped than most. I'll see what we can do."

Clay left the room and found his way down the stairs back to the main lobby. There he found Erika, Tanner, and

Corissa talking. When Erika saw him, she said, "Clay, look what we've found here in the bowl for business cards. This one was right on top. It says 'John Grisham, Dell Publishing, Random House, Inc.' Do you think he was here?"

"Hmmm. It appears he was, and recently. I'm sorry you missed him, honey. I know how much you like him."

"It's true," she said to Clay. "But I love you. Let's go. It's been a long day, and you and I have to go back to the hospital." She'd already paid for dinner, so there was nothing more to do. "You can tell us what just happened on our way to Tanner's car."

"*It's been a long day*," Clay agreed as he nodded his consent. A lot had happened. He had lots to think about, and apparently he now had two mysteries to solve in the town of Fenton.

Chapter 9

Butch Casserly had been the Fenton Chief of Police for slightly longer than two years. It happened completely by default. He had served in the military as an officer until 2002 and became a policeman when he was discharged simply because he couldn't think of anything else he might be good at. He could be hotheaded, and he could be a bully, but what he was best at was giving orders. His ex-wife and two estranged children had bitter memories of family life with Butch. He had a younger sister who was pursuing a semi-successful singing career and wanted nothing to do with him. Every partner he'd ever had on the police force had asked for a transfer. But Butch wasn't a quitter. One doesn't learn about quitting in the military, and eventually he outlasted everyone in the Fenton Police Department. The current city police department included four rookies and eight second or third-year officers. There was no one willing to take over such an inexperienced department, except Butch. He felt his main talent—giving orders—made him adequately qualified for the position.

Casserly wasn't particularly highly thought of—except by himself—so he hated that there was a crime spree in his precinct and he was making no progress in solving the crimes. The injury at the Speedway Gas Station was the single biggest break he had had thus far, so he was pursuing the case with total gusto. He received the videotapes from the gas station the day before. The camera at the exit door wasn't operating, but the other four cameras clearly showed the thief with a knit University of Michigan hat, navy pants, and a U of M jacket. The cameras at the cashier's counter showed the cashier putting money and a magazine in a bag and the thief quickly walking out of the store. As he passed the ice chest containing bottles of Starbucks coffee, Red Bull, and some other variety of iced caffeine, he stumbled and fell toward the exit door to the right of the fire extinguisher.

At that point, the camera at the doors wasn't working, so the best footage he had was of the stumble, a stumble that caused a collision with the door. Then, Lyle Riddick found the man unconscious outside the building, lying injured in the parking lot. It was a cut-and-dried case, and the district attorney saw it the same way. Eddie, the cashier, had no memory of what the thief looked like, and the thief had managed to keep his face out of camera view, but Eddie claimed that the thief had a gun and had told Eddie to stay where he was and not call the police. Shock, fear, or maybe stupidity would have been Casserly's best guesses as to the memory failure except that there were three previous robberies, and no one seemed to remember anything about them either. A problem concerning the Speedway robbery was that Carlton Thomas had no gun, nor did he have a bag full of money, and that left only two possibilities as far as Casserly saw it. Either Thomas had an accomplice who got away with the loot and the weapon, or someone in the parking lot stole them. The coincidental second robbery seemed far-fetched, even to a cop who was overzealously seeking a conviction, especially since he'd heard the news that there had been another robbery at a local barber shop which was similar to all the previous ones. So Chief Casserly was going on the assumption that there was an accomplice who was continuing the crime spree, and Lyle was the only known person in the parking lot. Casserly had shown up at his place of business to ask him a few questions. It was Tuesday, about noon.

Butch Casserly wasn't fond of anyone that he could think of, but he was especially not fond of Lyle Riddick for three reasons. First, Butch believed *he* was responsible for his sister's singing career, but she always gave Lyle credit. Second, Lyle made a lot of money using a gimmick about ghosts in his place of business, and Casserly didn't like anything about ghosts. Third, years ago, when his business was faltering, Riddick was bailed out by someone else's money. Casserly felt he'd never been given a break in his life, and he resented that Riddick got one he didn't deserve. The chief silently hoped Riddick was involved in the robbery, so he smiled his fake, toothy smile, flashed his badge at the pretty receptionist, and bellowed, "I need to see the proprietor of this establishment!"

"I think he's in the kitchen. Would you like me to go get him?"

"That'd be just dandy," he replied. His best people skill was avoidance, but he couldn't use that one presently. She hesitated as a man and woman entered the doors. "Now would be a good time to get started, young lady!" he snapped. Giving orders was his second best people skill. He had a lot to learn about people skills. He impatiently tapped his foot and glared at the couple that was waiting in the lobby.

Finally, the receptionist reappeared with her boss. Casserly continued his glaring. "We need to talk."

"Well, good afternoon to you too, Chief." Casserly made no attempt at niceties. He was glaring even more menacingly—at least that's what he thought. Riddick rolled his eyes, but he led the chief to the most convenient location that wasn't his office—the banquet room.

Casserly cut straight to the chase. "Lyle, I'm a busy man and more'n likely you are too, so lemme get straight to the point. What were you doin' in the Speedway parking lot on the night of the robbery?"

"I was pumping gas, Chief. That is, I was pumping gas until I noticed a critically injured man outside the store."

"Why were you there?"

"At the gas station?"

"Aren't we talkin' 'bout the same thing, Lyle?"

"Yeah, but I already told you I was pumping gas." Casserly's interviewing skills were admirable.

"You didn't happen to be there with Carlton Thomas, did you?"

"Didn't I just tell you that I found him lying injured outside the store? Are you taking notes, Chief, or are you just goin' by memory?"

"D'you know Carlton Thomas?" the chief asked, ignoring Lyle's sarcasm.

"I know of him now, but before the incident I didn't."

"D'you happen to take anything from him on the night of the robbery?"

"Listen, Butch. The only thing he had was a wallet and a credit card that I found in his hand. I assume he was going into the store to make a purchase when he got bashed by the door."

"That's not the way I see it. We got him on video robbin' the place. What I'm tryin' to figure out is what happened to the gun and the money. D'you take 'em?"

"Of course not. Did you? Or that cop of yours that showed up?"

"No need to be disrespectful, Lyle. When was the last time you had this place inspected?"

"Instead of wasting your time threatening me, maybe you should talk to his son. Carlton Thomas was at the Michigan game with his son and grandson. After it ended, Carlton was following his son home, but he stopped for gas on the way. Carlton and I were both at the pumps at the same time. No way he had time to go in, steal money, and come back out before I noticed him on the ground. There was a sports car—some shade of red—in the lot at the time of the robbery. Maybe the person you should really be looking for was in that car."

"Whoever helped him pull this off is who I'm really lookin' for, Lyle. Maybe it was his son, and maybe it was you. Just know that if it was, I'll be back with a warrant for your arrest."

***

Clay and Erika were once again sitting in Carlton Thomas's room in intensive care. The doctors had just left the room after telling Clay how desperate the situation looked. All indications were that Clay's father's condition was deteriorating, and he didn't have much time.

"We were gonna tell him about my abilities," Clay said. "I've gone my whole life lying to people, and the one person I respect the most is never gonna know the truth."

"You're beating yourself up over nothing, Clay. You did what you thought was right based on your own moral values. Not everything's black and white. You chose not to use your powers, and you chose to keep them a secret, knowing that people would always suspect you were manipulating them if they knew about you. You're a good person. There's no reason to regret the choices you've made."

"Maybe you're right, but it doesn't feel right when I'm about to lose him, and I know he never really knew me."

In a comforting gesture, Erika held his hand and smiled that smile of hers that said "I love you" even when she didn't say it. "I'm gonna run and get somethin' to drink. D'you want to come?" she offered.

"No, thanks. I really don't need anything, and I just wanna stay here with him," Clay said as he nodded toward his father.

Erika quietly left the room, and Clay bowed his head once more to pray. He'd lost his mother when he was thirteen. He'd lost his wife just two years ago. He didn't want to lose his father too. He was beginning to think that anyone he loved was cursed. He was tired of trying to be strong and trying to figure out why God allowed such tragedies to happen. As he began to ask God, once again, to spare his dad and bring him back to health, there was an odd movement and an unusual silence in the room. Clay fearfully looked up and understood immediately the difference. His father had just peacefully passed away. Carlton Thomas's body had relaxed and the anguish that seemed permanently etched on his face had finally disappeared. He looked to be at peace.

Tears welled up in his eyes as he reached out and used his thumb and middle finger to close his father's eyes. As he did so, an electrical feeling started in his fingertips and flowed through his arm, up to his shoulder, into the back of his skull, and all the way to his eyes. It was then that he saw a person approaching a glass door. The person had a knit University of Michigan hat pulled low and a Michigan jacket similar to his father's. Clay was sure it was the last thing his father had seen—the thief from the Speedway Gas Station. The thief stumbled and crashed into the door, swinging it violently open. The vision went black, but Clay had been given a brief glimpse of the thief's face.

Tears slid down his cheeks as Clay hugged his father. He, for the first time in several days, looked like his dad again, and Clay knew he was done suffering. For that he was grateful, but his sorrow lingered because he was so disappointed that they'd never discussed the truth that Clay had hidden throughout his lifetime.

"There's no need for tears, Son. I'm happy now."

Clay jerked his head up from his father's chest. It was his dad's voice that he had just heard. He looked at his father, lying completely still on his back, his eyes closed. He didn't appear to have been talking to him.

"That's not me, Clay. That's just my temple. It's just the body that housed my spirit all these years. I'm standing right here."

Clay looked in the direction of the voice, but he couldn't see anything. "Make yourself visible to me, Dad," Clay pleaded. "There's something that I need to tell you. I think God's giving me a chance."

"I don't know how."

"Do you want me to see you?"

"Yes." As he said the words, his body materialized, and Clay could see it.

"Dad, I love you. I'm so sorry."

"Don't be sorry, Clay. I'm happy. I already know I'm happy. I'm on my way to see my Savior, and when I'm done, I'm gonna find your mother. I've missed her so much all these years, and now I get to see her. I'm sorry to leave you and Tanner behind, but you have your own chance to love like I did."

As Clay responded, Erika slid quietly into the room. "I already did, Dad. I loved Jessie like that. I miss Mom, and I miss Jessie too. You're all gone now, and my heart's broken." Erika watched as tears formed in her eyes. She could tell that Carlton had died, just as easily as Clay could tell. She also could tell that Clay was having a conversation with his father.

"I'll find Jessie and tell her that. She knows you loved her, and she knows you miss her." Erika couldn't hear Carlton; however, she stood still during the pause in hopes that she didn't disturb anything, but she felt guilty listening to Clay.

"Dad, I can't explain it all, but losing Jessie—I loved her so much, Dad—was the consequence of me doing something I shouldn't have done. I never told you, but I'm getting a chance right now. Ever since I was a boy, I've had powers to manipulate people's minds. I did my best to not use my abilities, but I failed. A person that I humiliated killed Jessie to get even with me. It was my fault—I'm responsible for Jessie's death. I've gone through my whole life keeping my abilities secret, even from you. I was going to tell you last weekend, but you got hurt before I had the chance."

"Clay, I love you, and I've been proud of you my whole life. When you were born, we thought you might die, and we thought you might have brain damage. Instead, God chose to spare you. You're my gift, and he must've given you a gift too. Then He miraculously spared Tanner too. Your life is blessed. Whatever mind powers God gifted to you, you need to use them for good. You shouldn't be ashamed. You're perfect the way you are, and God didn't make a mistake."

"Sure, He gave me gifts, but He took Mom, and then He took Jessie, and now He's taking you. It must be His way of punishing me for my sins."

"Now, you know better than that, Son. God took us when it was our time. He'd taught us what we needed to know, and He'd let us experience what He wanted us to

experience. When we reach the point that He has planned for us, He takes us home, complete. You're looking at life through your own filter. It's time you looked at it through God's."

"I miss Jessie. Our problems were gonna be fixed. She finally knew about me too, and she'd made up her mind to trust me and make our relationship work. God took her before we had a chance. I'm afraid I can't love Erika like I loved Jessie because Jessie will always be a part of me; she's always in my memory, and I can't forget. I love Erika, but I'm afraid God'll take her too. I'm afraid to give her my whole heart."

Erika's tears started flowing. She loved Clay. She loved him in high school. She had visions of a long, happy life with him now that they were finally together, but now she was hearing things that hurt her terribly. She was hearing only part of the conversation, but what she was hearing was too unpleasant to bear.

Carlton responded to Clay: *"He took her away so He could give you Erika. Just like always, God has a plan for you, and that plan includes that beautiful woman who is standing at the doorway. That plan includes her, Clay."*

Clay turned his head just as he saw Erika leaving the room.

He was torn. He wanted to go to Erika, but he wanted to finish his conversation with his dad. He looked his dad's way in desperation. *"It's time for me to go home now, Clay. He's calling me home. I love you, and I love Tanner and Erika too. Tell them for me. Goodbye, Son…"* And just like a dad, he spoke his final words. *"I trust you to do the right things."* He smiled and faded away. He was gone, and so was Erika.

Jeff LaFerney

Chapter 10

After a full day of making funeral arrangements and doing paperwork that he had no interest in, Clay was in a deep dark place. Erika had been by his side to support him, but her joy and energy, the things besides her fantastic beauty that made her so unique and so absolutely attractive, were missing. He'd asked her to dinner in hopes of discussing what she'd heard in the hospital, but she had declined. Part of the conversation that they'd had kept replaying in his head:

"After the funeral, I'm going to visit my parents in Florida."

"Why would you do that when I need you here more than ever?"

"Really, Clay? Do you even know what you need? Do you have any idea what
 you want?"

"I want to find the person who's responsible for my father's death. I want to keep
 my word to Bosley Pemberton and find his murderer. I need to grieve my father's
 death."

Clearly, Clay was a moron. As he thought about it, he'd realized that wasn't what she was talking about. She was talking about them. She had heard him say things that made her doubt how he felt about her, and he was too dumb to figure it out until after she walked out on him a second time. So now, in an attempt to keep his mind off his father and his problems with Erika, Clay was at a fall league baseball game at Genesee Fieldhouse watching a Fenton area travel team. The weather was decent, so the game was being played outside. He came to watch Ace Royster, who was at the top of his list of star pitchers to recruit for his U of M baseball team. He was a good all-around player, but he had a great arm, and Clay had gotten word that he would be pitching.

Clay's attempt to be alone and inconspicuous was amazingly ineffective. He wore no Michigan gear advertising his baseball team, and he stood as far away from the parents as he could. He didn't feel like talking to anyone, and he wanted time to think. He hid his small radar gun in his jacket sleeve, and he hadn't even taken out his stopwatch to time the pitcher's move and delivery because after two innings, Ace hadn't given up a base runner. Nevertheless, the crazy man who had been yelling at the umpire since the first pitch was standing over his right shoulder, trying to read his radar gun.

"Eighty-nine?" he exclaimed. "There's something wrong with that gun of yours, Coach."

"The gun's fine. I've been noticing that the kid does a pretty good job of mixing up his speeds. Top speed of 93, low of 85. Change up clocked at 79 and 81 the two times he's used it."

"I'm the kid's dad—Matt Royster. We got lots of schools looking at him. Where you from?"

"I coach at Michigan." Clay could smell alcohol on Royster's breath.

"We don't know if we're goin' there, Coach."

"Well, I haven't offered a scholarship yet, Mr. Royster."

"You will; I can guarantee that," he said with unshakable confidence. "And we'll let you know what we decide. Gonna be lots of offers."

Clay didn't like the man already. It could have been because he was in a bad mood, but more likely it was because Matt Royster was unlikable. "You know, Mr. Royster, when we recruit players for our team, we look at more than just what kind of arm they have. Academics, citizenship...family," he emphasized. "They say that the apple doesn't fall far from the tree." Clay was a bit testier than usual.

"Don't matter to me what they say. When it comes right down to it, you'll be offerin' a scholarship." He walked away to harass someone else.

The odd thing was that Clay really did want to offer Ace Royster a scholarship on the spot, but when recruiting pitchers, he tried to wait until during the spring season to be sure that the kid's arm wasn't injured or the kid wasn't going into the draft. Belligerent parent or not, the kid was incredibly gifted, and Clay was sure he had the stuff to be successful in college.

By the time the third inning was completed, Ace's team was up 3-0, and Matt had spread the word that Michigan was at the game and ready to offer a full-ride scholarship. Becca Fonteneau's son was the left-fielder on Ace's team. He'd driven in two of the three runs with a double. Out of curiosity, she wandered over to Clay.

Clay saw her coming. She was tall—maybe 5'10" or a bit taller. She was dressed attractively in a stylish leather jacket and tight-fitting jeans. She had intense looking, big, brown eyes with beautiful, long eyelashes. Her less-than-shoulder-length blond hair was spiked and streaked in an eye-catching manner. She had a rolled-up magazine in her hand. She tripped over something in the grass and appeared a bit embarrassed as she looked to see if Clay saw the stumble—which he did. Matt was in the middle of a tirade against the umpire who had called ball four, putting a runner on base for the first time in the game. Apparently, Ace Royster only threw strikes, and the umpire must have been conspiring against Matt Royster's boy.

"Hi, there. I'm Becca Fonteneau. Excuse my klutziness. I hear you're from U of M. What do you think of our star pitcher?"

"I'd say he's pretty impressive, Becca. I'm Clay Thomas, and it's nice to meet you."

"What do you think of his father?"

"I've only spoken to him once, so I'm gonna reserve judgment."

"Oh, how refreshing. You're choosing to show restraint. I like it."

"That was a horrible call, Blue!" Royster yelled at the umpire. "You just cost my son a perfect game! Get a clue, Blue! I got me some glasses I could loan you. Wait, when you're blind, glasses wouldn't do any good, would they?"

"Is he always like that?" Clay asked Becca.

"Sometimes worse. He seems to think that the more abrasive he is, the more calls he gets from the umps. He also seems to think you have a scholarship in your pocket and the only reason his son hasn't signed it is because he's waiting for a better offer."

"Believe it or not," Clay smiled, "I don't walk around with scholarships in my pocket. It keeps me from tearing them up when I meet abrasive fathers."

"I like you, Clay Thomas. Makes me feel a bit guilty that I initially came here for selfish reasons."

"What reasons? I don't mind…really." Clay rather liked talking to the woman. She made him forget his problems for a minute. There was something about her that was familiar, but he couldn't put his finger on it at the moment.

"Well, my son's the left fielder. He's a good player. Certainly not Division I like Ace, but someplace smaller…Division II, NAIA, Community College. What's your opinion of him?"

"He's the kid that doubled in two runs, right? Good swing. Left-handed bat. Runs well."

"Very observant! I'm impressed. You not only have good looks and a sense of humor but outstanding skills of observation to boot."

"And on top of that, I'm a nice guy."

"I'm not so concerned that you're a nice guy," she flirted. "If I give you my number, will you call me to talk to me about his future? Or maybe you could call me to talk about our future?"

Clay actually blushed a little. She was very pretty, and Clay wasn't used to a female being so forward. "I'm sure your husband wouldn't be too happy about that."

"Oh, I'm not married. Never have been. How about you?"

"I was married, but my wife was killed nearly two years ago. I've been in another relationship for nearly a year."

"I'm sorry about your wife. And I'm sorry about your girlfriend too." Her eyes were stunning, and Clay couldn't help but look into them. "I'd like for you to be interested in me. Do you mind if I stay and talk with you?"

Clay smiled. It felt good to be encouraged. He found that he really did feel interested, even though he knew nothing would come of it. He was dating the perfect woman, and he wasn't willing to screw that up. Nevertheless, he spent the rest of the game talking to Becca. Her son had another single and a stolen base and made a nice running catch on a fly ball—one of the few well-hit balls against Ace Royster. The game ended with Ace's team ahead 7-0. He gave up a bunt single, an infield single, and two walks in six innings. Apparently the umpire was getting tired of being verbally abused, so he seemed to be aiding Ace with several questionable calls. The kid was good and didn't need the help. Interestingly, just like Matt said, Clay wanted to offer Ace a scholarship.

***

Zander Frauss rose from his knees where he was praying once again for forgiveness and wisdom. He'd been packing things in his office all day after hearing from University officials who had pulled financial backing for his Department of Perceptual Studies. His latest grant proposal had already been rejected, but the University money would have been enough to keep the laboratory operating until he could find another source of funding. With the latest news, he knew he had no chance of survival. The ironic thing was that Zander had learned what he'd set out to learn and had subjects who could prove his theories, but they weren't willing to cooperate or even to share the knowledge of their abilities. He was being shut down for not doing what he had actually done.

The door to his laboratory opened as Zander rose. He turned toward the doorway, and his blood pressure immediately rose to dangerous levels. Walking into his lab was Tanner Thomas. "Going somewhere, Doc?" Tanner asked as he observed the boxes and covered equipment.

"The lab's been shut down, Tanner. What do you want?"

"I want to know what's going on, Zander."

"I don't know what you mean. Nothing's going on."

"Except your lab's being shut down. You won't return my dad's calls. You ignored his request for help and advice when my grandpa was in critical condition in the hospital— he died yesterday, by the way. Your wife thinks you're having an affair. And I saw you leaving the scene of a crime in Fenton last Saturday. Besides that, and the fact that you look terrible, I suppose it's possible that nothing's going on, but I doubt it."

Zander cringed at Tanner's words. Everything he'd said was disturbing, but Zander ignored his guilt and common sense and decided to defend himself. "Tanner, you don't have any right talking to me like that. I'm a professor at the University, and you're just a student. My relationships are none of your business. And I'm sure you're mistaken about the crime scene accusation. I was in Ann Arbor Saturday evening at the game and at a tailgate afterward, and then I went home."

"You're lying. If my dad wouldn't be so disappointed in me, I'd make you tell the truth. There's another option, you know. You could tell us, and maybe we could help."

"You can't help me. Any problems I have are my own, so I'll deal with them myself. Please go now. I'm sorry about your grandfather. Please tell your dad I'm sorry. But please just leave me alone."

Jeff LaFerney

Chapter 11

Clay left the game with his thoughts swirling. Though he was grieving his father's death, he was excited about a terrific recruiting prospect. He couldn't understand why his best friend had abandoned him, and he was worried about his relationship with Erika, but strangely enough, he found himself thinking about Becca Fonteneau, with whom he had exchanged numbers at the ballgame. With all that was going on in his life, how in the world did he find himself interested in another woman? Shaking his head as if rattling the marbles loose, he did the most prudent thing, however, and gave Erika a call. He made small talk about the baseball prospect that he had just scouted, but just as he was about to ask Erika to meet with him again, his phone beeped from another call. "Hold on just a minute, Erika. I'm sorry, but I've got another call...Hello."

"Hi, Clay, it's Becca."

"Oh, hi. I didn't expect to hear from you so soon. Is there a problem?"

"No...There's no problem. I just wanted to tell you how much I enjoyed talking to you today. I was thinking about you, so I figured I'd call. I hope you don't mind."

"No, I don't mind. I enjoyed talking to you too. Normally I just stand alone when I'm scouting. It was nice to have some company."

"Thank you. I know I'm being forward, but would you be willing to meet me for a drink?"

"Today? No, I'm sorry. I have a date already…At least I'm on the phone with my girlfriend, *trying* to line one up. She's a bit upset with me right now." Clay felt guilty that he actually liked the idea of talking to Becca more than Erika at the moment.

"Oh, yes. The lucky girlfriend. Well, I have your number, so I suppose I can try again some other time."

"I don't know if that's a good idea. I'm in a committed relationship."

"Yes, you told me that already, but I told you that I'd like you to be interested in me. And since I can be hard to resist, I thought I'd call and see if I got lucky."

Clay couldn't help but smile and be flattered. The only time he'd smiled in the past couple of days happened to be because of her. He was glad he was in the car away from Becca. And with Erika waiting on the phone, it made her request a bit easier to turn down. "Well, you have my number, and I promised to make some calls for you about your son, so I'm sure we'll talk again. In the meantime, have a great day."

"Oh, I will. I always have some exciting adventure or another planned. I'll try again some other time. Goodbye, Clay."

"Bye, Becca." Clay switched the phone back over to Erika. "You still there?"

"Yes. Who was that?"

"Oh, it was just a parent of a ballplayer I'm recruiting. It was nothing. Listen, I'm almost home. Let me hustle in and change, and then I'll come get you. We need to talk."

Clay turned the corner on his street. There in his driveway was a police car. "What the…? There's a police car in my driveway."

"What's going on? Is everything all right?" Erika asked.

"I don't know. I'll get back to you." He hung up just like that, making Erika feel left out once again.

***

Bosley Pemberton hadn't heard from Clay in two days, and it put him in a chilling mood. He was impatient to find answers, yet at the moment, he couldn't be sure if he'd ever see Clay again or not. The thought of fulfilling his purpose and finding his murderer was obsessing him more than usual, and his mood reflected his anxiety.

Bosley was one of four ghosts in the Fenton Hotel. There was an odd bearded man who rarely appeared, and when he did, he simply looked around. He didn't communicate with anyone and seemed mournful and distantly curious. He liked to look through windows, and in the old days was known to occasionally look inside a second or third story window from the outside of the building. Lyle put a stop to the sightings by boarding up the windows, so the bearded man only occasionally wandered around with nothing to do.

There was a playful young boy as well. He liked to run through the restaurant and lobby but stayed out of the bar as if he knew he didn't belong there. He liked to knock menus onto the receptionists' heads, open doors, set signs and lights swinging "all by themselves," and play pranks like moving silverware or blowing out candles or opening the cash drawer. He was harmless, and Bosley enjoyed having him around.

In Bosley's opinion, the final ghost was evil. She was angry and despondent and frustrated. The ghosts in the hotel hadn't shared their purposes with each other, but Bosley always felt that the angry woman needed to forgive someone or maybe get some sort of revenge. Maybe both. When she revealed herself, she would pull wineglasses by their stems off their perch and throw them across the bar. She would knock hanging pots and pans to the floor in the kitchen. She would bump or grab customers or take money from paying customers and disappear. She spent a lot of time in the women's bathroom, which was cold year around, and she would play with the hair of women in the far third stall of the ladies' room. Bosley figured that all ghosts were unhappy, but the woman in the Fenton Hotel was more unhappy than the rest.

On this particular evening, Bosley was in a sour mood. He wanted a drink, so he sat down on the far end bar stool and waited for the bartender to notice him. Maggie was not working, which was good for Bosley. Maggie didn't really believe in ghosts, so she couldn't see him, but the fill-in, Lonnie, believed, so he occasionally served Bosley a drink. He walked over and said, "Can I get you something?"

Bosley always ordered a Jack Daniels on the rocks. He didn't know why. It was his drink of choice, and even though he was unable to actually drink from the bar, he got a bit of pleasure from making the order. Lonnie turned away from Bosley and prepared the drink, but when he returned, the ghost had disappeared just like he'd done many times in the past.

"Hey," Lonnie asked a man on a barstool several seats down, "did you see where that guy went?"

"What guy?"

"You didn't see that guy on the end who ordered a Jack Daniels?"

"There ain't been no one sittin' there since I came in. You must be mistaken."

"No, I talked to him and everything. Weird. I gotta tell Lyle about this. It's happened before, you know."

"Yeah, real weird, Lonnie. Can you get me another beer?"

Though he enjoyed spooking Lonnie, the fact that he couldn't drink his whiskey put Bosley in an even more somber mood. He wandered farther into the Tavern and observed the evening's entertainer singing at the hotel's piano bar. There was something about the live entertainment that made him sad, but he often stood and listened anyway. If the song was right, sometimes he even joined in. After four or five songs, Bosley heard the familiar introduction of a twelve-string guitar. The unusual sound evoked an eerie mood that fit the lyrics perfectly. "The Invisible Host" was the song of choice for the female singer. Bosley slipped in beside her behind the microphone. When she got to the words "You're not heaven, and you're not in hell," he joined in the singing.

A few customers began looking around when they heard the male voice coming through the speakers. The hired performer gave no sign of recognition, but simply continued into the chorus. Bosley joined in:

> "Welcome to the world between two worlds
> It's a lonely place
> It's a fall from grace
> Plenty to learn, but I'll be your host
> Years to burn…you've become a ghost."

Again, a few patrons seemed to be looking for the singer's male counterpart. After the chorus, Bosley discontinued his singing. People accepted that the voice must have been a taped background track or some such thing.

They continued eating, drinking, talking, and laughing. But finally, the song hit the last verse and Bosley joined in again:

"The one thing I remember
Was floating through the door.
I looked for a place to go
A place I knew before.
'Sir, what am I?' I asked
To a near invisible host. He said,
'Can't you see you're floating there?
Can't you see you're now a ghost?'"

Bosley actually had a good voice. It seemed natural to him to join in with the singing, like he knew what he was doing. His anxiety at the moment added a bit of desperation to his singing, however, and he belted out the last two lines more forcefully than he should have. Many of the folks in the Tavern felt the desperation of the words and again looked anxiously around. Lonnie, at the bar, had heard the voice before but never in a way that made him feel so uncomfortable. He now had two stories to share with Lyle the next time he saw him.

***

Clay pulled into his driveway and climbed out of his car. Butch Casserly was just returning to his car after ringing Clay's doorbell. A second officer was standing beside the police cruiser and seemed a bit jumpy as if he expected some action.

"Is there something I can do for you, Chief?"

"Yes, sir. We came all the way from Fenton to have a chat. Do ya mind if we ask you a few questions."

"I guess not. What's this about?"

"We're hoping you'll be cooperative."

"Now, why wouldn't I be cooperative, Chief?"

"I don't know. You tell me."

"Is that one of your questions? I actually have something to do this evening, so could we move this dialogue along?" Clay asked.

"You betcha. Where were you at 12:08 AM on the morning of Sunday, September thirteenth?"

"I was in my car about five miles north of Owen Road on US-23."

"How're you able to answer that question so specifically?"

"Because I was on my way home from the Michigan-Notre Dame football game. My father was following me because he was going to stay with me overnight and spend some time with my girlfriend and me on Sunday. I happened to look at my clock when he pulled off to get some gas. It was 12:03. That means about five minutes later I would have been about five miles down the road. Is there a specific reason that you're asking me that question?"

He ignored Clay's question. "So you weren't in the parking lot at the Speedway Gas Station is what you're saying?" Chief Casserly asked.

"The Speedway is where my dad was, but I was driving down the expressway."

"Hmmm. That's interesting, Clay. We already have confirmation that you actually were at the game with your father. The two of you were together that evening."

"Until the game ended. Then we departed in separate cars. He was following me home until he stopped for gas."

"The two of you pulled off at the Speedway together. Isn't that correct?"

"No, it's not."

"We have a witness that saw your car at the gas station."

"No, you don't. I already talked to Lyle Riddick too, in hopes of finding out who really robbed the gas station. Lyle thinks there was some sort of sports car of some shade of red in the parking lot. But it wasn't me."

"We also have a witness that claims the thief had a gun. Your father doesn't own a gun, Clay."

"Exactly. So he wasn't the thief."

"But you have one. And a concealed weapons permit to go along with it. Did you have your gun that night, Clay?"

"It was in a case, unloaded, in the trunk of my car. I didn't take it into the game, obviously."

"We have your father on video, robbing the store clerk inside the store. He fell while exiting the crime scene and injured himself. Because he was discovered without the money or the gun, the logical assumption is that someone took the gun and escaped with over six hundred dollars in cash. We believe that person is you."

"Chief, that's absurd. First of all, my father was not the thief. Secondly, I was not there. And thirdly, you're suggesting that as my father's accomplice, I sent him in to rob the store and then left him with a life-threatening injury so I could get away with not enough cash to buy a good personal computer. You have a strange way of investigating a crime. Why don't you try to find out what really happened?"

"We have a warrant to search your house for the cash. We would ask that you kindly let us in to search the premises."

When Clay let the men in, they went directly to his bedroom. Within ten minutes, they had found a Dort Federal Credit Union envelope with cash that Clay used for spending money. In it was seventeen twenties, eight tens, and four five dollar bills for a grand total of $440.00.

"That about clinches it. Clay Thomas," Chief Casserly said, "you're under arrest as an accessory to armed robbery. You have the right to remain silent. Anything you say can and will be used against you in a court of law. You have a right to an attorney. If you cannot afford an attorney, one will be appointed for you. Do you understand your rights, Clay?"

Clay had the mind power to end the ridiculous charade right then and there but decided against it. "Yes, sir, I do. But mark my words, Chief. You're gonna be mighty embarrassed when this case is over."

Jeff LaFerney

Chapter 12

Clay rode handcuffed in the back seat of the police car to the Fenton City Police Department. He was upset by the stupidity and impatience of the Fenton police chief, who was more interested in getting an arrest than in finding the guilty party. He was escorted into the building before he was freed from his handcuffs. He was then taken through the humiliating process of being photographed and fingerprinted. His valuables were documented and inventoried and taken away in a bag. His gun and the money taken from his house were labeled and put into evidence. A good hour and a half after his arrest, and two hours since his earlier call to Erika, he finally was allowed to make a phone call.

"Hello," Erika answered, unaware that the call from Fenton was coming from Clay.

"Erika, it's Clay."

"What's going on? Why haven't you answered your phone?"

"I couldn't answer it because I've been arrested."

"What? For what?"

"The amazing Chief Casserly is bound and determined to pin accessory to armed robbery on me. Doesn't matter that

I was never even at the station or that my dad's innocent. He just wants an arrest."

"Why you?"

"Because I have a gun. I had over four hundred dollars of cash in the house, and I have a red sports car. Plus he believes my dad is guilty, but since he didn't have any cash or a gun, Casserly assumes he had an accomplice. My dad was with me at the game, so the chief figures I arrived at the station with him."

"Everything's circumstantial evidence. He can't possibly prove anything, can he?" asked Erika.

"I don't know, but I'll be spending the night in lockup. They'll take me to the Genesee County Jail tomorrow, where I'll have to wait for a bail hearing in front of a judge. I need you there to post my bail, and you need to bring my lawyer with you."

"Your lawyer? Who's that?"

"Jasper, of course. Call the little guy and bring him to the courthouse tomorrow, okay?"

"Jasper? Are you sure? Does he have any criminal defense experience?"

"Doesn't matter, Erika. I'm innocent. He'll defend me in court, and when I get out, Tanner and I will find proof. We'll find whoever did this to my dad, and I'll make sure he pays for it."

"I'm so sorry you're going through this, especially now. What're you gonna do about the funeral home viewing?"

"Hopefully, I'll be out before then. And call Tanner for me, okay? This is gonna tick him off, and I don't want him to do anything impulsive."

"Jasper's more impulsive than Tanner," Erika said.

"Maybe so, but he has a law degree. He'll get me released, and that's all I need. Please, just give him the facts and have him find out the hearing time. Then just make sure both of you are there, okay? Everything'll be all right."

***

Erika called Jasper, who was nearly hyperventilating when she reached him.

"It's nice to hear from an old friend," Jasper wheezed. "To what do I owe the pleasure?"

"What's that horrible sound you're making, Jasper?" Erika asked.

"Um, I've been running," he suggested without conviction.

"Do you have asthma?"

"No, I think I have asphyxiation."

"Caused by what?"

"Running?" he choked out even less convincingly.

"Running with a bag over your head or what?" Erika asked.

"I wish. It might keep the horrible smell away."

"You're running from a smell?"

"I've been running from the skunk that sprayed the horrible smell."

"A skunk was chasing you? I've never heard of such a thing."

"Actually, I was chasing it...hence the running. It was squatting under my porch. But we barely got a good trot up before he stopped and started spraying. I tried to avoid it—did a back handspring and everything—but it got me. I ran into my unattached garage and stripped my clothes off to shed the smell. Problem is, now I'm naked, and the clothes are still with me in the stinkin' garage, and, again, I'm naked, so I can't leave...and I basically can't breathe either, which should explain the wheezing."

"Sounds like you have a problem, but I'm calling 'cause Clay has a worse one."

"Erika," Jasper choked out the words, "if his problem is worse than a stinking, naked midget with no way to get home, it must be something big. Let's hear it before I expire from my own stench."

"He's been arrested as an accomplice to armed robbery. He's innocent, of course, but he was booked in Fenton and will be transported to the county jail in Flint for his arraignment in the morning. You need to make some calls and let me know when to pick you up so you can be there for the arraignment."

"I'm honored that he wants me, but I'm not a defense attorney, you know."

"He asked for you. Find out the hearing info and call me back. Oh, and good luck getting into your house," she giggled. "Jasper, Clay's innocent. He'll prove it. He just needs you to get him out of jail."

Chapter 13

District Court Judge Jonathon Leskowski presided over Clay's arraignment. An associate for the district attorney, Monica Grey, was present at the hearing. Per request by Jasper, Clay was allowed to appear in person rather than via video from the county jail.

After sitting on a guarded bench outside of the courtroom with Erika, Clay's name was announced, and he was directed to meet with the judge. Erika breathed a sigh of relief when Clay and Jasper entered the courtroom. Jasper still smelled like a skunk. Upon entry, a court bailiff announced the case. "The people verses Clay Thomas."

The judge, with a document in his hands, said, "Are you Clay Thomas?" He glanced at Jasper, but ignored him.

"Yes, sir," he responded.

"You've been read your rights?"

"I have."

"You understand that you have the right to an attorney, and if you cannot afford one, one will be appointed for you?"

"Yes, sir. I have an attorney."

"Then I assume that he was informed of the arraignment time. Are you planning on proceeding without him?"

"Jasper here is my attorney, Your Honor."

The bailiff handed the judge a document. The judge read the paper, finally giving Jasper a closer look. He looked a bit skeptical as he spoke to the little person. "You're Jasper Bugner?" he said to Jasper.

"Boo."

"Did the midget just 'boo' me?" he asked the bailiff.

"Did you just call me a midget?" Jasper gasped. "My name is pronounced 'Boog-ner'," he said. "And I'm feeling a bit disrespected at the moment. I'm a little person, Your Honor," he said sarcastically as he climbed up on a table to improve his stature. "One would think you'd be a bit more politically correct in your position."

Monica Grey giggled as the conversation continued.

"My sincere apologies, Mr. Bugner. And would you please step down off that table. I'm feeling that any climbing on furniture in my courtroom—by a person of any size—is a bit disrespectful of me. Now, may we continue?"

Jasper jumped from the table that he had angrily climbed upon and said, "We may." Clay shook his head. Monica smiled. Jasper's antics were unpredictable, to say the least.

The judge scrunched up his face and looked to the bailiff. "Joe, could you identify that horrible smell for me?"

"Your Honor, I believe it's Mr. Boooogner," he said with extra emphasis.

The judge raised his eyebrows. "Explain," he demanded to Jasper.

"I was sprayed by a skunk, Your Honor, and I've been unable to completely rid myself of the smell. I apologize for the inconvenience. My intent is to end this hearing quickly, so I can take my aroma and my client home. He's been subjected to a night in jail for a trumped up charge. He should be released immediately."

"He isn't here to stand trial, Mr. Bugner. He's here to have his charges read to him, to make his official plea, and to determine whether bail is necessary. Then I'll set a preliminary hearing date. I've already decided that there's sufficient evidence to make your client stand trial on the charges filed. So, again, may we continue?"

Jasper nodded.

"Clay Thomas, you've been charged as an accessory to armed robbery. The robbery took place at 12:08 AM on Sunday morning, September thirteenth, at the Speedway Gas Station on Owen Road in Fenton, Michigan. How do you plead?"

"My client is absolutely not guilty."

"That remains to be determined, Mr. Bugner. Now, in regard to bail, what are you recommending, Ms. Grey?"

"The charges are felony armed robbery, Your Honor. The people recommend you set bail at $10,000." It was obvious that she spoke the words without conviction, but it rankled Jasper nonetheless.

"I object, Your Honor!" Jasper shouted out. "Mr. Thomas has no priors. He's an upstanding citizen with ties to the community. This was not a violent crime, and he is not a flight risk. For Heaven's sake, sir, his father is in a funeral home, awaiting his funeral, and his son is a college student at the University of Michigan. He's got no interest in running from a crime that neither he nor his father committed. I respectfully request that you release him on his own recognizance."

"It's not appropriate for you to object in an arraignment hearing, but I tend to agree with you. Your client may be released on his own recognizance, and I apologize for the time that you've already been incarcerated, Mr. Thomas. If there are no further objections, Mr. Bugner, I believe we can skip a preliminary hearing and move to a speedy trial.

Monday, September 28, is available. What do you say about that?"

Jasper looked to Clay, who knew there was no real evidence linking him to the crime. Clay shook his head yes. He just wanted to get out of jail so he could get to the funeral home. After the funeral, he would find the answers to the mystery, and he would find the person responsible for his father's death. "That's acceptable, Your Honor."

"Good. Your case will be sent to Circuit Court where you'll be assigned a judge for your trial. And Mr. Bugner, I would recommend that you do not show up smelling like you do today. You're dismissed."

***

Clay was led back to the County Jail, where he was forced to endure the release process. He was given his clothes, and eventually he also reclaimed his personal effects. While Erika and Jasper waited patiently, Erika used her phone to research how to get rid of skunk smell on skin, and she gave the recipe to Jasper. "I don't want you near me again until your smell is bearable. A quarter cup of baking soda, a quart of hydrogen peroxide, and a teaspoon of liquid soap. Mix it up and then lather up in the shower. Let the mixture sit for five minutes before you rinse it off. Do it again if it doesn't do the trick the first time. I found a separate recipe for getting the stench out of my car. It's basically a fumigation bomb. Thanks, Jasper. You reek."

"I'm gonna need a couple of those bombs for my house and garage," Jasper said.

When Clay finally emerged, he gave Erika a long, long hug, actually lifting his gorgeous, tiny girlfriend off the floor. "You know, normally, I love smelling you, but I have to say, you smell like a skunk. Just tell me that we're gonna ship Jasper home in a box. We don't have to ride with him all the way to Durand, do we?"

"Ha, ha, Mr. Funnyman. I'm the one suffering here."

"They kept my gun and money as evidence, Jasper. I need to get the gun back."

"We've got other more important things to worry about than that. We have to start planning your defense."

"I'll give you a list of things to do. While you work on my defense, I'm gonna find the real thief. That's why I need a gun."

"Just settle down, Big Guy. There'll be no need for a gun."

Just then Clay's phone started ringing. "Hello…Oh, hi," he said pleasantly… "Um, I had to deal with a situation where I didn't have my phone…No, I can't. I'm with Erika and a friend. I'm sorry…We'll see. Listen, I have to get going, okay?"

Erika didn't like the tone of his voice.

"Okay, sure," he said. "Goodbye." He had a stupid grin when he turned back to Erika and Jasper.

"Who was that?" she asked.

"Just a parent of a recruit. No one important."

"Yeah, right. No one important except she got you to have that stupid grin that was on your face. And you talked to her in your sweet voice."

"Sweet voice? What're you talking about? I don't have a sweet voice."

"Oh, yes you do. Is that the same parent that called you yesterday when you were on the phone with me?"

"Yes, but it's nothing to worry about. I already told her about you."

"Oh, you've talked about me. What is this? Lemme see your phone."

Clay handed it over, and she looked at his call record. "She called you seven times since yesterday evening when you were thrown in jail. You have nine missed calls. Two

109

from me on Wednesday evening and seven from her. What's her name?"

"It's Becca Fonteneau. Her son was playing in the game I watched on Wednesday. I told her I'd make some contacts for her to help her find a school for her son."

"You said that she was the mother of one of your recruits. That's what you said Wednesday too. What's true, Clay?"

"He's not one of my recruits."

"And what can't you do with her because you're with me and Jasper?"

"Um, she wanted to get together and go over my list of names. She's just a bit overenthusiastic is all, Erika. I guess she's a go-getter, you know?"

Erika stared into Clay's eyes. "You're actually interested in this woman, Clay. I'm not stupid. I can tell."

Clay looked at her apologetically. He knew what she was thinking. He shook his head no, but Erika just turned and headed to her car. It was going to be a long ride to Durand and back, and with Jasper along, the drive was going to stink in more ways than one.

Chapter 14

The county prosecutor, Irving Morrell, was talking with his associate, Monica Grey, when Chief Casserly arrived for a scheduled Friday morning meeting. "Morning, Butch," Morrell said.

"Mornin', Irv. Got any coffee?"

"Help yourself," he replied while organizing a pile of papers. "Butch, are we going to have a problem when Thomas's attorney shows up today for discovery evidence? You said this case is cut and dried. Monica, here, says her gut tells her he isn't guilty. What do you say about that?"

"First of all, Irv, I ran this by you before I arrested him, and you agreed with me. Secondly, we have his father on video robbing the place. We have an eye-witness that claims the thief had a gun. Carlton Thomas was with his son, Clay, at the Michigan football game, and even Clay admits that they were in separate cars but traveling together to Flint. But when we discovered there was a robbery, there was no cash and no gun. Clay Thomas had both, and we have another eyewitness that admits to seeing a red sports car on the scene. That's what Clay drives. He must have taken the cash and the money with him and fled the scene. He's scum if he left his father like that. I wanna nail the monster."

"Okay, the video evidence is pretty damning, so let's stick with it. His attorney is scheduled to be here any time. Do you have any other evidence at the moment?"

Morrell's desk phone beeped as Casserly pulled out a file. Morrell answered his phone. "I'll come out in just a moment," he said. "What's in the file, Butch?"

"It's the information about all the other mysterious robberies that've occurred in the last few weeks. I believe Clay Thomas had something to do with them, as well."

"You might want to keep that under wraps, for a while, Butch...at least until we investigate and look at the evidence." Morrell then opened his office door and stepped into his lobby. Monica had warned him about what he was about to see, but Morrell was still a little surprised. Seated in his waiting area was a midget. He was sitting all the way to the back of the chair, and his feet barely hung over the edge of the seat. He had curly, reddish hair and was wearing suspenders, a long-sleeved white shirt, and a big orange bow tie. His face, neck, and hands were an acid-burned red from the baking soda and hydrogen peroxide baths he took to remove the skunk smell. He looked like a clown. He scooted his butt forward in the chair until his legs were dangling, and then he jumped down to the floor. He had crooked front teeth as he smiled and held out his hand.

The D.A. spoke first. "Mr. Bugner, I'm District Attorney, Irving Morrell. We've been waiting for you. Welcome. May I get you a cup of coffee or some water?"

"No, thanks, Irv, and you can call me Jasper. I just crashed your party soze you can give me the tiny bit of circumstantial evidence you have, so I can get to work makin' you and your office look remarkably stupid. Clay Thomas and Carlton Thomas are innocent. The next time you see me, you'll be droppin' the case and tryin' to figure out what to do so we don't sue you for false arrest. My client spent the night in jail during which both his and his father's names have been defamed. I'll be thinkin' of a really big number for our settlement. I'm hopin' you'll be thinkin' of a similar figure 'cause otherwise we'll be makin' a big noise in the papers. I was seein' that you're up for reelection in November. That's not too far away now, is it?"

"You talk really big for a midget," said Casserly. "We'll prove he's guilty."

Jasper had been anticipating Casserly's quick tongue. "I have two issues with you, Chief," replied Jasper as he turned his attention from Morrell. "First of all, I don't particularly like being called 'midget.' It tends to make me angry, and you won't like me much when I'm angry. Second, I believe you have the burden of proof in this case. That burden's going to be a bit more than you can bear—even on those broad shoulders of yours—I fear. But that's what the courtroom is for. I don't believe that's what the newspapers are for. Yet, somehow, I have an article right here which names both my client and his father as the guilty parties for the Speedway robbery. It also says right here...um, just a minute...it says, 'An investigation has commenced in an attempt to link Carlton and Clay Thomas to the other unusual robberies that have occurred in town in the past three weeks." Jasper paused for effect. "Now the way I see it, once the case is dropped, there'll be a defamation lawsuit against you, Chief Casserly, which coincides with our wrongful arrest lawsuit against your D.A."

Casserly's face was moving to a shade of red nearly identical to Jasper's. The district attorney spoke first, however. "I was unaware of any article, Butch."

"He's guilty, and so is his father!" Casserly shouted. "And I'm not gonna let some little red dwarf try to bully me. I'll prove he's guilty if it's the last thing I do!"

"It may be the last thing you do in your current line of duty, Butch, because my client's innocent, and you made a colossal mistake arresting him." Jasper turned to the district attorney. "Irv, I'm here for my discovery evidence package."

Morrell pulled the package from his desk and handed it to Jasper. Jasper smiled and said thank you. "Before I leave, Irv, I expect information for each of the other robberies for which your chief of police is accusing my client. Clay and his father had nothing to do with any of those either, which will be even easier to prove than the Speedway robbery—not that that their innocence in that robbery won't be easy to prove too."

The D.A. reached out his hand and glared at Casserly, who put his file folder in it. He then leaned out of his doorway and told his secretary to copy all of the contents of the file to give to Jasper.

Jasper had a satisfied smile, but before he left, he turned to Monica Grey. "Ma'am," he said, "you're a very attractive woman. Please accept these as a token of friendship." As he spoke, he pulled a bunch of flowers from his sleeve, just like a circus trick. Monica couldn't help but smile.

Casserly couldn't resist. A hot temper and a loose tongue happened to be two more of his personality flaws. "Look at him. He's nothin' but a circus clown. When we get to trial, ain't no one gonna take this midget seriously."

"We *ain't* goin' to trial," Jasper mocked. "And someone's gonna take the fall for this, Butch. It's unlikely that it'll be the District Attorney, and it certainly won't be the pretty Monica Grey. And Butch," he added, "just so you know…you've gone and made me angry." Monica smiled again as Jasper excused himself and left the office to get his additional copies from Morrell's secretary.

***

The funeral was on an overcast, gray, misty day. Nearly every bad memory Clay had in his life was somehow associated with rain, but since her death, it always fondly reminded him of Jessie. So, as his windshield wipers slid across his windshield, Clay thought of Jessie once again. Tanner would arrive from school for the funeral, which was in Haslett, Michigan, where Clay grew up and his father lived. It was at the Pioneer Baptist Church that his father attended. Depressingly, Erika was also driving separately. She was planning on visiting her son at Michigan State University after the funeral. She was going to let him have her car while she flew down to Tampa, Florida, and visited her parents. Somehow Clay would deal with his grief alone while trying to figure out what happened to his relationship with Erika. Solving two crimes, hopefully, would keep his mind off his problems.

The majority of guests were from the church and from Haslett. Carlton's family consisted of Clay, Tanner, a brother from Iowa, and a sister and brother-in-law from Battle Creek, Michigan, and their three kids—Clay's only cousins. It was a terribly small family, and made the loss of his father even more devastating. The pastor was a nice man, even younger than Clay, and apparently he'd invited the whole church and half the town of Haslett. The church was packed.

There was a nice simple message about salvation and about how Clay's father was so respected. Clay was barely listening. He was supposed to speak, and he was worried about breaking down. There was a hymn, "Amazing Grace" maybe, but Clay wasn't paying attention. The program said that he was next.

He climbed the steps to the pulpit, and set some notes on the dais. His hands were shaking a bit. He looked at Tanner who sent him a message. *"Take a deep breath and relax."*

"*I know that,*" he thought back and then smiled because it was all so pointless. "*Forget about the notes and speak from your heart,*" he told himself. He pushed aside his notes, looked out into the packed auditorium, and began.

"My dad was my hero. After my mother died, he was pretty much my whole family. He did everything he did, just for me. Today, as I stand before you, I'm broken-hearted. But my father is not. My father taught me about Jesus, and he always told me that 'to live was Christ, but to die was gain.' He meant it. He looked forward to Heaven and always felt he was just an alien living here on Earth. His real home where he belonged was Heaven, and he's there now. My dad only loved one thing more than me here on this Earth, and it was my mother. She passed away almost thirty years ago, but he was never interested in another woman. Now he's with her again. My father died a tragic death, and I'm going to miss him terribly, but it gives me joy to know that he's finally where he belongs. He's at peace, finally experiencing life abundantly, just like he wanted. I know there are people here that are grieving just as I am, but what we really should be doing is celebrating. He lived his life thinking of others before himself, and his reward was to be yanked from this world and deposited right where he's always wanted to be. I'm—we all are better people for having known him. It's time we celebrated that Carlton Thomas finally got what he wanted all along. I love you, Dad, and I'm going to do my best to make you proud the rest of my life." Then he thanked his audience and sat down.

For the next thirty minutes, various people stood and told of the unselfishness of Carlton Thomas, but Clay wasn't listening. He'd spoken from the heart, and it was time for him to begin moving on with his life.

There was a very short reception, but again, it went like a blur. Finally, at the end, Clay was faced with Erika and her decision to leave.

Erika Payne was not a particularly complicated woman. She was smart. She was joyfully enthusiastic. She was beautiful. And she wanted to be loved. Everyone wants to be loved, but Erika didn't go through life gloomily wondering what was wrong or what she wanted; she knew what she wanted. She wanted to be loved, and she wanted to be loved by Clay. Clay wasn't like other men in her life who claimed they loved her because she was so beautiful. Clay treated her with respect and honesty, and Clay was a committed person—committed in everything he did. But she knew deep down in her heart that Clay needed time alone to figure things out. Once he did, he'd be the person she was willing to wait for, but she wasn't willing to watch while he went through the process. She needed to leave, so he could struggle through it alone and make up his own mind. So she sat down with him for a moment and held his hand. "I'm going to visit my parents. I'm long overdue, so this is a good opportunity. When you're done with all you have going on, you know where to find me."

"I don't want you to leave," he said.

"I know you, Clay. I know you struggle through things on your own, and while you struggle, you help people. You're just like your dad. Except he always knew exactly what he wanted and exactly why he did the things he did. You've kept things so bottled up for so much of your life, sometimes you lose track of why you're doing the things that you do. But when you figure it out, there you are, putting yourself second, and doing all the right things. You've got some people to help and some thoughts to sort out. I've no doubt that when you're finished sorting, you'll do the right thing like you always do. I just hope it includes me. But I

117

need you to love me completely. Until you can do that, I'll be in Florida. I have to go now. I'm meeting Logan, and he's taking me to the airport."

"This isn't how it needs to be, Erika."

"Yes, it is. For me, at least. I have to go." She gave Clay one of her signature hugs—the one that made Clay not want to let go, but he did. He listened to people he loved, and whether he agreed with Erika's choice or not, he believed she had the right to make it. He would consider what she said, and when it was time, he'd know exactly what to do.

With tears in his eyes, he watched her go. His heart was aching. What more could happen to him? She walked away without even looking back—proud and determined to do as she had planned. What he didn't see were the tears flowing down her cheeks. Erika's heart was aching too.

***

A large crowd had gathered at the nearly sold-out Ivan Williams Field for the Fenton verses Brandon High School football game. Linda and Mona were taking tickets at the main gate as the clock wound down toward the end of the second quarter of play. Only a few occasional stragglers were still entering the stadium.

"Let's start bundling the money, Mona," said Linda. "We'll be closing the booth in just a few minutes."

Mona looked up. "Hello," she said pleasantly to a new Fenton Tiger fan. "If you're willing to wait until halftime, we won't have to charge you."

"*Let me wait inside the booth with you,*" both women heard inside their heads.

"Why don't you wait inside here," Mona suggested. "It's chilly out there."

"Come on in through the side door," Linda said.

Linda and Mona watched the door open and welcomed the stranger into their ticket booth. "Hi. It should only be a few minutes. The second quarter's almost over."

"Hand me your money, please. I'll be taking it with me," Linda and Mona heard.

"We were just bundling the money for deposit at the bank, but how about we just leave it in the money box for you?"

"No, thanks. Just put it all in this carry bag, please."

The women began stuffing the bag full of money. It was a busy night. Nearly 3,000 fans had entered the stadium at their gate, paying five dollars per person. They were going to hand over something near $15,000.

Once they handed over the money, they heard, *"You won't remember me. You won't remember any details of the robbery. All you'll remember is that a man you've never seen before robbed you."*

Two men saw the thief exit the ticket booth. They heard, *"You don't remember seeing me."* They watched the thief stroll away. The older gentleman of the two said, "It's halftime. Let's help gather the money from the ticket booth." They knocked on the door and then entered. There was Linda and Mona, but there was no money. "What happened?" asked the older man.

"We were robbed. A man took the money. Did you see anyone?" Linda asked.

"No," the younger man answered, "and we were standing outside the booth the whole time."

Jeff LaFerney

Chapter 15

Clay made some phone calls, watched a video, and endured a nearly sleepless night, tossing and turning with too much on his mind to rest peacefully. The grief he felt at the loss of his dad was magnified as he remembered funerals for his mother and wife, and he felt alone knowing Erika was in Tampa. When he couldn't take it any longer, he got up and prepared a nice breakfast for himself and Tanner, who had considerately spent the night.

When they sat down together, Tanner noticed the weariness in his father's eyes. He didn't know what to say, so he skipped the small talk and went right to the plans he had for the day. "I brought my own personal box of detective materials. I got some things from my professor at school. It's time we put an end to this whole robbery thing."

"What do ya have?"

"A tape measure, a camera, and some chemiluminescence solution." He smiled when his dad wrinkled his forehead. "I'll explain that later. I also brought some evidence bags, a blood test kit, and a small tape recorder. Jasper sent a copy of the video of the robbery and gave me the list of all the robbery locations in town. I watched the video, and I think we need to go to the gas station first."

"I watched the video last night too, and I made a couple of phone calls from that list of Jasper's. There're some people on the list that we'll be able to talk to today if we want." Clay paused, and let loose a stream of sad, frustrated breath.

"You okay, Dad? D'you wanna talk?"

Clay hesitated. The mixture of feelings he had was hard to verbalize. He had spent a lot of years not talking to his son, but now that they shared mental powers, their relationship had improved tremendously. At the moment, Tanner was the only person to talk to, so he inhaled deeply again, and spoke, "I'm just really, really discouraged right now."

Tanner could have asked the stupid why question, but he wisely kept his mouth shut and let his father continue in his own way.

"I feel like God is just heaping more on me than I can bear. I just buried my dad. He and I are accused of a crime we didn't commit. I've hurt Erika, and she's left me alone to figure my life out without her input. And I went most of my life without a close friend, so when I finally had a friend that I could be honest with, it hurts that Zander's abandoned me too. I just don't feel strong enough to handle it all at once."

Tanner waited patiently until he was sure his father was done. "I don't remember you telling me what to do very many times in my life, Dad, but I remember you giving me advice quite a lot. I actually listened once in a while," he said with a smile. "It seems to me that when I had problems you said things like, 'the fire tests the quality of our works.' You said that 'all things work together for good for those who love Him.'"

"I remember saying those things. I remember believing those things, but this just seems like more than I can bear all at once."

122

"No, it's not. What was the verse? 'He'll never give us more than we can bear.' Dad, what I remember most about all those words of wisdom is when you said, 'When God begins a work in us, He'll carry it on to completion.' You said that God has an endpoint planned out for us, and he has a place for us to be eventually. The trials make us mature and complete, but they're never more than we can bear, and we can always know that until we get to that point, we're bulletproof. You're bulletproof, Dad. Everything that's happening has a purpose to get you closer to completion. If there's more for you to accomplish, then you're not complete, and you're still bulletproof. You have God's promise that you're stronger than these trials, so let's set them aside, and solve them one at a time. Don't you think that's what you need to do right now?"

"I'm not Superman, Tanner. I'm just a man."

"But you can do things that an ordinary man can't, and you've been given things that ordinary men couldn't handle. Take those gifts and solve your mysteries. And Dad? You've always been Superman to me. You're gonna be all right."

Clay couldn't help but smile. "I know you were taking about my powers, but my greatest gift is you. You're right. It feels strange taking advice from my son, but you're right. Let's head back to Fenton and start putting the pieces together, and let's do it together."

***

Butch Casserly was furious. There was no way some little, red-faced midget was going to get the best of him. He was sure Clay Thomas had helped his father rob the gas station and was determined to prove it. He also had a hunch that Clay had some part in the other robberies. He'd assigned a department employee to research everything about Clay's background and was currently reading the file that was produced. There was nothing.

He was a star high school athlete who had graduated with honors. He received a football scholarship at Eastern Michigan University, but he dropped off the team his sophomore year and focused on getting a teaching degree. He was a high school math teacher and baseball coach for several years while earning a Master's degree in math, which led to a teaching and coaching job at Mott Community College in Flint. Two years back, his wife had been killed. Clay took the varsity baseball coaching job at the University of Michigan. He still lived in Flint. He had no criminal arrests or record, no financial problems—not even a poor driving record. His only child, Tanner, was a star college basketball player at the University of Michigan.

Clay was squeaky clean except for a run-in with a criminal named Jack Harding a couple of years back, and a run-in with a couple of bad guys named Marshall Mortonson and Dan Duncan about a year ago. Dan Duncan happened to be a cop. Both he and Mortonson were currently serving time in the state penitentiary. A police detective in Flint by the name Lance Hutchinson was named in the Jack Harding report, and the police chief in Durand by the name of Luke Hopper was named in the Mortonson and Duncan arrest reports. With nowhere else to turn, Butch decided to contact the police officers.

His call to Flint and Detective Hutchinson came up empty. All he learned was more details about Clay's wife's death and the amazing ability of Tanner as a basketball player. There was a foiled kidnapping and a murder, but Clay appeared to be a victim, not the perpetrator. His call to Durand was a different story, however. Luke Hopper explained how Clay solved a seven-year-old mystery with his "special talents." When asked what he meant by "special talents," Hopper suddenly had very little to say. He vouched for Clay being a stand-up guy. He admitted to not trusting

Clay initially, but then he spoke to a doctor friend of his at the University of Michigan—a Zander something or other. The doctor spoke highly of him, and sure enough, Clay turned out to be a trustworthy person. The cause of the disappearance and death of a man named Adrian Payne was discovered by Clay, and he helped put two men into jail for a very long time.

Casserly couldn't pry any more information out of Hopper, but he had a name—a lead. He checked the University faculty directory at U of M. There was only one Zander, as he suspected—Zander Frauss. He was a neuroscientist who was in charge of a special division called The Division of Perceptual Studies. Apparently, Frauss studied elements of parapsychology: mind control, telepathy, extra sensory perception, telekinesis, clairvoyance, hypnosis, and precognition. Pertinent questions started arising in the chief's mind, which was an entirely unique experience for the man. Somehow the victims of the robberies weren't able to remember any details about the perpetrator. What if the thief could somehow control their minds? He momentarily forgot about his desire to pin the robberies on Clay. Maybe Frauss could tell him if his theory was possible, and in the process, maybe he could also find more out about Clay Thomas. It was time to head to the campus at U of M.

***

Clay and Tanner pulled into the parking lot of the Owen Road Speedway Gas Station in Fenton. Tanner reviewed what he had in mind with his bag of detective tricks.

When he was finished, Clay said, "Okay. I don't know what chemilumajiggy solution is, but you're the aspiring criminologist. You lead the way."

"I'll let you hold the tape measure so you don't feel insignificant," Tanner joked.

"Gee, thanks."

Tanner had his focused look—the one he had when he was playing sports. He had an intensity that was admirable. That, as well as his tremendous confidence, which made him an unusually effective leader, was a big part of the reason he was such a fabulous athlete. He seemed to be focusing that same intensity on the investigation. He walked through the entry doors, followed by his father, and walked right up to the checkout counter. "We need to measure the height," he said.

Clay pulled the tape from the tape measure and placed the end on the floor. The counter top measured exactly thirty-four inches. Tanner jotted the number down. "Why're we measuring this?" Clay asked.

"Because I can do a mathematical equation and figure out how tall the thief is from the video that Jasper sent me. If the thief and Grandpa were different heights, I can prove it."

He then turned and walked back to the exit door. He looked at a picture that he'd printed and touched a spot on the glass of the door. "Measure how high this is above the floor," he directed.

Clay measured it out at forty inches. Tanner recorded the number. Then, without a care in the world about what customers at the gas station might think, he stepped back, walked toward the door and fell into it. As he lay on the ground, half-way in and half-way out of the doorway, he told his dad to measure where his head was resting. "Two feet, three inches," Clay said.

Tanner sat up and wrote down the number. Then he stood up and stepped outside of the doorway. He looked over at Eddie, the cashier, who was watching him with the same interest as several customers. He pulled the door open a couple of feet and held it against his temple. "This measurement won't be accurate because there's nothing on the video to show where Grandpa was standing when the door hit him, but the door flew open when the thief hit it, and the door hit him in the temple, so it was probably about this far open when it hit him. Measure to my feet."

Clay did it. "Two feet exactly," he said. "How do you know it hit him in the temple?"

"Because he was only bleeding from one place on his head—at his temple—and when I got here that night, there was blood on the door edge. We'll get to that in a minute," Tanner said confidently. Next, he pulled out a spray bottle and a camera. He handed the camera to his dad. "It's pretty easy to work. Just turn it on and then snap a couple of pictures of the door both from the inside and out."

Clay followed directions and then asked Tanner what he was doing.

"I have a homemade blood identification system. I got some luminal powder from our lab at school. I mixed ten milliliters with ten milliliters of hydrogen peroxide and point one grams of potassium ferricyanide. I'm going to spray the solution where blood might be. If the solution contacts blood, it'll cause the iron in the blood's hemoglobin to catalyze and there'll be an oxidation reaction. For uneducated people like you, what I'm saying," Tanner smiled, "is that if the solution makes contact with blood, there'll be a reaction which makes the luminal glow blue. When it happens, take some pictures. You'll have about thirty seconds."

"Sounds fun. I'll try to keep up."

First Tanner sprayed the edge of the door. Immediately, it glowed blue. Clay snapped several pictures. Tanner then got out a couple of Q-tips and dabbed at the solution, making sure he had a couple of blood samples. Clay photographed the procedure. Then Tanner put the swabs in a plastic bag and labeled it. Next, he opened the door a couple of feet to get an estimate and sprayed the pavement near the bottom of the door's edge. It lit up in several small dots. Clay took numerous pictures of the blue glow. "Blood spatter from the collision with the door," Tanner explained.

Then he estimated where he thought his grandpa's head was lying. After a couple of sprays, he quickly found the spot where the blood had pooled. Clay snapped several more pictures. Then Tanner grabbed a rock that was lying against the side of the building and sprayed it. It immediately glowed blue, so Tanner set it exactly in the middle of the pool of blood on the spot that wasn't bloody. Clay took some more pictures. When he was done, Tanner said, "Now, measure the distance from the doorway to the rock. This is where Grandpa's head was lying."

Clay handed Tanner the camera and stretched the tape out, measuring six feet, two inches from the doorway. "That's about four feet past where the thief's head would've been when he fell, Tanner. Anyone can see that my dad didn't rob the store, then fall through that doorway, hit his head on the outside of the door and then fall on a rock more than six feet outside of the store."

While he was talking, Tanner took out a several more Q-tips and swabbed the ground where the blood had pooled and the rock that caused the serious injury to his grandpa. Clay took pictures, and then Tanner bagged the evidence and labeled it. He re-sprayed the blood spatter on the pavement, and they went through the same process to bag the evidence. "All we have to do now is test the blood to prove that it's Grandpa's," Tanner said as he got out his test kit. "I looked at Grandpa's chart in the hospital. His blood type is AB positive. That's not all that common."

Just then Clay's phone started vibrating. He answered the call from Jasper. "Hello."

"Clay, I just got confirmation from the credit card company. Your dad finished pumping his gas at 12:09 AM.

That's when the transaction ended. That proves he wasn't in the store at 12:08. I'll bet if we check his wallet, the receipt'll be in it, but it doesn't really matter 'cause I'll have the company confirm the time of the transaction."

"That's great news, Jasper. We've gathered some evidence also that'll prove he wasn't in the store. We've got some other things to do, but I'll get back to you when we're done."

After he ended the call, Clay looked at Tanner, who said, "This blood is AB positive, so at least we have proof that it *could* be Grandpa's."

"Well, that's one more piece of the puzzle, and Jasper has confirmation from the VISA company that my dad wasn't in the store during the robbery. I think it's about time we went inside and had a little conversation with Eddie."

Jeff LaFerney

Chapter 16

Zander Frauss was sitting in his faculty office at the University, perusing four of his patient file folders as he was prone to do, when his secretary entered and announced, "There's a Chief Casserly from the Fenton Police Department here to see you, Doctor."

Zander stood quickly as his pulse quickened and his blood pressure increased dramatically. Casserly pushed his way into Zander's office and asked, "Dr. Frauss?"

"Yes, I'm Zander Frauss...I don't recall having any appointments today. Is that correct, Janie?" he asked his secretary. "You never schedule me for appointments on Saturdays."

"That's correct, Dr. Frauss, but he just barged in anyway," Janie said defensively.

"Maybe it's inconvenient for you, Doc, but it's police business, and I'm gonna speak to you whether I'm on your calendar or not," Casserly said. Bullying was his specialty.

"It *is* inconvenient. Set up an appointment with Janie, and come see me when I'm available." Zander's heart was beating double-time.

"I could do that, Doc, but I'm a busy man. How 'bout we have a chat right now?"

Zander already didn't like the man, but Casserly was used to that reaction. There wasn't much to like about him. Zander took a deep breath to try to relax and finally sat back down on his desk chair. "It's all right, Janie. I'll talk to him." He was flustered when he set the file folders on his desk. Two names remained hidden, but the folders fanned out a bit, and there on the top two folders were two names that Casserly recognized—Bosley Pemberton and Clay Thomas.

Casserly shook off an initial feeling of shock when he saw the file folders. He was there to ask about mind control, but when he saw Clay Thomas's name on the tab, he said, "Is there a specific reason that you're reading Clay Thomas's file?"

"Is there a reason that you're asking?" Zander said a bit too defensively as he gathered the files back up and stuffed them in a desk drawer.

Casserly felt defensive himself, for some reason, but tried to remain composed. "I happen to be here on account of Clay Thomas," said Casserly. "Fellow cop in Durand mentioned that Clay had some, and I quote, 'special talents.' Seems he's associated with you, and it seems you're associated with a department that studies parapsychology. How 'bout you tell me how he's been usin' his special talents to rob numerous places of business in Fenton?"

"You're looking for the wrong person," Zander blurted out. He wasn't thinking clearly. He'd asked God to get him out of his mess, not get him further *into* trouble.

"Now, how would you know that, Doc? You know somethin' you're not tellin' me?"

"I know that Clay Thomas would never use his powers for selfish gain." There it was. Zander had no intention of saying what he'd just said, but he'd said it anyway. It was the first time he'd ever betrayed Clay's desire for secrecy.

The words hung in the air like a bubble in a cartoon, waiting to be reread and comprehended.

"What kind of powers does he have, Frauss? How's he gettin' away with all those robberies? Can he make people forget who he is? 'Cause none of the victims seems to remember a thing. Is that how he's doin' it?"

"He's not 'doing' it."

"He's been arrested in connection with an armed robbery at the Fenton Speedway, and he's goin' down, Doc. If you're withholding evidence in a felony, you're goin' down too. Since that robbery, his phone records say he's made exactly seven phone calls to you. Maybe you know more than you're sayin'."

"You're making wild speculation, and you don't know a thing, Casserly. I have a hunch that it's contrary to your personality, but you'd be wise to look in a different direction. I think you should go now."

"Clay Thomas ain't gonna know what hit him when I'm done with him. No little midget man is gonna embarrass me like that lawyer of his. Clay did it, and I'm the man to prove it. And I suggest you stay outta my way, or I'll run you over too."

"There are people in this world that actually have integrity, Chief," said Zander as he stood up behind his desk to make himself somewhat more imposing. "Clay's one of those people. You'll find out you're wrong. I don't have the power to see the future, but I'm guessing that when this is over, the person who'll be damaged the most is you. Now, get out of my office."

Casserly left, and Zander literally collapsed onto his knees on the floor. "The person who may be damaged the most is me," he said to himself. Once again he began to pray. "I deserve it, God. Instead of helping me out of this, you're gonna make me pay, aren't you? I'm watching my life fall apart around me, but it's my own fault. I pray to you, and my prayers don't make it past the ceiling. Tell me what you want me to do. I don't know what to do."

***

Clay and Tanner once again walked into the Speedway Gas Station. A female with a badge that said "Connie" was restocking candy. Clay approached her. "Is there any way we could pry Eddie, over there, away from the counter?" Clay pointed his thumb in Eddie's direction as he spoke.

"Who are you?" she asked.

"We'd like a few minutes to talk to Eddie about the robbery about a week ago."

"Are you cops? 'Cause if you're not, he's workin'."

"Is there a manager here?" Tanner asked.

"I'm the assistant manager. Eddie said the cops said not to talk to no one."

Tanner shook his head sadly and then controlled Connie's mind. "Well, if he can't talk to no one, he must be able to talk to someone. I happen to be someone. Tell Eddie someone's here to talk to him. It's okay for him to talk to someone, Connie."

"Eddie, take a break. I'll cover for ya. Someone's here to talk to you."

"And, Connie," Tanner smiled and pointed to his dad. "This man is nobody. If any cops come here and ask if anyone came to talk to Eddie, don't tell them someone was here; tell them nobody was here, okay? You can't remember someone. You'll only remember that nobody was here." Tanner was enjoying slinging indefinite pronouns around.

She went off to work the cash register. Clay smiled at Tanner's sense of humor. "Do ya think Eddie'll be as weak-minded as Connie was?"

"More'n likely."

Eddie slowly approached the men. "Who are you?"

134

"We'd like to talk to you a few minutes, Eddie, about the robbery about a week ago."

"Are you cops? 'Cause if you're not, I have work to do."

"We asked your manager," Tanner said.

"She ain't the manager—she's just the assistant—and the cops said not to talk to no one," he replied.

Tanner looked at his dad. "Do you think I saw into the future? I'm pretty sure I already had this conversation. Does everyone in Fenton speak in double negatives?" Tanner rolled his eyes and shook his head again and then controlled Eddie's mind. "You can't speak to no one, but you can speak to someone. I'm someone. He's nobody, so don't concern yourself with him." He looked at his dad who was shaking his own head with a grin. "Let's go into the office."

They sat in chairs in a small office space. Tanner flipped on the tape recorder.

"I'm tape recording our conversation, Eddie, okay?"

"Okay."

"Good, now tell my dad what you remember about the robbery last Saturday night."

He turned and looked into Clay's eyes. "I remember comin' in to work. It was busy at first but was slowin' down a little before midnight. I was ticked that I couldn't see the end of the Michigan game, but I was just sittin' at the counter, readin' a magazine. Then the chick I was workin' with rang up a sale and went to put some cash in the drawer. There was a couple bills in there, but it was mostly empty. She asked where the money was, but I didn't have a clue. I didn't have it, and we couldn't find it. So she ran out and brought the cop in and told him we was robbed."

Clay was reading his mind to see what he left out, but there wasn't anything. He asked, "You don't remember anything about the robbery?"

"Nope. Nothin'," Eddie replied.

"But you identified the thief. You said he had a gun."

"I saw the dude on the video. That cop with the flat top showed it to me. He was wearin' a Michigan hat and jacket. I gave him a sack of money and a magazine, and he left. Then he fell into the door and got hurt, and they found him in the parking lot."

"Look me in the eyes," Clay said. "You don't have *any* memory of what the thief looked like?"

"I don't remember anything except what they showed me in the video. Except he had a gun, and he threatened me about callin' the police."

"How do you know he had a gun?"

"I just do. I mean, I didn't see one—not that I can remember, at least. But I just know somehow."

"There was no gun in the video," Tanner said. "There wasn't even any evidence that anyone ever talked. Your lips never moved, Eddie. Did you talk to the guy?"

"I don't know. Maybe. Maybe not."

"Did he say he had a gun?"

"Not that I remember. I just had a feeling, I guess."

"Look me in the eyes one more time," Clay ordered. "Now, I want you to picture exactly what you saw during the robbery, and tell me about it."

"There's nothin' there, Dude. Only thing I remember is what I saw on the video."

Tanner flipped off the tape player. They let Eddie go back to work, and they left the office and store and got in Clay's car. "Did you see anything when you read his mind?" Tanner asked.

"Not a thing."

"He's a doofus, Dad. Maybe he was scared and he's repressing the memories."

136

"No, there's nothing there. That's the weird thing. His memory's a complete blank. It's like it's been completely erased."

***

She was in the parking lot at Target. Shirley Maxwell set a sack with a new four-slice toaster, a four-pack of Chapstick, a birthday card for her mother, and some Hall's cough drops onto the back seat of her car. She closed the back door, opened the front door, and climbed into the front seat of her green, 2009 Toyota Camry.

As she turned the keys in the ignition, there was a tapping on her driver's side window, so she pulled back the automatic window button and let it sink into the door. "I'll be needing this vehicle, Ma'am. Please get out of the car and step aside."

The woman climbed out of the car. Once the car thief entered the car and moved the seat back a bit, Shirley actually asked, "Will I get it back?"

"You don't even remember speaking to me, and you won't remember your car is missing until you get home. How far away do you live?"

"Five or six miles."

"You'd better get walking then."

The woman nodded her head, looked for traffic, and walked across the parking lot on her way home. The car thief smiled, started the car, pulled out onto Owen Road, and headed for North Leroy Street. The idea was to drive to some local fast food restaurants and rob each of the drive-through windows. With a hooded sweatshirt, a Braves baseball cap, and some reflective sun glasses, the driver's first stop was Burger King. When the Camry pulled up to the menu board, a chipper voice said, "Welcome to Burger King. Are you ready to order?"

"Um, I'll have a Whopper, small fries, and a Diet Coke."

"Will that be all?"

"Yes."

"Okay, your total is $5.49. Please pull up to the second window."

At the window, the cashier leaned forward and said, "That'll be $5.49, please."

The cashier smiled pleasantly at the driver and heard in her head, *"When you bag my order, also fill the sack with the money from your register."* The cashier then took the ten dollar bill that was offered her.

She slid the window closed temporarily, then returned and handed back $4.51 in change. She then handed over the heavy food sack filled with money.

"Thank you!" the driver said.

In her head, the cashier heard, *"When I drive away, you won't remember me at all."* Except for a vague memory of a mid-sized, light green, sporty-looking car, the girl's memory was completely erased.

"You're welcome. Have a nice day!"

"I'm having a wonderful day, thank you."

After a quick stop at the McDonald's and the Subway, each time successfully cleaning out the restaurant's drive-through cash register, the car was returned to the Target parking lot. The keys were left under the front mat, and the door was left unlocked.

When the robberies were discovered, three mystified fast-food employees told nearly identical stories to the police authorities. No one remembered a single significant detail, save the one vague memory of the light-green sedan which "might" have been involved. In total, nearly $700 was neatly removed from the tills.

Chapter 17

A waitress at the Fenton Hotel Grille brought Cokes and a spinach and artichoke dip appetizer for Clay and Tanner to snack on. They were rehashing their most recent interviews, but Clay was also keeping a sharp eye out for Bosley's ghost.

Clay had a notepad and pen out. "Okay, so before the Speedway robbery, there were reported robberies at Café Aroma, Gerych's Distinctive Flowers, and the Fenton Kar Wash, all on West Silver Lake Road. Since then we know of two others at the Mug and Brush on Silver Lake Road and the Fenton High School football ticket booth off from the stadium on Owen Road," Clay recounted. "We don't really have any idea if the thief has gone outside of Fenton, but if not, every robbery has been right in town."

"That could mean that the thief is from here," said Tanner.

"But it would have to be someone unknown or the person is taking a huge risk of being seen and recognized."

"Or he has stones the size of bowling balls."

"True. Or it could mean the thief is from nowhere around here."

"Then why so many robberies from this one town?"

"Maybe the thief has something against someone here...like the police chief. He's a moron, Tanner. I wouldn't mind takin' him down a notch myself," said Clay.

"So you have that notepad. What're you thinkin'?"

"Nobody remembers a thing at the Speedway, the café, or the flower shop. Even the one lady from the football game doesn't remember. And it's not that they're hiding something from the cops. I wondered if they were stealing from their own places and it was just coincidence that all the robberies happened so close to each other. Or maybe they were all scared and were hiding the thief's identity. But their minds are erased. I've read them all, and there's nothing there to remember. It doesn't make sense. They can remember right up to and right after the robberies, but nothing whatsoever about the robberies."

"We told them not to lie, and you read their minds, so it seems like we didn't learn a thing," Tanner said.

"Sure we did. We learned that someone's controlling people's minds. I can't think of any other explanation. Can you?"

"Maybe someone that we haven't talked to yet will remember something."

"I doubt it. I'll find the kid at the car wash and ask him the same questions, but I have a feeling his story's gonna be the same."

Just then Clay got another phone call from Jasper. The waitress returned with Tanner's sirloin burger and Clay's fried cod sandwich. "I've been making calls quite a bit today," Jasper explained. "I've got your Verizon phone records and credit union withdrawal slip. I got some help from Chief Hopper out in Durand to get GPS tracking records, and we can prove that you texted and called Erika from your house in Flint at 12:26. I can prove that you didn't have time to get home if you robbed your father from the parking lot."

"Thank you," said Clay. "We all knew it was just a matter of gathering all the facts to prove it, but it's still a relief to know it's all coming together."

While they were sitting at the table, Tanner was studying the video of the robbery. He had taken his dad's notepad and was doing some calculating. "Here's a couple of other things, Dad," Tanner said excitedly. "I blew the picture up so I could do some measuring. Since the counter top is thirty-four inches, I can figure out how tall the thief was—well, almost. Grandpa's six one and a half. The thief, with stocking cap and all, is only six feet tall. If it was Grandpa, figuring some height enhancement from the hat he was wearing, he'd be about six foot three, but the thief is about three inches shorter than that."

"That's more good news…"

"There's more." Tanner cut off his dad. "Look here. The thief had on tennis shoes! I can't believe no one noticed that before. Grandpa had on loafers. Does Grandpa even have tennis shoes? You're free and clear, Dad. And Grandpa's name'll be cleared too."

It felt good to have some good news, but before Clay could even comment, sitting to his left with a discontented scowl on his face was Bosley's ghost. He was tapping his fingers on the table impatiently. "*So what have you learned*?" he asked.

***

Matt Royster was in his bedroom reviewing his bank accounts and bills. In walked his wife, and the nagging began. "What're you doing? I asked you to rake the leaves today. Why can't you just do what I ask?"

"I told you I'd do it."

"When? In November? What's so important that you can't just do one simple task for me?"

"Nothing…nothing's more important than you! Why can't you just let me live my life without you nagging all the time? I swear you're giving me a brain tumor. My head hurts all the time."

"That's not the only thing I'd like to give you. You drink all the time; you never pay the slightest bit of attention to me. You're out doing who knows what when you should be home helping out around here. Are you gambling again? Where's all the extra cash coming from?"

"What extra cash?" That was a lot of questions. Too many to answer, so Matt just focused on the one that indicated an invasion of his privacy.

"All the cash that's hidden in your sock drawer. What'd you do, rob a bank?"

"That's my money that I've been saving up. Don't you dare touch any of it."

"Something's going on, Matt."

The migraine headache was back. There was an agonizing pain in the back of his neck which shot all the way to his forehead. "Just leave me alone, okay? I'm sick of you prying and meddling in my life!" He was rubbing his temples furiously and felt sick. Matt rushed to the bathroom and threw up in the toilet, relieving some of the pain in his head.

"Are you okay, Matt?"

He turned and looked into her concerned eyes. "Just go away, would you? Just go away!"

His wife turned and walked away, and Matt collapsed on the bathroom floor. Something had to change, or she was going to literally drive him to an early death. He needed to get away and get away soon.

***

The waitress at the Fenton Hotel Grille returned and asked Clay and Tanner, "How's the food today?"

"It's great," said Clay.

"Is there anything I can get you? Would you like a refill on your Coke?" she asked Tanner.

"Sure, that'd be great. Thanks."

"I'd like a Jack Daniels on the rocks," said Bosley.

The waitress nodded and disappeared. "You can drink?" Clay asked as soon as the waitress was out of ear shot.

"Course I can drink," said Tanner. "What're you talkin' about?"

"Not you. Bosley. You're a ghost, but you can drink?"

"No, but it doesn't stop me from ordering one. I get cravings for Jack Daniels once in a while, so I ask. Can't drink it though."

The waitress returned and set Tanner's Coke on the table. She grabbed the glass of whiskey and looked toward Bosley's ghost, but he wasn't there any longer. "Where's the man who ordered the drink?" she asked.

"You must be mistaken," Clay said, feeling badly for the girl. "There's no one here but the two of us, and I didn't order anything."

"I swear a man ordered a drink. That's so weird..." She walked away shaking her head, and then Bosley was sitting at the table again.

"Well, what have you learned?" Bosley asked again.

To Tanner's surprise, all of a sudden, there was a person in the seat to his left and to his father's right who was staring right at him.

"*If you can fly, I want you to hover right over the table*," Tanner thought. Bosley started floating over the table.

"What the heck!" said Bosley. "Why am I up here?"

"Is that the ghost you're talking to?" Tanner asked. "Floating above our table?"

"Yep. That's Bosley. Bosley, that's my son, Tanner. You wanna stop fooling around and stop floating up there. You're not scaring anyone."

"You can stop floating," Tanner thought to Bosley. And Bosley sank back down and seated himself in his chair.

"What was that all about?" Clay asked. "Are you done fooling around?"

"I didn't do it on purpose. I don't know what got over me," Bosley said.

"You?" Clay sent a telepathic message to Tanner.

"Uh huh," Tanner smiled and thought back.

The anxiety he'd been feeling seemed to slip away as he fought back the urge to laugh. Tanner's mind powers were incredible; he could even manipulate ghosts it appeared. He turned to Bosley. "One of the reasons we're here in town today is to start your investigation, Bosley. It's been a tough week for me, but I'm ready to go now. As soon as I get done eating, that is."

"Well, I have a lead for you. A lovely lady by the name of Bonnie Webster was in here this week. Heard her say she ran the Fenton Museum. Seems she sees herself as some kind of town historian. Besides, Lyle Riddick, she seems like the next best person to start talking to." And just like that, Bosley was gone.

When their waitress returned, they learned that Lyle wasn't expected at the hotel until about 2:30. She knew where the Fenton Museum was when they asked. They were on North Leroy and just had to head south. It was right across from the police department on South Leroy. Clay paid for the meals, left a good tip, and the Thomas men headed out the door to continue their detective work.

Chapter 18

Chief Casserly was fuming. While he was in Ann Arbor, three calls came in from restaurants just down the road from the police station. There had been three more robberies and no one had any information about them. No one remembered a thing except for a ditzy girl at Burger King who thought she remembered a mid-sized, sporty-looking, light green car. When asked if the thief was in the car, she didn't remember.

Then there was a call-in from the husband of a lady named Shirley Maxwell who claimed to have lost his wife's light green 2009 Toyota Camry. The husband claimed his wife arrived home from shopping at Target without her car and without her packages, and she had no idea why she left them. Considering the walk was more than five miles, Mr. Maxwell assumed the car had been stolen, but Casserly's men found it in the Target parking lot. It matched the description of the airheaded girl at Burger King who couldn't figure out why her cash register was empty, but it seemed to be just a strange coincidence.

What made Casserly angry, however, was that while talking to an employee at the Subway store, he saw Clay Thomas drive by in his red Camaro. In Casserly's mind, the fact that Clay was in Fenton was evidence enough that he'd just committed three more robberies, but there were no eye-witnesses, and no one knew how the money was stolen, so he couldn't just cuff him and throw him back in jail like he wanted. Casserly figured Clay's criminal success must have something to do with the "special talents" and brain "powers" that he supposedly had. Whatever connection there was, Casserly was hell-bent to figure out how to use it to put Clay behind bars—not to mention shutting the little midget clown's mouth.

***

Bonnie Webster was a retired librarian, who was once the long-time Fenton city mayor. She'd been on nearly every town committee and had read every historical book about the town she loved. Bonnie was now efficiently running the Fenton Museum as a volunteer and writing her memoirs. When Clay and Tanner entered the museum, she was carefully dusting an exhibit at the rear of the building. She turned her attention to the door, and a smile crossed her face while she walked toward the men.

"May I help you?" she asked pleasantly. She was in her mid-sixties, but looked much younger—possibly as much as fifteen or twenty years younger. There were remarkably only the fewest of wrinkles around her eyes and only moderate graying that had been colored nicely. She was slim and shapely, and her active mind was still as sharp as ever.

"Hello. My name is Clay Thomas, and this is my son, Tanner. We'd like to ask you a few questions if you don't mind. We heard that you're something of a town historian."

"Certainly," she said as she shook each man's hand. "I'm Bonnie Webster. What can I do for you?"

"Well..." Clay hesitated. He hadn't given much forethought to the interview. "I guess what I'd like to know first is what you know about a man named Bosley Pemberton."

Tanner started wandering around the museum. It was small enough that he could hear the conversation, but he left the questions to his father.

"Bosley Pemberton. There's a name from the past. He died on New Year's Eve—New Year's Day, actually. What was it? 2001?"

"He died in his sleep, I believe. What do you know about him?"

"The Fenton Hotel changed owners quite often between 1950 and 1992 when Lyle Riddick bought the place. In the early seventies, Bosley was hired to bus tables, do laundry, et cetera. His father was a drunk who died in a car accident after bar hopping on St. Patty's Day. His mother was a somewhat accomplished singer who ran away with a boyfriend as soon as Bosley graduated. I don't think her head was right. Rumor had it that she was abused by both her husband and her new boyfriend and she eventually got mixed up with drugs and such. Happens to so many 'entertainers,'" she said as she made quotation marks with her fingers and editorialized. "It's a rather sad story, actually. Bosley, however, was meant for the hotel and restaurant business."

"Did you know him?"

"Oh, of course. He was a soft-spoken boy who grew into a responsible adult. He loved the hotel. Between the early seventies and the early nineties, the hotel ownership must have changed five or six times. I could look it up if you'd like."

"No, that's not necessary," Clay said as he glanced over at Tanner, who seemed to be engrossed in his perusal of the museum.

"Well, anyway, each and every new owner kept Bosley on. He was given a permanent room to live in sometime in the mid-seventies, and he lived there until the day he died."

147

"I assume he didn't continue as a busboy and laundry worker all those years."

"Certainly not. He became the caretaker of the entire facility. Custodian…hotel manager…Stories are he kept that place together nearly single-handedly."

"What do you mean?" Clay asked.

"The hotel was originally built in 1856. It was falling into disrepair. Bosley loyally attempted to keep the hotel operating, but until Lyle took over, prior owners steadfastly refused to put money into repairs. In the eighties, the third floor was closed down, and by '95, I believe, the hotel was closed permanently and became just a bar and restaurant."

"Bosley always lived there, you said?"

"Oh, yes. And a few of the rooms were kept in order for special guests, family, and so forth. Two of the rooms were turned into offices. But as much as Bosley tried to keep the building he loved running efficiently, the hotel part of the facility was eventually shut down."

Tanner was reading a placard on the wall with a sort of blank stare on his face, but Clay turned his focus back to Bonnie. "Do you know anything about his personal life?"

"Oh, goodie. I thought you'd never ask. That Bosley was quite a lady's man" A good-looking man he was. But his most attractive feature, besides possibly his wonderful singing voice, was his kindness—his genuine politeness. He was a charmer…and his eyes! Many a woman looked into those eyes and was smitten. And his home was a hotel room. Isn't that convenient?"

"So he didn't have a regular relationship?"

"He had two that I'm aware of. I'm not sure how faithful he was, but that would be purely speculation. What I'm sure of is he was engaged two separate times."

"I suppose you know all about each?" Clay asked with a smile. He genuinely liked this energetic lady.

"I most certainly do, young man." She returned the smile with an obvious twinkle in her eyes. "His first marriage proposal was in the summer of '94. Remember, Bosley was quite the lady's man, and several women were extremely disappointed. No date for the wedding was announced, and the engagement dragged on for years. As I said, the third floor of the hotel was closed down in the eighties—Bosley would always be more married to that building than to any person—but after the second floor rooms were closed down in late '95, Bosley seemed to have lost interest in the wedding, and rumors emerged concerning other women. Then, in the late nineties, he met the woman of his dreams. She was a singer, hired for singing engagements on the weekends. She was remarkably good, and business was picking up. I recall several times myself, sitting in that restaurant watching Bosley obsess over that woman."

"His charms weren't working on her?"

"Oh, yes they were, and from what I've heard, did that ever cause problems."

Tanner was still wandering curiously around the museum. Clay glanced his way again and saw that curious intensity in his eyes that showed he was focused on something. He made a note to ask him what it was when he was done with Bonnie Webster.

"I'm curious about the problems you mentioned. Do you care to elaborate?"

"Most certainly. This is such a delicious conversation. Bosley took to singing with his new love interest on occasion, and one night, love in his eyes, he announced to the audience that he was newly engaged."

"You didn't say anything about him breaking off his original engagement."

"That would be correct. His fiancé learned the news second hand and the ripples from that big splash began to spread. It had been news around town for ages that Bosley's fiancé was medicating. She was clinically depressed, possibly bi-polar, and had been greatly distraught for years as the rumors swirled about Bosley cheating on her. His infatuation with the singer put her nearer to the edge, but it was the announcement that put her over the edge completely. Her love of Bosley became an obsession. In June of 2000, she entered the hotel one evening to plead with Bosley once again. He ignored her pleas and her advances and went to his room. Early the next morning, a passerby, Old Maid Johannson, saw Bosley's ex-fiancé hanging with a rope around her neck outside the second floor ballroom window. She had committed suicide."

"You're kidding!" Clay said in shock.

"Rumor has it that she still haunts the hotel to this day. But there's more, Clay. Apparently, Lyle, one of the town's most eligible bachelors for years, was and is madly in love with his bartender, Maggie Royster. But Maggie only had eyes for Bosley's newest fiancé. Maggie, if you don't mind my saying so, is gay."

"That explains how she was looking at Erika," Tanner interjected from the far side of the room.

"You noticed that too, huh?" Clay said.

"You bet. Hard to miss."

The room got eerily quiet as Tanner held a telephone in one hand and picked up a lamp in his other. Bonnie glanced over at him and noticed a curious look on his face. "Are you okay, Tanner?" she asked.

Tanner shook his head, seemingly clearing it of cobwebs. "Yes...yes, ma'am, I'm fine. I'm just having a look."

"At that telephone? You know, that nightstand, the telephone and the lamp, and that chair were all items from Bosley's room. It's interesting that you happen to be looking at them."

"Did Bosley keep a journal?" Tanner asked out of the blue.

"Rumors have always existed that Bosley kept a journal, yes. But no one's ever seen it. It either wasn't true, or he kept it hidden someplace."

"I know where he kept it," Tanner said. He set the items back where he found them and found a seat next to his father. "I have a question for you, Ms. Webster."

Bonnie was curious about Tanner's comment, but politely responded to what Tanner said. "Okay, ask away."

"Would you tell us the names of Bosley's two lady friends?"

"I haven't said?" Bonnie replied. "Hmmm. I guess I haven't. The fiancé who Bosley was engaged to first—the one who committed suicide—was Rachel Fonteneau. The singer, who left town shortly after Bosley passed, she was our very own police chief's little sister, Kayla Casserly."

Clay's jaw practically dropped open. Finally, he had something to work with.

Jeff LaFerney

Chapter 19

Maggie Royster showed up for her shift just moments before her brother showed up at the bar. "It's too early for you to already be drinking," she said.

"I'm not here to drink," he stated. "I need a favor."

"You need a favor from me? That's something new. You're always doin' your big brother thing and tryin' to help me even when I don't want it. This is new. I'm listening."

"I'm plannin' on leavin' for a coupla days. I've got some money, and I've tracked her down. I'm gonna convince her to come back."

"Who, Matt?"

"Who else would it be? Kayla. I can convince her to come back. You gotta let me do it."

"That's the favor? Then forget it. I mean…I want her to come back, but I want her to come back on her own. Don't do it, Matt."

"Maggie, my head won't stop hurtin'. I got a wife that nags the life outta me. I got scouts wantin' me to decide where to send Ace to school next year. I been drinkin' too much…I know that, but all I can think about is how to get that woman back to you. I know where she is, so I wanna go talk to her, at least. You gotta let me do it."

"No, Matt. I love her, but she doesn't love me. Stay out of it. Besides, I know where she is too, and if I wanted to talk to her, I could do it myself. Once Bosley's funeral was over, she was outta here, and she ain't comin' back."

Matt nodded at his sister. His headache started pounding once more, but he was determined to help her. Regardless of what Maggie said, he left the store determined to get Kayla back in town.

***

When Clay got his thoughts together, he turned back to Bonnie Webster. "Let me ask you something. Let's just say that just maybe Bosley didn't die a natural death. My question is…who would benefit?"

"Are you a cop, Clay? A private detective?" she asked. "Are you trying to solve a murder?"

"I'm just an interested party. Do you believe in ghosts, Bonnie?"

"I don't know, but I've heard rumors that Bosley is haunting that hotel. If someone killed him, that someone should pay. Is Bosley really haunting that hotel?"

"All I can say, Bonnie, is I can't help but wonder if there was foul play. What do you think?"

"I've had some ideas of my own, Clay."

"Well, then who do you think might have benefited most?"

"Lyle Riddick."

"What? You'd better explain." Clay didn't actually have any suspects of his own, but Lyle Riddick?

"Bosley lived in that hotel for nearly twenty years. He boarded there rent free. He ate most of his meals in the restaurant. He was putting away money his whole life, and when he died, he left it all to Lyle. His money had been put in a trust, and everything he owned was given to the Fenton Hotel. Lyle could use Bosley's money at will, as long as it

154

was used to improve the Fenton Hotel Restaurant and Grille. Lyle has spent Bosley's fortune remodeling, upgrading, and improving his restaurant. With Bosley alive, Lyle had no access to that money. And clearly, Lyle had access to Bosley while he stayed in his hotel room. I'm not saying he committed a murder, but you asked who benefited most. In my opinion, the answer is Lyle Riddick."

"What about Becca Fonteneau?" Bonnie added.

"Becca? I know her," Clay said. "How would she benefit?"

"I don't know how she'd benefit, but it was Bosley who dumped her sister. Then Rachel Fonteneau committed suicide. Maybe Becca did it for revenge?"

"These are great theories, but what we need is proof." Clay rose from his seat. Bonnie stood as well. "It was a pleasure meeting you, Bonnie. You've been tremendously helpful."

"You're going to walk right on out of here without telling me about ghosts or about why you're asking these questions or about how he," she pointed at Tanner, "knows where the mysterious missing journal is?"

"Unfortunately, yes. I'm sorry. We came in here to learn about Bosley, hoping it would help us solve a possible mystery. Right now, practically all we know is what you just told us."

"Well, that's a bit disappointing, but I enjoyed talking to you this afternoon. Maybe you can let me know what you find out someday."

"I'd be glad too. Thank you again."

"It was nice to meet you, Ms. Webster," Tanner added.

"Same to you, honey. Stop by anytime." Bonnie took up her dust cloth again and energetically picked up her dusting right where she left off.

Clay and Tanner stepped outside of the museum and found themselves looking face-to-face with Micky Kidder of the Fenton Police Department.

"Hey, Tanner," Micky said. "Hey, Mr. Thomas. Sorry to hear about your dad."

Clay nodded and said thanks. Tanner said, "W'sup, Micky?"

"Saw your car, Mr. Thomas, when I was drivin' back to the station. Just wanted to tell you that there were three more robberies today. McDonald's, Burger King, and Subway. Casserly saw you drive by and 'bout burst a blood vessel, he was so mad. He thinks 'cause you're in town, you must be guilty. I ain't the most experienced cop in the world, but anyone who thinks you'd rob your dad and leave him to die at the gas station is outta his mind."

"I appreciate hearing that," Clay said. "Why is he so determined to prove I'm guilty?"

"I think it has more to do with some midget he keeps talking about than you, but mostly I think he doesn't have any other answers. The man's so stubborn and hardheaded, though, that I don't see him giving up."

"We've talked with several of the previous victims and no one remembers a thing. Anything different about today's robberies?"

"Nope. No one remembers nothin'."

"Micky," Tanner interjected while controlling his mind, "sooner or later, we're gonna find out what really happened and find who's responsible for injuring my grandpa. You just haveta keep Casserly out of our way. We need you on our side." Clay couldn't tell if he was manipulating the young cop's mind or not. He'd learned with Tanner, it was sometimes best not to ask. Tanner had a sense about things that Clay didn't understand.

"I got your back," Micky said. "No need for any other innocent people to get hurt." He hesitated a minute. "When this is over, I'll be watchin' you play, Tanner. You make sure my Wolverines have a great year."

Tanner smiled. "I plan on it." They shook hands, and Micky Kidder drove away.

Jeff LaFerney

Chapter 20

Erika Payne was lying on a lawn chair beside the swimming pool at her parents' house. She looked at her phone for about the hundredth time that day, looking for a call or text from Clay, but there was nothing. He hadn't called since she left. She knew what Clay was like. He was extremely focused. She'd told him to solve his mysteries and to sort out what he wanted in life, and she had no doubt that was exactly what he was doing. He'd focus on his relationship again when he'd accomplished what needed to be done. She'd never met anyone more capable.

In the meantime, she was sadder than she'd been in a long time. Her mother walked out onto the patio. Erika wasn't close to her parents. They were another of a long line of relationships in her life that just didn't seem to work. Clay was the first relationship she'd ever had that actually *had* worked, until recent events made her wonder if she had just been being hopeful. But her parents loved her, and her mother seemed to realize that Erika needed some encouragement.

"Hi, honey," her mother said. "I brought you some lemonade. How're you doin'?"

"I've been better, but I can't complain about the sunshine and lemonade."

"Has he called?" her mother asked.

"Not a single time."

"You should call him, don't you think?"

"Maybe, but I won't. I love him. I think he can love me the same way, but he needs to figure it out himself without me pressuring him."

Her mother sighed. She wasn't really good at talking to Erika. "You're a good person, honey. I don't know why bad things happen to good people, but that seems to be the way of things in our family. But *you've* always been an overcomer. Somehow you always seem to rise above your circumstances and not let them defeat you. Why is that, Erika?"

"It's because I have faith, Mom. It's because I have hope for my future. I don't just live one day at a time...I live for my future in a different place. This life is only temporary."

Conversations in general made her mother uncomfortable, but conversations about faith and hope and eternity were more than she could handle, so she patted her lovely daughter on the shoulder and took away Erika's empty glass, leaving her with her replacement drink.

Just then Erika's phone rang. Her heart skipped, hoping to hear from Clay, but instead it was Jasper checking in. She may not have been willing to call Clay, but that didn't mean she didn't want to know what was going on.

"Hello, Jasper. How's Clay?"

"What am I, chopped liver?"

"Compared to Clay, you are. So are you planning on answering my question?" There was a clunk and a long pause with no response. "Jasper...are you there?"

"Yeah, sorry. I was changing my bandage and dropped the phone."

"I'm sure I'm gonna regret asking, but what happened?"

"I fell."

"That's it? You fell?"

"Well, I fell into a tree house."

"You mean you fell *out* of a tree house, right?"

"I wish. It woulda hurt less. And caused less damage. The tree house happened to be in the tree I was climbing. I fell into it from above. Right through the roof. From maybe fifteen feet. But the good news is I got the umbrella I was after."

"I've heard enough, Jasper. I'm not even gonna ask. What's goin' on with Clay?"

"Thanks so much for the sympathy. While I'm not so sure about me, Clay, on the other hand, will be all right. We'll be meeting the district attorney and his cute assistant on Monday morning at which time I'm certain they'll be dropping charges against Clay and clearing Clay's dad. We have more than enough evidence to prove that it couldn't've been Clay. Other than that, Clay and Tanner are in Fenton right now doin' something. Clay's pretty determined to find answers. From what I've seen of that man, I wouldn't bet against him. Whatever he's doin', he's doin' it well."

"That's Clay, all right. Thanks for the call, little friend. Keep in touch. And Jasper, I'm certain there are easier ways of getting an umbrella than to climb a tree for it. Be careful, okay?"

"Awww. I'm not chopped liver after all. Take care, Erika."

***

As soon as they got back in Clay's car, Tanner spoke up. "Dad, I had a vision in the museum, but it was different than any other one I've had. I'm almost positive it was a vision of the past."

"Retrocognition? I read about that recently. Seems like every time we start spending lots of time together, our abilities improve. What did you see?"

"I saw Bosley in a room sitting in a chair. He looked drunk or doped up or something. He seemed to be nodding off occasionally and fighting sleep while he was writing in a book. There was a lamp and a phone on a night stand just like in the museum. He closed his book and then answered his phone. I couldn't hear sounds, so I don't know who it was or what was said, but it was a short conversation. When he was done, he staggered across the room and hid the book in the bottom of his closet."

"Hid? Like he buried it under some things?"

"No, like he pulled up a corner of carpeting, pulled up a section of the floor, and placed it in the flooring. He covered everything back up, staggered back to his bed, and turned his light off."

"You didn't happen to notice anyone else in the room did you?" Clay wondered out loud.

"No, but Dad, we have to go back to the hotel and find that book. It has to be a clue, don't you think?"

"Probably. You always have visions of things that are important. I need to talk to Lyle again, anyway. And maybe Maggie. Maybe you can find the book while I keep them occupied. His room was number 206."

The drive back to the hotel was only about a mile. They were quickly back in the parking lot, heading into the building, when another police car pulled up. This time it was Chief Casserly.

"Thomas!" Casserly called out. Clay stopped. "I see you're in town. D'you have any idea what I been doing all morning?"

"Eating donuts?"

Casserly scowled at Clay. "No, but I been hangin' out at some fast food restaurants. How 'bout you?"

"We actually ate in the Hotel today. You should try to eat healthier, Chief."

"You can make all the jokes you want, Thomas, but I think you been messin' with people's minds, and that's why they don't remember you robbed 'em. Three more robberies today with you in town seems like quite a coincidence."

Clay didn't like what he just heard. Where would he come up with a theory like that? "What'd you say about messing with people's minds?"

"Spent a little time with a Dr. Zander Frauss this morning while you were on another crime spree. The good doctor of parapsychology was readin' your file...and Bosley Pemberton's, for some reason. After Chief Hopper in Durand said something about your 'special abilities' helpin' to solve one of his crimes, I couldn't get 'im to say anything else. But he mentioned Frauss's name. Frauss was pretty adamant that you'd never use your 'powers' to steal. But he knows something he wasn't tellin' me, and he couldn't wait to get me outta his office."

"Maybe that has more to do with your personality than your line of questioning. That wouldn't be too hard to believe."

"He was hidin' somethin'...probably somethin' inside that folder. I once knew Pemberton. What Frauss has to do with him, I don't know. But I think I know what it has to do with you. You're messin' with people's minds, aren't you?"

"Chief, I had nothing to do with any of the robberies you're tryin' to pin on me...and we can easily prove that my father and I had nothing to do with the one at Speedway. You're wasting your time on this. The real thief is out there somewhere, and I'll find him if you don't."

"I think I already found 'im. Won't be long before I can prove it." He hopped back in his car and pulled away.

"That dude's an idiot, Dad," said Tanner.

"Obviously...but what's the deal with Zander? Why in the world would he tell him I have mind powers? Sooner or later, I'm gonna find out what's the deal with him. But for now, I need to talk to Lyle, and you need to find that book."

Chapter 21

Lyle was in the lobby when they entered the building. He smiled, and then immediately remembered the recent funeral, and the smile left his face. He stepped forward and shook Tanner's hand, then Clay's.

"I'm so sorry to hear about your father, Clay...and your grandpa," he said to Tanner. "I sure wish it'd turned out different."

"Thanks, Lyle. I never really got a chance to thank you for what you tried to do for him," Clay responded.

"I didn't do anything, but if there's anything I can do for you in the future, you just let me know."

"There actually is something you might be able to help me with, if you don't mind. Is there some place we could talk?"

Lyle led Clay to the same little banquet room where he had talked to Chief Casserly. Tanner didn't follow. Instead, he went up to the check-in counter where Corissa was working again. He made a bit of small talk with her. After just a couple of minutes, Corissa had to seat a couple of guests in the Grille, and as soon as she was out of sight, he scampered up the stairs in search of room 206.

Clay knew that the conversation he was about to have was a delicate one. If Lyle truly was a suspect, Clay didn't want to let him know that he was investigating the murder.

"Can I get you something to drink?" Lyle said as they entered the room. "Are you hungry?"

"Well, I ate lunch here just an hour or so ago, so not really. Thanks anyway."

Lyle excused himself for a minute, stuck his head into the kitchen anyway, and told his cook to prepare him a Shrimp Sizzler. When he returned, he said, "I ordered a little something anyway. I think you'll like it. So how can I help you?"

Clay hesitated. "Well, Tanner and I have been doing a little investigating on our own, trying to figure out what really happened that night...trying to figure out who really robbed the Speedway. Anyway, as we've asked some questions, the name Bosley Pemberton came up."

"Bosley? What in the world for? He's been dead, what, ten, eleven years?"

Clay finally had an idea about how to get information from Lyle. "I need you to be open-minded for me, okay? When I met Erika about a year ago, I went into her workplace—the Durand Depot. There were rumors that the Depot was haunted. Well, I heard a voice that no one else heard, and eventually we figured out that I was hearing a ghost. That ghost helped me solve how Erika's husband disappeared and died." He paused. "This is where you're gonna have to be open minded...I've heard voices here in the hotel."

"Ghost voices?" Lyle asked skeptically.

"Yeah...you and even some of your employees have said this place is haunted. What if it really is?"

"There're some strange things that happen around here, I admit...but ghosts? I don't think so. It's just a gimmick owners here have taken advantage of for decades to generate interest in the restaurant and grille."

"Well, one of the ghosts I heard actually told me that you didn't believe, and neither did Maggie. But what if other people are right and there really are ghosts here? Do you have any ideas about who they could be? Could one be Bosley Pemberton?"

"How would I know that? What causes a ghost to exist...*if* they exist?"

"Well, from my limited experience, they hang around to achieve some purpose before they can move on. I think most ghosts' lives end unexpectedly...tragically. Whose life ended here in the hotel tragically?"

"Bosley's did. And his ex-girlfriend too. There are rumors of some others, but I didn't own the place during any of those events, so I don't know very much."

"Tell me about the ex-girlfriend."

"Her name was Rachel Fonteneau. She was engaged to Bosley for several years, but Bosley showed less and less interest in the marriage as the years passed. He truly loved this hotel more than he loved her, and as it fell more and more into disrepair, it seemed to affect his personal life more and more. But then we hired a singer. She was very talented—and very attractive. Bosley fell for her, and Rachel lost it. Started taking anti-depressants...drank too much. When Bosley announced his engagement to Kayla, Rachel committed suicide. Hung herself from the ballroom window upstairs."

"What can you tell me about Bosley?"

"Well, he was a good man. He worked here at the hotel for several different owners before I bought the place, and they all kept him on just like I did. He could fix just about anything. He could cook, work the bar, clean, do some accounting. This place was his home."

"What was unique about him that I might recognize?"

"I don't know. He drank Jack Daniels on the rocks. He liked the ladies, and the ladies liked him. He liked to sing. After he fell for Kayla, he'd actually sing with her sometimes."

"Would you say he was well-liked?"

"Overall, yes, but not by everyone. I mean, the fact that the ladies were so enamored with him irritated a few people." As Lyle was talking, an employee brought in the appetizer that he had ordered. "What exactly are you trying to find out, Clay? And what does it have to do with your father?"

***

Tanner made it to the top of the stairs unnoticed. There were a couple of offices at the top of the steps, but there were no numbers on those doors and his dad had said the room was 206. There was a hallway straight ahead that led to an open ballroom that was filled with a bunch of junk. He backtracked and noticed another short hallway that went off to his right. At the end, on the left, after stepping carefully around the many objects that were littering the hall, he found a door on the left that said 206. He turned the doorknob and found the room to be unlocked. He entered. There was a light switch, so he flipped it up, but no light came on. There was a window, but it was covered on the outside, and only a moderate amount of light filtered in at the edges. The light from the hallway didn't help much.

Tanner moved slowly along the edges of the room, looking for the closet. When he found the door, he slid it open along a track. Then he got down on his hands and knees and worked his way into the corner that he saw in his vision. It was remarkable to Tanner that clothes were still hanging in the closet, and shoes and boxes were on the floor. He found an edge of the carpet in the front left corner and pulled it up. He felt along the floor, but there was nothing to grab onto, and the light was even worse in the closet. Finally, he felt a crease, but it was too small to get his fingers in it. He took his car keys from his pocket and slid one end of a key—he had no idea which one—into the crease and pried, and it came up. Luckily, it wasn't heavy.

Tanner reached inside and pulled out the book. It was leather, hard-covered, and about the dimensions of a piece of notebook paper. Tanner slid the flooring back in place, re-covered the spot with the carpeting, rose from the floor, and slid the closet door shut again. As he was about to slip back out of the bedroom, he began to wonder if it was a good idea coming from the second floor with an old book in his hand, so he looked around the room for something to hide it in. In a waste basket—another item that had never been removed from the room—he found a folded paper sack, so he grabbed it and slid the book inside. It was time for him to try to make his way unnoticed back to the first floor.

***

A kitchen employee walked into the banquet room and set the Shrimp Sizzler on the table in what looked like a "to go" box. Clay's phone began ringing. He looked, and once again, it was Becca calling. Clay ignored the call, but noted the coincidence that he'd just been talking about her sister. He was going to have to talk to her again sooner or later.

Clay grabbed a shrimp and popped it into his mouth. It was delicious. Lyle was staring at him, his question still hanging in the air. Clay grabbed a second shrimp, trying to decide how to continue. "I'll ask you again, Clay. What exactly are you trying to find out?"

Their eyes locked. Clay began controlling Lyle's mind. "Okay, if you really wanta know. I wanta know who might've wanted Bosley dead. Tell me, Lyle, who could be a suspect for Bosley's murder?"

Lyle couldn't control what he was saying. "I've often wondered if this day would ever come. If someday someone would suspect foul play. I wondered if someone declared his death a murder, who would be a suspect."

"Tell me who, Lyle."

"Sherman Tankersley for sure."

"Who's that? And why him?"

"He's a gigantically huge, powerful man…from out in Holly somewhere. His wife wanted to work here. She could sing, but I had Bosley scheduling our performers, and he wouldn't have her. Tank had a terrible temper, and he didn't like Bosley at all."

"Who else?"

"I hate to say it, but Maggie…she loved Kayla Casserly. Kayla cared for her, but not the same way. And once she fell for Bosley, Maggie had no chance. With Bosley out of the way, she at least had a chance."

"Anyone else?"

"Well, Becca Fonteneau. Bosley dumped her sister. Rachel couldn't take the rejection, especially the way Bosley made it so public. Rachel's suicide would be a good motive."

"There's more?"

"Long shot, but Matt Royster."

"Ace Royster's dad?"

"Yeah, that's the guy. Complete lunatic. Only cares about himself, his son, and his sister, Maggie. Maggie wanted Kayla, and Bosley was in the way. Remove Bosley—and you'd have to be crazy to do it—but Maggie has a chance again."

"I get the feeling you're holding off on me, Lyle. Who else? Tell me."

"Me, okay. I would be a suspect." His eyes dropped from Clay's and his voice got quiet. "Bosley had too much

170

control of the place, but I owned it. I paid his salary. I let him live here. Plus, I've always wanted Maggie for myself. Kayla wasn't interested in the kind of relationship that Maggie wanted. I don't think she could ever love Maggie back, but with Bosley gone, it made sense that Kayla would leave to begin pursuing her career. I admit, once Bosley was dead, I thought I might have a chance. I wondered if Maggie would give up hope, but she never really has."

"That's a flimsy reason. There's no other way you would benefit?" Clay already knew about the trust fund, but Lyle was no longer looking in Clay's eyes. He'd dropped his head. "What about his money?"

"I didn't know about his money until after he died, Clay, I swear. And I didn't kill him—if *anyone* did it. I pray to God that no one killed Bosley. You have to believe me."

"There's more to this story than you're sayin', Lyle. I think Bosley was murdered. I don't know if all this is linked somehow to the Speedway robbery, but I'm gonna find out."

Lyle's head was down, staring at the table when Clay rose to leave. Clay looked back at the Shrimp Sizzler, held his arm out and the box flew into his hand, "to go." That's when Tanner popped his head into the room, the sack folded under his arm. Clay motioned that it was time for them to leave, so they walked directly out of the hotel.

***

On their way to the car, Tanner checked the time on his phone. "Do you want me to keep the book and go through it, or do you want to?"

"I've pulled you away from school so much this week, I'm feelin' kinda guilty. I'll take the book. Once you get back to school, you have some catchin' up to do, but before we even think about what's inside that book, we need to stop at the drugstore and print the pictures I took. I'll need to take them and the other evidence we gathered to the prosecutor's office Monday. Jasper texted and said we have a meeting Monday morning."

"Do ya think this book's gonna help you figure out what happened to Bosley?"

"Don't know, but it called out to you…let you find it. My guess is it'll tell us something."

Tanner held the book while they climbed into the car and pulled out of the parking lot. At the drug store, Clay caught him up on his discussion with Lyle while they printed their pictures. He told how Lyle mentioned Maggie, Sherman something or other, Matt Royster, and Becca Fonteneau before he mentioned his own problems with Bosley. He caught Tanner up on who Matt and Becca were. He was unaware that he'd actually met Sherman at the gun range.

Ironically, as they were leaving the drugstore, there was Becca behind the pharmacist's glass with her cell phone in her hand. Clay's phone began to ring. It was Becca calling again.

"Hello," Clay answered while looking at Becca, who apparently hadn't noticed the men.

"Hi, handsome. You're a hard man to reach. I've been wanting to see you again."

"Well, look to your right. You prob'ly can't miss me."

"Oh, I miss you all right," Becca said as she turned and looked. A sneaky smile crossed her lips when she saw Clay. Then a bit of disappointment registered as she realized he was with Tanner.

Father and son walked to the pharmacist's window, and Clay introduced Tanner to Becca. "It's nice to meet you," she said sweetly. "Now go away while I talk to your dad."

Tanner looked at her, amazed at what he'd just heard. But for some reason, he did as she said. Why hang with such a rude person anyway?

As soon as he was out of earshot, she leaned forward and lowered her voice. "You're planning on taking me out tonight, aren't you?"

Clay wanted to take her out, for some reason, but he was somehow put off by her at the same time. Erika was away in Florida, waiting for the man she loved to sort out his feelings, but whenever he was near Becca, he had a hard time doing that. "I'd like to do that...maybe some other day. But today I have some important things to do with my son." He looked over his shoulder and noticed he was missing. "Where did he go, anyway?" He hesitated, like he was unsure of his next move, but with his eyes still averted, looking for his son, he said, "It was nice to see you again, but I need to get going."

He found Tanner eyeing some candy bars hungrily. "She's rude," he said.

"Really? I didn't notice. There's something about her that's dangerous though. I mean...I can't think straight when I'm around her. We need to get going. You want a candy bar?"

"Nah...I'll eat the rest of your shrimp. Let's get outta here." When they got back to the car, Tanner said, "So that's Becca Fonteneau. Nice lookin' lady, but Erika doesn't have to worry about her. You'd never go for someone like that."

"*Why?*" Clay thought, but thought better of verbalizing the question.

After the pause, Tanner said, "*That* woman is *my* number one suspect. She's manipulative...and she's dangerous all right."

All of a sudden, Clay felt tired. It was getting on toward evening, and he was ready to call it a day. They both agreed to have Clay drive Tanner back to his car which they'd left in the Target parking lot at the beginning of their day in Fenton. Once there, Tanner said goodbye and exited the car.

He left the packaged book on his passenger seat and closed the door. Clay patiently waited to be sure Tanner got in his car and got it started before he finally reached over and grabbed the sack in his right hand. He gasped as a vision shot into his mind.

Chapter 22

What is it that makes going to church alone so miserable? Clay felt lonely and couldn't wait to escape as soon as the final prayer was voiced. He didn't have anyone to sit with and didn't feel the need to talk to anyone. He just wanted to get home. There was so much on his mind that he got very little sleep during the night and couldn't remember a thing about the sermon. His mind kept reviewing Bosley's journal/log book. Then he would consider all the other facts he'd discovered the day before. But mostly, he couldn't get the vision of Bosley's face out of his head.

Clay had come to the realization that the more time he spent with Tanner, the more their abilities grew. He'd studied enough that he knew exactly what happened to Tanner and him in Fenton. Tanner had experienced retrocognition when he was able to view past events. That was a new ability, but it was what led them to Bosley's journal. Then Clay had his vision. He knew immediately that he'd experienced what the books called "psycometry." For the first time, he had learned the history of an object that he had touched. He had learned the history of a paper sack.

The paper sack had snapped open and several objects were lowered into it. A bottle of Jack Daniels, a couple of candy bars, a toothbrush and toothpaste, a small bouquet of flowers, and a bottle of sleep aid pills. He could see them clearly in the vision. There was no question in his mind. He saw them being pulled back out of the bag. Then—and this is the part that he was having a hard time getting out of his mind—he saw the bag being slid over the head of Bosley. Bosley's eyes were closed. Clay got the impression that he was lying down, but he wasn't sure of that. What he *was* sure of, however, was that the bag was removed from Bosley's head, folded, and then it fell. Next, it was set inside what seemed like a wastebasket. It was circular, dirty, and littered with other papers, so Clay was pretty sure. Then the sack was removed from the wastebasket, unfolded, and a book was slid into it. It was the same book that he later removed from the bag. Tanner had brought him Bosley's journal in a sack that had been a resting place for Bosley's head!

Speaking of heads, Clay needed to clear his own. He put on a jogging suit and his running shoes, and headed out for a run. His first thought was that he missed Erika. With everything he had to think about, he found he cared most about his relationship with her. As he briskly ran toward the end of his street, his mind began to focus temporarily on Zander Frauss. His behavior—or lack thereof—was unsettling, but *why* would he ever tell Casserly about his mind powers? Why was he in Fenton on the night of the robbery, and why did he refuse to return Clay's calls? Tanner said that Zander's lab was being shut down. That would be disturbing to Zander, but it wouldn't lead him to abandon their friendship.

As Clay approached the end of the street and took a right, his mind changed gears. How was he going to find the real Speedway thief, and what was he going to do when he found him? Part of him wanted revenge for the death of his father. That would be wrong, but it would feel right, Clay thought. It appeared that someone was manipulating minds, but who? Would Zander have any idea?

Clay was running at a brisk pace when he took another right at the next corner, but it was his mind that was working overdrive. Both Bonnie and Lyle had given him names of people who might have reason to kill Bosley, but neither of those two had any idea what he had found in Bosley's journal. Bosley had bedded so many women that Clay's list of suspects had increased maybe tenfold. How he got so many women—most of them married—into bed with him, Clay had no idea. But the most unsettling revelation in Bosley's journal was that he was cheating on Kayla Casserly, and she had found out. The night of Bosley's murder, in his last journal entry, he had written, "I'm wasted, but drinking can't change the pain—it's still there. I love her so much, but she's going to leave me anyway. I feel like dying. I've abused my power, and now I'll pay the consequences. I don't deserve to live."

Clay neared the next corner and actually increased his pace. Did Bosley commit suicide? And though a huge number of people may have been angry enough to kill him, who had access to the hotel late that night? He died on New Year's Eve—well, New Year's morning. Who had been in the hotel that night? Even if Bosley had committed suicide, there was a person who was in the hotel that saw him dead in that bed. Did anyone come forward? Did a medical examiner make any discoveries? He was going to have to check that out.

Clay had rounded the last corner to the right and begun the homestretch back to his house. His active mind began to think of the meeting the next morning with the prosecutor. He and Jasper were confident they would leave with all charges dropped. Clay would get his gun back. He had begun to get used to it and felt a bit naked and exposed without it. He'd pick Jasper up in the morning, meet with the prosecutor, and then possibly seek answers from the medical examiner.

Clay finally slowed down in front of his house and put his hands on his knees as he struggled to regain his breath. He had practically sprinted down the straightaway back to his driveway. He walked toward his door, and as he entered his home, his mind completed its own "lap." His breathing was settling back to normal and his heart rate was slowing, but there was no denying that his heart was hurting. He missed Erika terribly.

Chapter 23

As they were taking the elevator to the second floor of the courthouse on their way to see District Attorney Morrell, Clay felt the need to give Jasper some advice.

"Jasper?"

"Yeah?"

"You're gonna be professional, right? I mean, we have the evidence. We don't need to make any enemies in the process."

"Me? Are you *kidding*? Clay, you have nothing to worry about."

Clay was worried. "Course not."

Irving Morrell's secretary led them immediately into his office. Jasper smiled when he saw Monica Grey, his assistant, and scowled when he saw that Chief Casserly was present. All of a sudden Clay wasn't just worried; he was uncomfortably nervous. He and Jasper shook hands with the DA and his assistant. "Please, sit down," he said. "We've all met, so we can get right to it. You have evidence, you say, Mr. Bugner?"

Jasper climbed up on a chair and glared at Chief Casserly while unloading papers from a briefcase. "Why is *he* here?" he asked.

"He's the chief of police in Fenton. It's his case. He's been investigating the crime wave in Fenton and believes your client is involved."

"Well, Buzz. I'm gonna prove how wrong you are!"

"My name's not Buzz," he growled at Jasper.

"Really? I could've sworn you were named after your haircut. That's how I remembered. It's not *flattop* is it? That just doesn't sound right."

"Jasper...remember our talk in the elevator? His name's Butch," Clay interrupted. "Let's just get to the evidence."

"I know his name, Clay. I got it written right here on this document wherein I'll be showing a Mr. Butch Casserly that we'll be suing the shirt off that broad back of his."

Clay just rolled his eyes and shook his head no to the DA. "I just want the charges dropped and my dad's name cleared."

Jasper took his stack of papers, licked his lips, and cleared his throat. "Okay, first of all...video evidence. I've looked at it. From that video, there's no way to identify Carlton Thomas, and there're no eyewitnesses to the crime. There's also no gun. The cashier..." He looked at his notes. "...Um...Eddie. We have a taped interview in which he admits that he couldn't ID Carlton, nor did he see any gun. Just had 'a feeling,' he said. That would be the tape that Clay there is holding for you to see. Then, let's see. Based on the counter being thirty-four inches, we can prove that the thief was nearly three inches shorter than Carlton Thomas and certainly not as broad shouldered." Jasper was just getting started.

"Next, we did a luminol chemiluminescence reaction test...The pictures are right here, Irving. The blood spatter on the ground and door edge prove that the *outside* of the door hit Carlton before he fell on the rock you can see there in the picture. Remember, the video shows a person banging into the *inside* of the door, but Carlton's body was found *outside* of the door. He actually hit his head over six feet from the doorway, but the video evidence shows the thief nearly running through the store—something Carlton Thomas and his bad knees wouldn't have done, certainly not without a limp. The thief stumbled into the door about forty inches off the floor and fell into the doorway, his head landing no more than two to two and a half feet outside the door. I have an affidavit from the hospital stating that Carlton took *two* blows to the head, not just one. That would be the outside door edge and the rock six feet from the door. Then Carlton was discovered with no money, no gun, no magazine, and amazingly, with no tennis shoes. Yes, the thief had on tennis shoes. You can see that in the video. Are a judge and jury supposed to believe that Clay ran up, took the bag from the robbery, took a gun that no one saw, and changed his father's shoes? Then he escaped the scene with about six hundred dollars while his own father bled from an injury so serious that he died!"

District Attorney Morrell loosened his tie. He was becoming quite uncomfortable.

"The blood type on the door, by the way...AB positive...matches Carlton Thomas's. Then we have a receipt that proves the moment Carlton hung up his gas pump—12:09 AM. The time stamp on the video for when the thief was given the money is actually one minute before Carlton was done pumping his gas. Lyle Riddick will swear that he saw Carlton at the gas pump, right where his car was found sitting after he was knocked unconscious by the door. I think it's safe to say that Carlton isn't your thief, but it gets better.

"Not only are there no eyewitnesses that saw Carlton *in* the gas station, but there are none that saw Clay *anywhere*. And no one saw his car. We have another affidavit right here...." He handed it to Morrell. "It's from Lyle Riddick who cannot say with any accuracy at all that the car he claimed to see even matched the make or color of Clay's.

"Let's talk some more about my client, Mr. Morrell. According to satellite phone records and GPS tracking, Clay called Erika Payne from his home at 12:26 AM." Jasper handed the phone records and Carlton's VISA receipt to Morrell. "Clay would have had to drive...what, Clay...an average of 109 miles per hour without any stops—including through the city and his subdivision—to get home in time to make that phone call if he actually robbed his father and left him to die."

"We found the money and the gun!" Casserly shouted.

"Well, we already established that no one saw any gun, spoke of any gun, or used any gun. The fact that Clay Thomas has a registered handgun holds no bearing on this case since there was no gun involved. But there *was* money is Clay's drawer. You or one of your officers removed $440 from a Dort Federal Credit Union envelope that was stored in his dresser drawer. Here is Clay's bank withdrawal slip, Irving. Clay withdrew five hundred dollars—nineteen twenties, ten tens, and four fives on Thursday, September 10, at 4:03 PM. The officers took seventeen twenties, eight tens, and four fives from that envelope and then arrested Clay, who still had forty-two of the other sixty dollars in his wallet. Estimates were that the thief stole over *six* hundred dollars. Clay's home was searched further with no other cash found and no *Cosmopolitan* magazine, which we all saw being put into the money bag. All of the, quote, 'evidence,' against Clay, by the way, is predicated on the assumption that he was the accomplice of his father, who obviously did not rob the store."

Casserly's face was a beet red, and sweat was beaded on his forehead when Morrell cleared his throat. "So what are you suggesting, Mr. Bugner?" he asked.

"Well, we can go through the charade of a trial. That's a complete waste of time—much like letting Chief Casserly investigate the robbery in the first place. I'm surprised your police chief is so incompetent. Did you do any actual investigating, Buzz?"

"I don't have to take his sarcasm!" Butch yelled once again.

"Hold on, Butch. Let him have his say."

Jasper smiled his crooked-toothed smile. "We want you to drop all charges, make a public apology, and suspend the Chief here, or we'll go through with the trial, embarrass everyone involved, and file charges of false arrest and slander." He looked Casserly's way. "I still have my copy of the news article naming Carlton and Clay Thomas—his so-called accomplice—as the thieves and accusing them of other robberies—robberies, by the way, that Clay can alibi out of. He could no more have committed the three prior robberies than the one at the Speedway Gas Station."

"He's got mind powers!" Casserly yelled. "He's committing the robberies somehow. I don't know how, but somehow he's doing it."

Jasper started laughing like a rodeo clown. "Mind powers? And they helped him rob the Mug and Brush while Clay was eating at the Fenton Hotel? Or at the Fenton football game while he was mourning the loss of his father on the day of his funeral? Come on, Buzz. You need a vacation. Your stupidity's overwhelming. One thing is for sure. The person who is committing the robberies is *not* Clay Thomas." He turned his attention back to the DA. "Well?"

"All charges will be dropped, Mr. Bugner. Mr. Thomas can go to the station in Fenton and pick up his money and gun. Chief Casserly will be suspended indefinitely. You have my word. I apologize for putting you through this, Clay. And you have my condolences about your father. I'm very sorry for everything."

"You can't be serious!" Casserly spat out. "He's manipulating you just like he's manipulating others. I'll prove it!"

"Chief, so far you have no proof whatsoever, and since you'll be suspended shortly, you won't be investigating the case any further," Morrell stated. "You're dismissed while Monica and I finish cleaning up the mess you've made."

"You'll be sorry, Thomas. And you better watch your back, you little midget!"

"Irving, we'll be filing a report concerning the Chief's threat before we leave, also. I believe we have four witnesses that'll verify that Chief Casserly is an incompetent lunatic who threatened two innocent citizens."

Casserly made a lunge for Jasper, who jumped right into the lap of Monica Grey. It was probably intentional. Clay stood his solid six foot two inch frame between Jasper and the rampaging police chief. He looked Casserly in the eyes. "Back off!" he shouted. "Back off," he said, his voice quieting, "before you do somethin' even more stupid. The real thief is still out there, and I'll find him. I assure you that, Chief. I'll find him." Casserly's mind was under the control of Clay, so he stopped. He collected himself while considering Clay's words. "And while I'm at it, I'm gonna figure out who killed Bosley Pemberton nearly eleven years ago."

Casserly recalled Bosley's name on the file in Zander's office. Somehow the three men were tied together, but not knowing how made his anger begin to boil again. He glared at Clay with hate in his eyes, but instead of acting on his desire to hurt Clay, his mind was still telling him to back off. So, instead, he turned and exited the room.

When Clay turned back around, Jasper was sitting in Monica's lap with a satisfied smile on his face.

Jeff LaFerney

Chapter 24

Before driving back to Fenton to get his personal items from the police station, Clay had something to do. He figured that somehow Jasper would make accomplishing his plans more difficult, but he was tagging along, regardless. Clay wanted a copy of Bosley's autopsy report, which, after more than ten years, would more than likely be archived at the Genesee County Medical Examiner's Office in Flint. They left the courthouse, drove down Beach Street and Third Street, and eventually found a parallel parking spot on Saginaw Street near the office.

"Repeat this to me again," Jasper said. "You're gonna do what?"

"I'm gonna go into that building and ask for Bosley Pemberton's autopsy report."

"And you assume they're gonna just give it to you? Just like that?"

"Yep."

"Why?"

"Maybe 'cause I have a smart aleck, dwarf-sized attorney with me who breathes political correctness and loves to file discrimination charges. Maybe 'cause I'm stunningly handsome. Maybe just because I'm gonna ask nicely. We'll see when we get there." They entered the front doors and were directed to the second floor where there was a window and front desk but no workers. Jasper stood on his tip toes, nervously trying to see over the counter. "Do you want me to lift you up?" Clay laughed. "There's really nothin' to see."

"This place makes me nervous. There's probably dead bodies in there somewhere."

"That's quite possible, Jasper. Just relax, okay? I'm just planning on lookin' at a file…maybe talk to someone."

"Speaking of dead bodies, did you know when I did some research on Lyle Riddick, his dad was a mortician?"

"Yeah, and Becca Fonteneau is a pharmacist. She'd know a little about medicine and death too."

"And that Zander Frauss. He's having funding problems for some Department of Perceptual Studies. He's a neuroscientist. He has obvious medical knowledge."

"But he's not involved, Jasper," Clay said. "At least not in any crime. That's not possible, but somehow he's involved with Bosley, so that's why I had you do a background check. Did you see any connection between the two?"

"Nothin' that I've been able to dig up so far."

Just then a lady in a flowery scrub top walked to the window. "Have you been helped?" she asked. She was slightly overweight, with a smooth, round face, but it was an attractive face and she had a pleasant smile.

"No, not yet," Clay responded. "We were hoping to talk to a medical examiner about an archived autopsy."

"Dr. Howard, the deputy medical examiner, is unavailable, but you could talk to one of our two autopsy assistants or the administrative secretary."

"Who has easiest access to archived files?" Clay asked, using his best smile. He wondered if it had any effect. She wasn't exactly throwing off her scrubs, so he wasn't sure.

"One of the assistants, most likely. I'll see if someone's available."

After another few minutes of Jasper nervously pacing the lobby, one of the autopsy assistants returned without the woman. So much for her infatuation with Clay.

"Good afternoon. I'm Lou Kirkus. How may I help you?" He was very polite. Made terrific eye contact. Clay was more than willing to share how the man could help.

He looked Lou squarely in the eyes and said, "You would like to show us an archived autopsy report."

"Yes, I would," he said.

"You'd love to stay with us to explain the findings, and then make us a copy that we can take out of here with us."

"I would love to do that."

"I thought so. My friend here was a little skeptical, but I was confident you'd cooperate."

"Aren't there rules or something about who can see the autopsy?" Jasper asked incredulously. He didn't like that Lou had begun leading them back behind the glass.

"Apparently not for us, Jasper. My name's Clay Thomas, by the way. And this is Jasper Bugner."

"It's a pleasure to meet you. So tell me, Clay. What exactly are you looking for?"

"We're looking for the report for Bosley Pemberton. He died on January first, 2001."

"Come into meeting room one," he directed. "If you don't mind waiting here for a few minutes, I'll look for the report." He left the men alone.

"What in the world!" Jasper exclaimed. "Don't you have to be a doctor or a cop or a member of the family or the President of the United States or some such thing to be given access to a report like that?"

"I just have a way with people, I guess," Clay said. "Look at *you* for cryin' out loud. You're a grumpy little pain in the rear, and *you* like me."

"You do have your moments...but your girlfriend's a goddess and I get to stare at her occasionally for bein' your friend. What does Captain Kirkus get? Aren't there *rules* to follow?"

"Aren't you the maniac I met when you threw a rock through my car window? Since when do you care about rules?"

"Good point," Jasper conceded. "But Kirkus clown ain't me."

"Nope. He's his own self, and he's sharing a file with us. And here he comes."

***

Zander Frauss pulled into a parking spot at the Meijer shopping center in Hartland with his eye on a car that had parked just seconds before. He was only a few miles from his home, on the way to another discouraging day of work, when he had seen a car that he recognized. He had been behind it at a stop light, one lane over and two cars back. He glanced at the license plate and recognized it. It was one of the benefits of having an IQ of 139. He remembered lots of insignificant things. Zander had kept his distance, but his curiosity compelled him to follow the car. It had proceeded to the Meijer store and pulled into a parking space just one row over from where Zander was sitting. He pulled his keys from the ignition as the driver exited the car. Zander's curiosity increased twofold when he recognized that the driver was wearing a disguise.

All of the previous robberies that had occurred in Fenton had gone extremely well. Except for the accident outside the Speedway station, they'd all gone off without a hitch. Local police hadn't managed to come up with a single meaningful lead to the real perpetrator. This robbery was going to be different, however. The crook entered through the doors of the Meijer shopping center which was several miles south of Fenton. This was intended to be the first robbery outside of the Fenton city limits. With a fake mustache, a short, black wig, loose Lee painter jeans, Chuck Taylor tennis shoes, and wire-framed glasses, the thief entered the shopping center—Zander Frauss following closely behind—and began searching for the manager's office. It was nowhere to be found. The thief began to get anxious. Didn't it have to be at the front of the store near the cash registers? After making two complete trips around the perimeter of the store, there was nothing resembling an office. Finally, out of desperation, the thief found an employee and asked for directions to the manager's office and was told it was at the complete back of the store, beside the restrooms.

At the back of the store, the office was still nowhere to be found, but there were some swinging plastic doors. Could it be behind the doors? The thief placed a hand on the left side door and pushed it in, hoping to get a glimpse of what was inside. Several customers and a store employee looked on curiously. Finally, the thief took a deep breath and entered through the doors. There was an office on the right, and a woman with a manager's badge was sitting behind a desk doing some paperwork.

She looked up in surprise. "May I help you?" she asked.

The thief looked her in the eyes and spoke firmly. "I need you to open the safe and give me your money."

"Yes, sir...but there's no safe in here," the manager responded hesitantly.

"What? I know you can't be lying to me. I said to open the safe and give me the money!"

"But...the safe isn't here."

191

"Where is it? Tell me the truth!"

"It's all the way to the front of the store. It's in a room to the back of One Hour Photo. I'll take you there if you'd like."

"Yes...let's go there now." Things were not going smoothly *this* time.

When they exited the employee area and stepped back out into the shopping center, several new sets of eyes rested on the thief, and two people actually appeared to be looking and laughing. One pointed at the thief's drooping mustache, which was hanging partly unattached. The thief, heart racing, casually reached up and reattached it. Things were going from bad to worse. Zander, who was doing his best secret agent imitation, ducked back when the two people re-entered the shopping area from behind the plastic doors.

As they reached the front of the store and approached the One Hour Photo, it became even more obvious that things were falling apart. They would have to pass numerous customers and employees inside the photo store to get to the safe—lots of people would see them go in. But the manager, under the thief's mind control, walked through the store and unlocked a small room. Cashiers working the Meijer check out isles glanced their way, recognizing that something unusual was happening. Zander kept a safe distance as he continued to spy.

When they entered the room, the thief gave the same command. "Open the safe, and give me the money."

"Yes sir...except, well...I *can't* open it. It opens with two keys. I have one of them, but the lock has to be turned simultaneously with our district manager. I can't get in it."

The thief began to panic. "Let's get out of here. You will *not* remember me asking to get into the safe or anything else about me. You were looking for my lost wallet."

When they exited One Hour Photo, there was a small crowd of people, accompanied by a store security guard. The security guard asked, "Is everything okay, Lois?"

The thief looked into Lois's eyes. *"Everything's fine. We were just looking for a lost wallet that we can't find."*

"Everything's fine," Lois said. "We were just looking for a lost wallet for this man. We can't seem to find it."

One of the employees said, "The lost and found is in customer service, Lois. Did you try customer service?"

The thief said, "Yes, we already checked there. I must not have lost it in this store. Thank you, Lois, for your help. Obviously, I left it somewhere else." He turned back to Lois. *"Say that you have my information, and you'll call me if it's found somewhere else in the store."*

"I have your information, Sir, so I'll call you if the wallet shows up somewhere else."

"Thank you. I appreciate your time."

With that, the crook looked up and happened to spot Zander. The not-so-super-sleuth looked awkwardly away and began to walk casually in the opposite direction. While his back was turned, the thief slipped out of the store. When Zander finally looked back and made his way discreetly back to the front of the store, he knew that he'd been given the slip. He considered hustling out of the store in another attempt to follow, but instead something seemed to click in his head. After all the prayer and consternation, it finally came to him what he simply *had* to do. Relying on himself to fix the situation he'd gotten himself into wasn't working out too well. It was time that he swallowed his pride and went to the one person who was most equipped to help him. Ironically, it was the person he had once told to stop relying on himself—that he had friends he needed to trust. That person—the one to whom it was time to talk—was Clay Thomas. It was going to be difficult for him, but it was about time that he did the right thing. He slipped out of the store and headed for his car.

While Zander was having his moment of clarity, one of the concerned employees checked to see if Lois had actually been to customer service, but she hadn't. The employee told the security guard, who asked Lois for the information that the man had given her, but Lois didn't have it. When he asked Lois if the man was trying to rob the store, she said, "We were just looking for his wallet." The guard checked the store videos and eventually discovered the two people walking out of the doors which led to Lois's office. The employee that had noticed the activity at the back of the store confirmed that he saw the two people together and commented that the unknown man was wearing a fake mustache. When the security guard asked her about it, Lois didn't remember talking to the man in her office. All she remembered was someone was looking for a lost wallet. The person was gone and nothing had been taken, so there was nothing else the guard could do except to wonder what exactly had happened that evening.

***

Lou Kirkus stepped through the doorway with a file in his hand. "Hmmm," he said. "Apparently, this autopsy you asked for was performed by me. Nearly eleven years ago. I don't remember much about it, but it's my signature on the report."

"I'm gonna get right to the point, Lou. Do you see anything on there that might suggest that Bosley was murdered?"

"Well, I marked it as 'undetermined/undetermined'."

"What does that mean?" asked Jasper.

"There are five possible causes of death that might be identified: accidental, homicide, suicide, natural, or undetermined. In order to declare it to be a homicide or

194

suicide or an accidental death, I have to be able to understand intent by the end of my autopsy. Maybe, if I could determine a sequence of events that leads to the death, I could determine intent. If the death can't be determined conclusively that it's natural, and I can't determine intent, then I have to call it undetermined."

"What does the other 'undetermined' mean?" Jasper wondered.

"I try to figure out the cause. But I also try to figure out the manner. Let's say someone dies from trauma to the head. I'll attempt to determine if it was accidental or a homicide, but I also try to determine the manner in which the blow to the head occurred. Maybe it was a baseball bat or maybe it was the pavement or something else. But if I can't determine the cause of death conclusively, I certainly can't determine the manner. Therefore, I can't make a determination, so I have to call it 'undetermined/undetermined'. But that also means that the issue can be reevaluated if new information comes to light."

"So what information did you actually discover in the autopsy?" Clay asked.

"The toxicology is unrevealing. There was a large amount of alcohol in his system, but it was New Year's Eve, a time when lots of people drink too much. Apparently, Mr. Pemberton was *known* to drink too much. On that particular night, his blood alcohol level was point two five. He weighed 179 pounds, so he consumed the equivalent of ten drinks of eighty proof alcohol. He was *very* drunk when he died. On top of that, there was nearly sixty milligrams of doxylamine succinate in his system."

"What's that?" Jasper asked.

"It's just simple, over the counter sleeping pills. One pill is usually twenty-five milligrams. He had more than two of them in his system. It's odd that he'd be as drunk as he was and still use sleeping pills, but maybe he didn't realize what he was doing. Maybe he thought he was taking aspirin. It certainly isn't a lethal dose, but it's plenty to put a person to sleep. Not enough to determine suicide or homicide, though, especially when I can't determine intent. It shouldn't be enough to kill him accidentally either, so I can't determine that."

"And you can't prove that he died naturally," Clay deduced.

"Exactly. It's undetermined."

"Is there any sign that he was suffocated?" Clay asked.

"There was no ligature…no markings…and generally, any kind of struggle causes marks."

"But if he was extremely drunk *and* overmedicated with sleeping pills, maybe he was too passed out to struggle."

"A person is going to struggle to get oxygen. A victim would have to be very, very drunk, and have the perfect dose of medication to not struggle."

"Would Bosley meet that criteria?"

"Hmmm…possibly. But if he was suffocated—with a pillow, for instance—there'd be some evidence of increased intravascular pressure. I just don't think it could be proved that someone suffocated him."

"What if he was deprived of oxygen in a different way?"

"Do you have an idea what that might be?" asked Lou Kirkus.

"What if a bag was placed over his head? What if someone secured a bag over his head, and he simply breathed until he ran out of oxygen?"

Kirkus thought for a minute. "You mean he breathed in his own carbon dioxide as he ran out of oxygen? It still seems logical that his body would struggle…unless, of course, he was extremely drunk and perfectly medicated." A light was flickering on in the medical assistant's head. "Is that how *you* think he died?"

"You might have a difficult time believing this, Lou, but after Bosley died, some of his bedroom articles were donated to a local museum, but everything else was simply left in the room. He had no family or such to get his personal articles. The Fenton Hotel already had stopped renting out rooms, and the owner never cleared out Bosley's. I have a paper grocery sack that was found in Bosley's waste basket. It was folded and dumped into the basket, but it's wrinkled like it was possibly bound around his head."

"So," Lou interjected, "he could have been so drugged up and passed out that someone could have secured the sack around his head and waited for him to suffocate in his own exhaled gases. Ingenious. You say you have the sack?"

"In my car."

"You know, I could test it. If there's any dried secretion inside the sack, I can determine if it's Bosley's. With that kind of information, the issue of his death can be reevaluated. We'd then have a suitable cause of his death. I could then determine the manner. That's why we call it undetermined/undetermined, by the way. It leaves open the possibility of a new determination if new evidence comes to light."

"Speaking of evidence," Clay said. "Is it possible to identify fingerprints from paper?"

"Oh, yes, definitely. I'll definitely test for that too, once I have the bag."

"There's one more piece of evidence, Lou. There was a receipt in the bag. Whoever purchased the items, bought Jack Daniels whiskey and sleeping pills."

Jeff LaFerney

Chapter 25

After delivering the sack to Lou Kirkus and leaving his cell phone number, Clay and Jasper walked back to the car and began to head to Fenton so Clay could pick up his money and gun.

"Tell me about Zander Frauss," Jasper said. "I know you're tryin' to find out who's pulling off those robberies because then you'll know who hurt your dad. I get that. But you're also tryin' to solve some eleven-year-old murder. That I don't get. And I don't get what Zander Frauss has to do with it."

"Zander was my closest friend—until recently. He's a neuroscientist at the University of Michigan, and he used to run the Department of Perceptual Studies, which is simply a research group studying the brain and what it has to do with extra-sensory abilities. Bosley, I guess, was an old patient of his, so somehow Zander has information that I need. But like I said, as of lately, he doesn't seem willing to communicate with me, and I find that suspicious. Plus, Tanner saw him at the gas station on the night of the robbery. I want to know what he was doing there, and what, if anything, he has to do with the robberies too."

Just then Clay's phone rang. It was Tanner. "Hello."

"Hi, Dad. You wouldn't happen to be with Jasper still, would you?"

"Yeah. He's right here. D'you wanna talk to him?"

"No...Are you kidding?" he laughed. "That surly little guy?"

"I heard that!" Jasper yelled at the phone. "Surly? Me? You don't even know what that means!"

Clay tucked the phone in tighter to his ear so Jasper couldn't hear. "So what's up? Besides that you got my attorney all riled up again."

"Any chance you've seen him sprawled in a bush during your adventure today?"

"Um, not so far. What're you sayin'?"

"There's a fender bender...didn't seem too serious in my vision. But then there was this *giant* shadow...I mean something literally blocked out the sun. I couldn't see anything clearly, until I saw Jasper lying half in and half out of a bush. I'm just callin' to warn you. Watch out because he's gonna make someone else angry."

Jasper heard that last phrase. "I heard that! What d'you mean someone *else* angry? Kids nowadays. They got no respect."

Clay ignored him. "Do you think that this has anything to do with our investigation? I mean, it seems so random."

"No idea, Dad. I just call 'em as I see 'em. You'd better watch his back."

After he ended the conversation with his son, he said, "Hard to figure, but he's predicting you're gonna get yourself into some trouble."

Jasper rolled his eyes at Clay. "Ha, ha...very funny." The rest of the drive to Fenton thankfully went smoothly and quietly, giving Clay a little bit of time to think. Apparently, there were loads of people that might actually have motive to kill Bosley, but the important question was who also had the ability and opportunity to kill Bosley that New Year's Eve? Who was there that night at the Hotel's New Year's Eve party, or if they weren't at the party, who had access to the building after it closed? Those were the questions that needed to be answered. Another troubling issue was that he was no closer to solving the robberies than he was at the beginning. The only things he knew for sure were that the thief probably drove a red sports car, probably stood five foot ten or eleven, appeared to be slimmer than his father, and wore Michigan gear. Another thing that he was reasonably confident about was that the thief *must* be able to control minds. That was one thing he wished he could talk to Zander about, but Zander didn't seem willing to talk to him.

He spotted the police station. The setting sun was in his eyes as he was turning into the parking lot, his mind focused on his mysteries. All of a sudden, he felt a collision. The metal on metal sound made his stomach sick. He'd turned into the parking lot and gotten into an accident—a fender bender, just as Tanner had seen in his precognition.

The sun was glaring in their eyes as Clay and Jasper stepped out of the car to see the damage. From the other car, a man slid out of his seat, and as he stood, he completely blocked out the globe of light. "Oh, my gosh, it's Goliath!" Jasper said.

A man the size of a department store stood in front of him, but all Clay could see was a dark shadow. "You!" he heard.

Clay squinted and then moved in hopes of seeing who or what he was dealing with. When he finally found an angle that gave him a clear view, he recognized that it was the mammoth man from the shooting range. It was chilly outside, but the man was wearing a short-sleeved bowling shirt with the name "Sherman" stenciled on the front pocket. A woman slipped out of the passenger side door. She was about one-fifth the size of her gargantuan husband who was glaring angrily at Clay. She had on an unzipped jacket, and Clay could see the name "Agnes" on her bowling shirt pocket.

"I'm sorry," Clay said. "I'm sure it was my fault. I'll contact my insurance company." Neither car had any serious damage, but the man was the size of moving van, and he was angry.

"You better believe it was your fault! Why, I oughta break your neck, right here and now!"

Clay lifted both hands in the symbol of surrender. Between the glaring sun peeking around his frame and the dark shadow he was casting, Clay couldn't see into his eyes, but before he had time to figure out what to do, Sherman punched him in the chest so hard he nearly blacked out. The pain was incredible. Clay, a strong, tough man, felt his knees buckle as he collapsed to the ground. Sherman, despite the screaming of his wife to stop, wound up for another punch to Clay's face. But as he pulled back his arm, Jasper the gymnast, did a cartwheel and a back handspring and somehow managed to leap all the way onto Sherman's shoulders. He grabbed Sherman in the face, and as Clay tried to get his breath and regain enough strength to stand up, it looked like he was holding on with one arm and punching the side of Sherman's head with the other.

Sherman reached behind his back and grabbed Jasper in one monstrous paw and yanked him off his back. He turned and hurled the little acrobat about twenty feet into a large bush. Jasper entered the foliage headfirst, his feet sticking straight up in the air. As Clay watched his friend spinning through the atmosphere and embedding himself like a lawn dart in the shrubbery, he managed to get to his feet. Sherman turned back to Clay. "How dare you embarrass me like you did" And now you wreck my car? I'm gonna kill you, Clay Thomas!"

Clay held his hand out as the man began to approach. He summoned all the strength in his mind that he could muster, and he held the man back. Sherman had a confused look on his face. He couldn't figure out why he wasn't snapping Clay in two at that very moment. And then he thought in his head, "*Clay Thomas is a friend.*" He shook his head. He didn't have friends. The only person who cared for him was his wife. During his pathetic adulthood, she was the only person he ever really cared for in return. In the background of his consciousness, he could hear her voice yelling for him to stop, but his mind said, "*There's no need to be angry. There's no need to hurt him; he's a friend.*" And bewildered, Sherman Tankersley stopped.

Agnes ran up to him and punched him in the arm, about as high as she could reach. "Stop it, Sherman!" she yelled. "Don't you dare hurt that man!"

Sherman glanced at his wife and then he looked back into Clay's eyes. "I'm sorry," he said. "I may have overreacted."

"You think?" Clay said with relief, still gasping for breath. He continued to look into Sherman's eyes, still manipulating him. "Maybe instead of you pummeling me, we could be friends."

He hesitated as if he was considering Clay's proposal. Finally, he reached out his hand for Clay to shake. "Maybe we could do that, Clay. Maybe we could."

"It's possible, Sherman," he said as he held his chest, "and right now's the perfect time to start." Clay sank back to his knees. His chest hurt like crazy, but he'd had broken ribs before from football, and he didn't think Sherman had broken any bones—miraculously.

Jasper was kicking and screaming, trying his hardest to escape the hedge that he was impaled in. Holding his chest, Clay started over to retrieve his little friend. Sherman, who was at least seven or eight inches taller than Clay, grabbed Jasper by the ankles and lifted him high in the air. As soon as his head emerged, he started flailing at Sherman, twice more striking him in the face. After the second punch, he dropped Jasper on his head and walked away. Clay gasped as he bent down to see if Jasper was okay. His face was scratched and bleeding lightly, and sticks and foliage were in his red hair, mouth, nose, and ears. He sneezed and began brushing off the debris. "How's your head, Jasper?"

"There's nothin' wrong with my head, Moron! I been dropped on my head lots of times!"

"I figured, but I also figured it'd be best if I asked anyway. Compassion, you know?"

"Where's the brontosaurus? Did you shoot him?"

"I haven't got my gun yet, but I don't think a bullet would work anyway. I talked to him nicely. We're all friends now."

"All of us? He's King Kong. He scares me, Clay."

"Then you showed amazing courage. Everything's all right now, though. Sherman?"

"Yeah, Clay?"

"Come over here and meet Jasper. Sherman…Jasper. Jasper…Sherman."

"Sorry about the toss, Jasper."

"It's okay. Happens more'n you'd think."

"This is my wife, Agnes."

"That wasn't fun at all!" she wailed. "We're gonna put you on Valium one day, Sherman. Nice to meet, everyone. All that anger and violence, honey, and there's *barely* a dent on the car."

As much as it hurt his rib cage, Clay started laughing. Soon everyone was joining in.

Micky Kidder, walked up in the middle of the hysterics. He was wearing the badge of the Chief of Police. "I hate to interrupt all the fun, but your cars are blockin' the entrance. Hey, Clay," he said as he noticed who he was talking to. "Would ya mind movin' your car?"

Clay saw the badge. "Aye, aye, Chief. The badge looks good on you, by the way."

"It's just temporary. Either Casserly'll be reinstated eventually, or someone with more experience'll be assigned. I'm just fillin' in."

"Casserly's suspended?" Sherman asked. "Good. Can't stand the man."

"We need to talk, Sherman," Clay said. "How 'bout we move our cars right now? I have to pick up some personal items in the station, but d'you have a few minutes?"

"I just stopped here to pay a parking ticket. We got bowling in a few minutes."

"You have a card or something so I can give you a call?"

Sherman took a business card out of his wallet. It read, "Sherman 'Septic' Tankersley Plumbing." Clay had to laugh. They shook hands, moved their cars, and the Tankersleys drove away. Clay went into the station, went through the process of picking up his belongings, and then gave Jasper a ride home. He still had more questions than answers, but it had been a productive day.

Jeff LaFerney

Chapter 26

Matt Royster had taken the day off work and left early Tuesday morning for Nashville. He told his wife he was making a college visit to the University of Tennessee to meet with the baseball coach. She knew so little about college recruiting that she didn't even ask why Ace wasn't going with him. He drove straight through Nashville to a town off I-65 called Brentwood. That was where Kayla Casserly lived on 1665 Frierson Street.

He nervously sat in his car on the street in view of the house. He chugged a beer for some liquid courage. It was an awfully long drive for her to say no. Finally, he put the car back in drive and pulled into Kayla's driveway. He stepped out of the car and climbed the porch steps before ringing the doorbell. There wasn't an immediate response, but just as he was raising his hand to try again, the door opened, and there she was.

She was just as beautiful as when he'd last seen her almost eleven years before. Her curly blond hair hung just short of her shoulders, and her light blue eyes were just as sparkling as he remembered. She smiled a friendly smile. Matt had aged and his hair was graying a bit. He had a short, scruffy beard, and his belly was getting pudgy, so Kayla didn't recognize him. No one spoke. The pause, only a few seconds in actuality, seemed to go on and on to Matt, so he spoke first. "Hi, Kayla. I'm Matt Royster...Maggie's brother."

"Oh, my gosh, you are! What in the world are ya doin' here?" she said with a touch of Southern accent.

Matt looked her in the eyes. It was the most sincere gesture he'd made in a long, long time. "I've been following your career, and I know your singing career's sorta on hold right now. I came to try to convince you to come back to Fenton for a while. You don't have to stay...you just have to come. That's all I'm askin'."

"Come on in, Matt. Let's have ourselves a li'l chat."

Matt followed her into her small but cozy home. The living room was the first room they came to, and Kayla suggested that Matt take a seat. "Kin I git ya somethin' ta drink?"

"A beer?"

"I don't believe I have any beer. How 'bout some tea?"

"Sure, sure. That'd be fine. Thanks." Matt's continuous headache was starting to pound once again.

When she returned, she sat down in a cloth chair opposite the couch that Matt was sitting on. Again, she didn't speak, so Matt cleared his throat.

"I talked to Lyle. He said you could sing again at the Hotel if you came back. He'd pay you just like before."

"Matt, you were right about my singin' career, but that's my own choice. It's on hold fer personal reasons."

"I have money." Matt looked again into her pretty blue eyes. "I got $10,000." He pulled out an envelope with all the bills rubber-banded together and handed it to her. "Don't tell Maggie that I gave it to ya, but it's yours if you come back to Fenton for a while. Please," he stressed. "Come back to your hometown for a visit. Say you'll come."

"Okay, I'll come," she said. She hadn't thought about coming home for a long, long time, but suddenly, it seemed like a good idea. She had family and friends there, and with the plans she had, she was pretty sure she wouldn't have another chance for a long time. "When would ya like me ta come? You seem ta have it all pretty well planned out."

"Today...tomorrow. Soon as you can."

"Yer timin' happens to be right on the money, Matt. I'll need a day ta git things in order, but it's awful hard ta turn down ten grand. I'll be there."

Matt looked her carefully in her stunning eyes and said, "It's not about the money, Kayla. I'll see ya again in a coupla days."

He left with an excruciating headache. Something was wrong that alcohol wasn't fixing. At least he'd performed a good deed. He hadn't done too many of those in recent days.

***

Sherman climbed onto the metal steps of the mobile home before knocking on the door. The owner opened her door and screamed before slamming it shut again. The steps began to bend under his weight and the handrails seemed to be closing in on his body. "Ma'am, I'm Sherman Tankersly!" he yelled through the closed door. "I'm the plumber you called!"

The door eased open once again. "I don't think you can fit in my bathroom."

Sherman stepped back off the steps that were beginning to fold under his weight. "What exactly is the problem, Ma'am?"

"How tall are you? How much do you weigh?"

"I'm nearly six foot ten, and last I checked...I was...overweight. What does that have to do with your problem?"

"It's just a little bathroom...with a doorway not designed for a mythical-sized being. The toilet leaks, it runs all the time, and it's flooding the floor."

"Do you mind if I take a look?"

"Do you really think you can fit?"

"How 'bout you let me give it a try."

She looked skeptical, but nodded and opened the door. Sherman stepped back onto the metal steps, which bent even more. He looked down just as the steps gave way under his weight and folded around his legs. The handrails squeezed into his waist and ribs as he sunk to the ground. He was stuck—trapped completely. He had about a hundred pounds of iron enclosing his lower legs and waist, and when he reached down to pull the rails apart, they wouldn't budge. The lady of the house stood on the threshold of her trailer with her mouth gaping open. "You wrecked my steps...my entire porch...you'd better pay me for that!"

Sherman was embarrassed, and he hated to be embarrassed. He usually responded to that by losing his temper. "Heck if I'll be paying *you*! I'll be *suing* you. Premises Liability. I know my rights. I got injured because of the hazardous condition of your personal property."

"You don't look too injured, and the only defect in my property was it wasn't designed to hold a million pounds." She slammed her door shut and left Sherman standing there, trapped.

He dialed 9-1-1, gave his address, and told them to bring the Jaws of Life. He couldn't see any other way to pry his body out from the metal. He had no choice but to sit on the ground, the trailer's porch attached to his body, and await his rescue. His phone rang, so he pulled it from his belt. "It's Tank! Who's callin'?" he nearly shouted in frustration.

"It's Clay Thomas. You wake up on the wrong side of the bed today?"

"If I woke up on the wrong side of the bed, Agnes'd be dead...squished flat and suffocated. I'm just sittin' around twiddlin' my thumbs, Clay. Barely a concern in the world. What's up?"

"D'you mind if I ask you some questions?"

"No problem...I ain't goin' anywhere...and I mean that literally."

"Thanks. Listen, did you happen to know Bosley Pemberton once upon a time?"

"Bosley! Hated the man, but yeah, I knew him. He got what he deserved...an early death."

"You live in a dark place, Sherman. You ever think about counseling?"

"You're a funny man. The guy was a womanizer...even had Agnes under his spell somehow. Agnes can sing, Clay. That little woman can belt out a tune, and she had a gig at the Fenton Hotel for a while. Then Bosley got his hooks into Kayla Casserly. He was determined to add her to his collection, I suppose, and since he was doin' the entertainment schedule, he dropped Agnes off the rotation and replaced her with Kayla."

"Did he ever hit on your wife?"

"Not that I know of...but he was prob'ly too scared of me to try."

"Probably true."

"More'n likely," Sherman said honestly, "but he got into her head somehow. Got her to believe that he was doin' the right thing pullin' her off the schedule. Agnes kept tellin' me how he was such a nice man who was doin' his job the best he could. I didn't buy it."

"From what I'm hearin', there were a lot of people who felt the same way about him. Is that true?"

"Heard rumors all the time that he'd seduced dozens of women. I never let Agnes outta my sight, so I'm sure she wasn't one of 'em. If I'd've known he touched my Agnes, he'd've been a dead man."

"Well, he *is* a dead man, and it could be that someone killed him. It seems it could've been anybody, though, especially if he'd seduced as many women as you're suggesting, but I don't know how to find out who had access to him that night."

"Heck, Clay, I could tell ya. Lyle threw a party that night. Closed down the Hotel early and had lots of folks there."

"How do you know that?" Clay asked.

"'Cause I was there."

"Seriously? Who else was there?" Clay asked.

"Well, let's see. We was there...me an' Agnes. She was doin' some catering for Lyle. That woman sure can cook."

"Yeah, I noticed. Who else?"

"Um, Lyle and a couple waitresses. Kayla Casserly was singin' and her parents and brother were there. Maggie's family was there—Matt and his wife and a couple others. Couple other friends of Lyle's...the old police chief, seems like. A music producer was there listenin' to Kayla. Bosley was there. I remember a tall, Amazon babe there. Hot. Don't know her name."

"You remember a lot."

"Listen, just 'cause I'm big don't mean I'm dumb. I wasn't drinkin' so that I could drive Agnes home safe, and I remember stewin' about that Casserly woman singin' all night. Bosley was drinkin' and joinin' in with the singin'. Then, of course, he died that night which kind of cemented most of the images in my brain. I guess I just happen to remember a lot of the details."

Just then sirens were heard in the distance, closing in and getting louder.

"I'm gonna have to let you go, Buddy. Those sirens are for me."

Before Clay could even formulate a question, he heard, "You the guy who needs the Jaws of Life?"

"Yeah," Sherman responded. "That'd be me."

"You're trapped in a car? You've been in a bad car accident?" Clay asked incredulously.

"No, had an accident with a porch..."

Another voice in the background started shouting, "You make sure that he pays me for my porch! I'm too old to be steppin' up into my home from down there! He destroyed my steps and railings both!"

"You better watch what you're sayin', Old Lady. I'll be suin' your pants off. I'm the one in distress here!" Sherman realized Clay was still on the phone. "Hey, Clay? I'm a little busy at the moment. I'm gonna have to let you go." He hung up.

Clay looked at his phone in wonder. He was now friends with the biggest and smallest men he'd ever encountered—both of whom had awful tempers. There was no telling what kind of mess that Sherman was in, but after knowing Jasper for almost a year, he knew to just shake his head and let whatever happens happen. He'd gone most of his life, distancing himself from people in an attempt to avoid manipulating them. Now, two of his friends were people that he happened to manipulate while in the middle of an attack. It made him miss the normal friendship that Zander provided. He was someone who understood Clay and let him be himself. And then, while thinking about Zander, his mind shifted to Erika. He realized in a sudden jolting admission, that *she* was actually his best friend, and it made him miss her all the more.

Watching his dad suffer in the hospital, getting arrested, and attending his father's funeral were all stressful events. He began to think of his father again. Losing his mother, then his wife, and now his father were easily three of the saddest moments of his life. However, as his mind processed his current condition, he realized his saddest moment was watching Erika leave for Florida. He recalled her words. *"You've got some people to help and some thoughts to sort out. I've no doubt that when you're finished sorting, you'll do the right thing like you always do. I just hope it includes me. But I need you to love me completely. Until you can do that, I'll be in Florida."*

It seemed to Clay that he was making progress on the murder mystery, but he didn't know what to do next. He felt that talking to Zander Frauss might be the next logical step so that he could solve the mystery and begin to work things out with Erika. Clay bowed his head for a moment and said a simple prayer, "God, if there's any way You can help me to work all of this out, now would be a good time to start. Amen." It was just then that his phone rang. He looked at his caller ID. It was Zander.

Chapter 27

Tanner stepped out onto the basketball court with a ball in his hands. He'd been meeting regularly with two of the freshman recruits, Earvin and Gervin Jones, to play some pick-up ball after weight training and conditioning. Earvin and Gervin were identical twins. They both were two-time first team All-State players while at Flint Southwestern High School, and they led their team to the state championship their senior season. They were voted number two and three—both would claim to be number two—for the state of Michigan's Mr. Basketball award. They made no bones about it; they came to the University of Michigan so they could play on the same team as Tanner. They had played against each other in one of the epic basketball games in Flint area history when Tanner was a senior for Kearsley High School, and they had maintained ever since that they would follow him wherever he went.

They both had grown some since that junior year when they first met Tanner, and now each stood at nearly six foot six. Both would almost certainly be in the starting lineup, and Michigan was getting pre-season attention as one of the better teams in the nation. They took turns warming up with some outside shooting. On one of Tanner's turns, he made nineteen consecutive three-point shots before the Jones brothers got him laughing so hard that he missed.

"Ain't never seen no one could shoot like you, man," said Earvin—or maybe it was Gervin.

"Yo, you mean no one besides me," said Gervin—or maybe it was Earvin.

"You? I meant besides me. Bro, you always had brain damage. You can't even count to as many as he's made in a row. You tryin' to count, man? You can't count that high."

"I ain't countin' shots. I'm standin' here amazed at how many passes you throwin' in a row. You be throwin' more passes right here, right now, than you threw the whole season last year. What it feel like to pass the ball, Bro? You actually pretty good at it."

"You talkin' to *me* 'bout passin' the ball? How you know anything about it when you never done it your own self?"

"Tanner...*Dude!* You ever gonna miss? Gervin here never went so long without a shot. I be worrying 'bout his mental state."

"Least I have a mental state, Earvin."

By then Tanner was laughing so hard he missed, which was probably the goal of the twins from the beginning. At least Tanner figured out who was who during the conversation. They both happened to be *great* passers and terrific all-around and unselfish players. Their only flaw was with their great intensity came lots of trash talk, and it got them in trouble occasionally. Tanner was the perfect leader and role model for the twins, and he loved hanging with them.

Gervin began to shoot and was putting together his own run of consecutive shots when Tanner got that dizzy feeling he got when he was about to have a vision. He'd been thinking about his dad a lot that day, hoping to come up with a way to help him solve his mysteries. He backed off the court for his own self-protection as the vision started to become clear. He saw a bottle. It was sitting on a shelf in a dimly-lit office next to a book called *Haunted Michigan* by Gerald S. Hunter. Tanner had to bend over and put his hands on his knees to steady his balance.

"You all right, Tanner?" he vaguely heard one of the brothers say.

He nodded his head yes, as the vision expanded, letting him see the office a bit better. There was a large, wooden desk and a high-backed, leather chair. There was some paperwork on the desk that he couldn't make out clearly, but one thing he could identify was a menu. Some items were crossed off; a few notations had been made in the margins. At the top, he could clearly read "Fenton Hotel Tavern & Grille." He was looking at the office of Lyle Riddick and a three-quarter empty bottle of Jack Daniels on his bookshelf.

As soon as the image was clearly identified, it went away. With it went the dizziness. Everything was fine, but Tanner knew that he'd discovered another clue. He'd tell his dad as soon as he was done working out with the Jones brothers.

"You okay, Tanner?"

"Yeah, I'm okay. Just got dizzy for a minute." Both of his friends were staring at him with genuine concern. They really were great guys to know and be friends with. "I'm fine." They still were staring. "Tell you what...either one of you girls beats me in one-on-one, we'll know there's somethin' wrong. Who's gonna lose first?"

"Oh, here he go," said Earvin—or maybe it was Gervin. "Makin' excuses even before the game. You know you got no chance, dizzy or not."

"I guess you just volunteered to be my first victim," Tanner responded.

"Now you talkin'. Game on, Airhead. I'll even let you have the ball first." He checked the ball and D'd up on Tanner.

"Rookie mistake," Tanner said. He let fly a three-pointer that hit nothing but net. "One zip. You can play better D than that, right?"

Both players and the other Jones twin—whichever one it was—smiled together. They were genuine smiles of respect.

***

Clay let his phone ring one additional time before he said, "Hello." Intentionally, there was no inflection in his voice.

"Hello, Clay...It's Zander." Clay didn't say a word in response. "Um...I guess you're gonna wait for me, huh? Well...I'm callin' because I need your help."

Clay still waited. Was he kidding? No apology. No explanation. Just "I need your help"? Finally, he decided to respond through the uncomfortable silence. "Where were you when I needed *your* help?"

"Clay, I'm sorry. I've got a lot of explaining to do, I know. But that's why I called you. When I'm done explaining...well...I've reached the conclusion that I need your help."

Clay felt himself getting angry. He had a right to be angry. He took a couple of deep breaths and tried to think logically instead of emotionally. He would suggest they meet, and once they did, he'd make Zander talk. He'd make him talk, and he'd read his mind, and when he was done manipulating him, he'd release him forever.

The pause while Clay was deliberating how he was going to treat his old friend was long enough that Zander became impatient. "Clay? I know I don't deserve your help.

I've been a horrible friend. But I'm asking you, please. Please, talk to me."

"I have some things to do in my office on campus, Zander. I'll stop by to see you. I'll listen, but I'm not sure if I'm willing to help you. Actually, there're some questions I need answered by you. If not for that, I'd be tempted to tell you to just take a hike."

"I understand," Zander said.

"It'll be about an hour and a half before I can get there."

"I'll be waiting in my office in the science department. Thank you."

Clay hung up. He tried to fight the anger he was feeling, but the urge to boil over was overwhelming. He went down to his basement and took fifteen minutes to pound his punching bag. His ribs were aching from the blow from Sherman, but he pounded the bag until he was exhausted. Then he took a quick shower, jumped in his car, and headed for Ann Arbor. It took nearly an hour to get there from his home in Flint. Just as he started heading south on US-23, he received another phone call. It was Tanner.

"Hello," Clay said.

"Dad, I had another vision," Tanner said. "There's a bottle of Jack Daniels whiskey on a shelf in Lyle's office at the Hotel. It must be evidence of some sort. We need to get it."

"We can't just walk in there and take it, Tanner."

"We probably could, but how 'bout we ask Lyle nicely. I think he'd do whatever I asked. Where you at, by the way? It sounds like you're in your car."

"I am. I'm driving down to the campus."

"Why're you heading out here?"

"Because Zander called, and I'm gonna meet him. I'm hopin' that I don't punch his lights out...or shoot 'im. Maybe you should come too, so I don't commit a crime."

"Where're you meeting?"

"In his office in the science department. Be there in about forty minutes."

"I'll meet you there. I'll try to make sure you don't melt his mind or something. Plus, I wanna see what he has to say about the night I saw him at the Speedway. And why did he tell Casserly you have mind powers? He has a lot of answering to do."

"He sure does. Should be interesting…Hey, I'm gonna let you go. I've got another call."

"Okay, I'll see ya soon."

Clay switched from one call to the next. "Hello."

"Is this Coach Thomas?" the unknown caller asked.

"Yes, can I help you?"

"Probably. This is Matt Royster. We talked about Ace a while back. I'm callin' to see when you're plannin' on makin' an offer to me."

"Well, Matt, here's the thing. I'm impressed by Ace. I really am. But the only offer I *could* make is for some sort of a partial athletic scholarship. He still hasn't pitched this spring, and I don't know how I'm gonna allot my monies, so right now I have no definite offer to make."

"You gotta be kidding! Everyone wants Ace. I got recruiters callin' every day. Recruiting's easy if you make the right offer. I'm on my way back from Tennessee, and I got proof of that."

"Proof of what, Matt?"

"That if you flash the right amount of money around, people'll do whatever you want. I went down there to get my sister's girlfriend to come back, and she'll be here tomorrow. Lyle Riddick's already makin' arrangements for Kayla Casserly to sing tomorrow at his Hotel…just like old times. I flashed a wad of money, and got right into her head. Had no trouble convincin' her to come home. Recruiting's that easy."

"That's not how I do it, Matt, but did you say Kayla Casserly's gonna be at the Hotel singing tomorrow?"

"Yep. Get there early. Place is gonna be packed. She starts at eight."

An idea started formulating in Clay's mind. "I'll tell you what. I'll show up tomorrow night, and we can talk. How about that?"

"I knew when we talked before that you wanted Ace. Wasn't too hard convincin' you of that."

"I guess you're right. I'll see you tomorrow night."

Clay hung up, but before he could sort his thoughts, his phone rang again. "Hello."

"Hi, Clay. It's Becca. How are you?"

"I'm fine, Becca. How're you doin'?"

"Well, not so good actually. I've been waiting to hear from you, and it seems you've pushed me to be the forward one. How about we meet for dinner?"

Clay couldn't help but smile. He'd made one small prayer and the floodgates were opening. "I'll tell you what. How about we meet for dinner tomorrow night? I heard Kayla Casserly's in town, and she's performing at the Fenton Hotel."

"That place makes me uncomfortable, Clay. I've been avoiding it for the last ten years. How about somewhere else?"

"I've already made plans...plans to be *there*. How about you come with me?"

She hesitated. She was used to getting what she wanted, and she wanted Clay. "Okay. What time?"

"How about 8:00? That's when the excitement begins."

Almost immediately after he hung up with Becca, his phone rang again. "Hello."

"Clay? It's Lou Kirkus. I've got some information that you'll be interested in."

"You've done your tests already?"

"Oh, yeah. And let me tell you, the evidence on that paper sack was very helpful."

"D'you find saliva traces in the sack?" Clay asked. His mood was improving minute by minute.

"Yep, we did. And guess who it belonged too? Bosley Pemberton. Inside of the sack, seven inches from the bottom. From the top of your head to the corner of your mouth is seven inches. If the sack was pulled over his head and secured to make it airtight, Bosley would drool seven inches from the bottom of the sack. His head was inside that paper bag, Clay."

"Finally, some actual evidence. Thanks, Lou. Any fingerprints on the bag?"

"Sure was. Pulled some good ones. There's more than one set, yours and, I assume, your son's included, but I sent the information to AFIS for identification."

"AFIS?"

"Automated Fingerprint Identification System. It's a database of all fingerprints taken and stored in the U.S. If the person's prints are in the system, there'll be a 'mostly likely' match soon."

"That's encouraging too. I've got some more news for you, Lou. There's a whiskey bottle—Jack Daniels—on a shelf in Lyle Riddick's office. I have reason to believe that you just might be able to pull some prints from that too."

"Excuse me for asking, Clay, but what would make you think that particular bottle is important in any way at all?"

"Did you trust me with the sack? You need to just trust me on this too. We need to get to that bottle and pull some prints."

"How do you plan to do that?"

"Well, what're you doing tomorrow evening, say around 8:00?"

"I don't have plans."

"How about you make some? Come to the Fenton Hotel. Get a good meal; some entertainment'll be provided. And bring your equipment because I'm gonna need you to pull some prints."

"Sounds like the kind of adventure I've been waiting for. I'll be there."

Clay was suddenly in a much better mood as he hung up the phone for the last time. He still didn't have any answers, but he had a really good feeling that he was about to figure some things out.

Jeff LaFerney

Chapter 28

Clay drove up and parked in a faculty parking space. He exited his car and walked into the science building where Zander's office was. Tanner was waiting inside the door. They took the stairs two at a time to the second floor and turned left down the hallway.

"How're we workin' this, Dad? We just gonna *make* him talk?"

"An hour and a half ago, I would've said yes. Just make him talk and be done with him. But I've had time to simmer down a bit, and I say we give him a chance first."

Tanner shrugged his shoulders as if to say, "Whatever." He was willing to give Zander a chance to come clean on his own, but if he didn't cooperate, Tanner had already decided that he'd make him talk.

They entered the offices' common area and walked down a short hallway to enter Zander's office on the left. He was sitting on a couch, and he looked horrible, so Tanner said, "You look like crap." He was just being honest.

Zander's normally stylish haircut was overgrown and undermanaged. His face was pale and his baggy eyes were swollen and bloodshot. He was even thinner than when Tanner had visited just six days earlier. What was most evident right away, however, was that Zander was hurting emotionally. Any remaining anger that Clay felt, just slipped away. All of a sudden, seeing Zander the way he was looking, Clay wanted to help. It didn't make sense, but that's how Clay felt.

It was Tanner, however, who said, "Holy cow, Doc. You look like someone who could use some help." He was an insightful kid. Clay and Tanner both took a seat and patiently waited to hear what Zander had to say.

Zander hesitated, took a deep breath, and began. "Back in 1996, I was a young, thirty-year-old neuroscientist and neurosurgeon, and I was ready to change the world. I got hired by the University hospital and started what I was sure was going to be a successful career. One day a patient came in to see me. He was having headaches that lingered and were affecting his sleep, his work, and his personality. He admitted that he drank to dull the pain. We did tests...CT scans...MRI...X-rays. What I noticed was that he had an unusual formation in his medulla oblongata. He'd fallen off a ladder doing repairs at his work and landed on his neck. He was alone, and the injury temporarily paralyzed him. Unable to move and with no one to help, he eventually fell asleep, and apparently he had a vision of me. When he awoke, he had movement again, and though the vision haunted his thoughts and dreams for the next two months, he never did anything about it. He finally looked me up and came to me when his fingers started going numb, and his headaches started getting worse.

"We were talking one day when I was going over test results, and he asked me if I thought that people could manipulate others with their minds. Apparently, he believed that he had the ability to do so. Then he also told me about his dreams and visions. He thought that if he wasn't going crazy, then his injury had somehow affected his brain. It was this patient—my first parapsychology patient—that led to me opening my Division of Perceptual Studies in 1998. I was working under the theory that this man's medulla oblongata had partially opened and made an unusual brain connection due to the injury.

"After enormous amounts of testing, observation, and interviewing, we reached the conclusion that the man had actual, though limited, mind control and clairvoyant abilities. The man regularly came to me for five years as my research began to develop and take shape and as my Division of Perceptual Studies began to get noticed. Then he died suddenly."

"Bosley Pemberton," Tanner said to no one in particular. He was just thinking out loud, but Zander nodded affirmation.

"You had his file out the day Chief Casserly came to see you. The day you told Casserly that I had mind powers," Clay said.

"That's one of many things that I need to apologize to you about. There've been a lot of reasons to be discouraged lately, but learning the Department was being shut down was the biggest reason. I wasn't producing enough information, apparently, and though my theories were all proved true by the two of you, I'd promised to keep quiet about you. I had four folders in my hands when Casserly barged in. I was trying to figure out a way to use the information I had recorded in them without breaking your trust and without getting myself in trouble. When I tossed the files on my desk, Casserly only got a look at your name and Pemberton's. Tanner's file and one other were buried under yours, Clay. He came into the office already talking about mind control, and when he accused you of using mind powers to commit crimes, I reacted and said you'd never use your powers for something like that. It just slipped out."

"Bosley's ghost haunts the Fenton Hotel, Zander," Clay informed the doctor. "I told 'im that I'd do my best to find out how he died. He believes he was murdered, but he doesn't have memory of his past. We've discovered that he was using mind control, and we know how he was using it. Did you know?"

"No, he claimed to me that it wasn't right to use his powers, and when he did, he felt guilty. He claimed that his headaches were a constant reminder to *not* use his abilities because when he manipulated people, the headaches got worse. I assume he lied, so what was he really doing?"

"He was using his powers to seduce women. He was a womanizer, and he kept a very lengthy and often detailed list of his conquests. As a result, he caused himself numerous problems, and he also made a lot of enemies—enemies that had a motive to kill him."

Tanner was admittedly fascinated by the fact that Pemberton was a patient of Zander's, but the discussion wasn't heading in the right direction, as far as he was concerned. "That information's all fine and dandy, Dr. Frauss, but I, for one, have questions about more pressing issues. For instance, what were you doin' at the Speedway Gas Station on the night my grandpa was injured? And why did you lie and tell me you weren't there?"

Zander bowed his head in shame. "I'm sorry about lying to you. Yes, I was there that night, but it was just coincidence. I stopped for gas is all. I saw the paramedics load up a patient into their ambulance, but I had no idea that the injured man was your grandpa, and I didn't know anything about the robbery either. I guess you saw me when I pulled back out. That evening is just one more thing to be ashamed of, and I've got a lot of explaining to do to my wife too."

Clay let the sketchy explanation slide for the time being. "Zander, Tanner and I've been doing our best to investigate all the robberies in Fenton lately. The one at the Speedway was just one of many, but we're comin' up short. Besides the videotape at the Speedway and one eye-witness account of a car at the station, the only thing we're sure of is that the thief is controlling people with his mind. He's forcing people to give him money, and he's erasing their memories. Do you know anything about that?"

"Remember when I said I had four file folders when Casserly came to visit me? The fourth folder is a file about the thief in Fenton."

***

Butch Casserly snapped his book shut and threw it across the room in an aggravated fit of frustration. Three times he'd pulled his personal handgun out of his drawer with the intention of continuing his mission to put Clay Thomas behind bars. If Clay wasn't the perpetrator, he had to be involved in some other way, probably manipulating others to do his dirty work. If Clay wasn't a criminal, he was certainly digging up information, and Casserly needed to find out what he knew. Each time Casserly pulled out the gun, though, he had second thoughts and replaced it in the drawer. He'd try to occupy his time and mind but would end up with the gun in his hand once again. Slinging the book across the room marked the end of another futile attempt to distract himself.

He rose from his favorite chair and headed for the refrigerator for another beer. No matter how unusually determined he was, he couldn't formulate a plan to arrest Clay. Casserly was probably the only person surprised at his own ineptitude. He never really perceived his flaws the way everyone else did, but his vanity often kept him plugging away at his job, and occasionally he had stumbled upon success in the past.

As he continued to wallow in self-pity and beer, his phone rang. "Yeah, it's Casserly!" he snapped.

"I see you're just as pleasant as ever," replied his sister, Kayla.

"Kayla?" Butch asked. "Is that you?"

"Yes. I just called to let you know I'll be in Fenton tomorrow afternoon. I need a place to stay if you don't mind."

"You haven't been back home for more'n ten years. What's wrong?"

"I was persuaded to return and sing at the hotel—special return engagement, sort of. I've run from my past long enough. I'm hoping that returning will rid me of my ghosts once and for all. It's time for me to move on to a new stage of my life."

Casserly wasn't listening. "I get to hear you sing again? Tomorrow? Course you're welcome to stay with me. Long as you want. I've managed to get myself a couple of days off, so I'll be here whenever you get here." Thoughts of Clay Thomas finally eluded Butch. Old memories of his sister's singing and of his dreams of her success replaced his feelings of aggravation and frustration. When the call was completed, he set out to get things prepared for her arrival.

***

"So who is it, Zander? Who's responsible for the death of my dad?" Clay said. "You've known all along? How could you keep something like that from me?" he asked incredulously as he looked his old friend in the eyes.

Zander paused to consider his reply. Finally he said, "Doctor/patient confidentiality."

"That's bullcrap, and you know it!" Clay fiercely responded. "*Seriously*? Not only is that an absurd lie, but I know what you were thinking. I read your mind, Zander. What do you mean that you got yourself into trouble, so you figured you had to get yourself out of it?"

Tanner stood up and started pacing the room angrily. "Don't lie to us, Doc." There was a burning intensity in his eyes. "You've lied long enough. We're playing by different rules now. Tell us the truth on your own, or I'll make you. I swear on my mother's grave; *I'll* make you."

Clay stared daggers into Zander's eyes. "*I'll let him,*" he said telepathically. The amount of intensity that the Thomas men were able to draw upon was a shared trait that was staggering.

Zander bowed his head in shame again. "I did something horrible. I convinced myself that I was doing it for the good of science—for the good of mankind. But I was lying to myself too. I did it for me. You two weren't cooperating, and I wanted to save my lab. I wanted to tell others what I'd discovered. I did it out of pride and selfishness. And once I did it, it backfired, and I tried to fix it on my own. I was ashamed of myself. Clay and Tanner, your hearts are so good...so genuine...that I just knew you'd be ashamed of me...and disappointed. Now the guilt just eats away at me. I couldn't see how you could forgive me when I couldn't even forgive myself."

"What did you do?" Clay asked impatiently.

"A patient came to see me. The patient had a medulloblastoma at the fourth ventricle which needed resecting. In layman's terms, there was a cancerous tumor on the medulla oblongata at the opening into the fourth ventricle. Unlike the two of you, the medulla was closed on this patient, but I theorized that if I cut another fistula—another opening—in the medulla oblongata, I could surgically create another connection in the closed part of that section of the brain. With a simple cut, I could open up the closed part of the medulla oblongata. So I deceived my surgical team, and I made the opening—an opening similar to the two of yours. Like some sort of modern Dr. Frankenstein, I created a monster.

"At first, my patient was cooperative, and I began to build a new set of data, but unlike yours, this data was going to be shared. Until my patient turned on me. You see, I didn't procure permission to do what I did, so I ended up between a rock and a hard place. My patient had become a monster, and I couldn't do anything without implicating myself. If I tried to turn the monster in, it could manipulate everyone involved, and the only one who would suffer consequences was me. I was too ashamed to come to you as I watched the consequences of my selfishness spiral out of control. And then when I realized that your father died at the hands of the monster I created, I withdrew from you completely." Tears filled Zander's eyes and began streaming down his face. "I'm so sorry, Clay. Tanner. Someone you loved was killed because of me. It was my fault."

The room was silent as Clay composed himself. Tanner was watching his father closely. Clay felt his son's eyes riveted upon him. He took a deep breath to calm the anger he was feeling. "One thing I've learned the last couple of years is that the only choices I'm responsible for are my own. I've experienced my own consequences, but I also learned that I'm not responsible for the choices of other people. You may have created your monster, Zander, but you aren't responsible for its choices. You're only responsible for your own." Again he took a deep breath, knowing that Tanner was eyeing him closely. By then the glare in his eyes had softened. "I can find it in my heart to forgive you."

Zander bowed his head and cried even more. "You're a better man than I am. Thank you."

"He's Superman, Dr. Frauss. You should've known," Tanner said proudly.

"But now it's time we stop your monster before someone else gets hurt. So give me the name."

Zander humbly did what he should have done a long, long time before. He slid open his desk drawer and pulled out the fourth file folder. The name was typed in bold on the tab. Clay looked down, and his jaw opened in utter disbelief. He knew Zander's monster.

Jeff LaFerney

Chapter 29

Clay was a big guy—six foot two and nearly two hundred pounds—but next to Sherman, he felt small. He was doing his best to keep a conversation going as he and Sherman were headed to a shooting station at the Williams Gun Club the morning after he and Tanner had talked to Zander. "You really put 'Sherman Septic Tankersley' on your business cards?"

"I'm a plumber…septic tank?…Get it?"

"Yeah, but aren't septic tanks, like, full of crap?"

"Ha, ha. You're a funny man, Clay. Don't you think I've heard that one before? Load of laughs, you are."

"How 'bout if I call you Septic instead of Sherman?"

"How 'bout if you call me Tank, like in Sherman Tank?"

"You're about the same size. It makes sense."

"And I'm about as indestructible and powerful."

"That too."

"Why you got yourself such a sissy gun, Clay?" said Tank as they were preparing to shoot at a target just fifteen yards away.

"It's small enough to fit in my back pocket. I have a concealed weapons permit due to the fact that I've had people try to kill me twice in the past two years...not counting your attempt with your bare hands the other day."

"I was just goofin' around, Clay."

"Good thing or my aching chest might've actually been caved in. Thanks for not takin' that punch seriously."

"The one thing that's serious is that you're one tough dude. In more'n one bar fight, I done knocked people unconscious with that punch."

Clay aimed and emptied his gun in a nice tight grouping on the target. He was pretty impressed with himself. Sherman then pulled out his weapon of choice. It was a Smith & Wesson .44 caliber Magnum revolver. The overall length of the gun was almost fifteen inches, and loaded, it weighed nearly five pounds. Sherman proceeded to blow the target to pieces with some nifty shooting of his own.

"I can fit the gun in my back pocket too," he said.

"Yeah, but you have much bigger pockets."

"How true that is," said Sherman. "How're you from thirty yards?"

They shot several more rounds, and Sherman proved to be quite consistently impressive. "You're one big, scary dude, Tank," Clay said as they finished up their last target. "Which brings me to part of the reason I asked you out here."

"You got somebody for me to scare?" he asked in all sincerity.

"Sort of. I want you to come out to the Fenton Hotel tonight at about 8:00. Casserly's sister's singin', and there's gonna be a lot of people there. I'd like you there, sort of as my body guard. I mean, there's probably gonna be some trouble there tonight, and besides my son, I can't think of anyone that I'd more rather have my back. How about it?"

"I don't know. Did you know that place is haunted? The last time I was there, a ghost with a tall hat and a long beard just appeared outta nowhere when I was about to get in a fight. He said, 'Leave...now!' So I left. He only had to tell me once."

"There's nothin' to be afraid of, and I need your help."

"Ghosts scare me, Clay."

"There's a quote I read once. It said, 'Courage is not the absence of fear, but rather the judgment that something else is more important than fear.' Like friendship, for instance. In the face of fear, you gather up your courage because there's something else more important to you. Can I count on you to be there?"

"If I can bring Agnes. Want me to bring Dirty Harry? That's what I call my gun."

"Yeah, just slip it in your back pocket."

Clay hadn't gotten into Sherman's head, but he still felt a little guilty manipulating Sherman to do something in which he wasn't comfortable, but he wanted his new friend Tank there for two reasons. The first was that he was still a suspect in the murder of Bosley, but the second was that Tanner had warned his father that guns were going to be fired. It was becoming a common theme in Tanner's visions to see someone shooting at his dad. What were Tanner's exact words? "For such a nice guy, you sure rub a lot of people the wrong way." Clay had to laugh.

He'd already talked to Zander earlier in the day. Apparently he'd come clean with his wife, who forgave him just as Clay and Tanner had. Lydia and Zander were planning on being at the hotel for dinner. He'd also called the acting police chief, Micky Kidder, and told him to come, possibly to make two arrests. Micky had some investigating to do but said he'd get it done as quickly as possible. With everyone and everything in order, Clay and Tanner were hoping to solve both mysteries in the same night. It was time to move on with his life, and he felt it would all start at the Fenton Hotel Tavern and Grille.

***

Lyle Riddick had worked himself to near exhaustion preparing for Kayla Casserly to arrive. The stage was set, the sound equipment tested and retested, and the lights prepared. She showed up at 6:30 with her brother, Butch, close on her heels and went through the process of her preparations. Maggie was a nervous wreck. Butch was trying to help but was just getting in the way. Lyle was trying to oversee it all while dealing with the evening dinner crowd.

Tanner and Lou Kirkus timed their arrival together at about 7:45 and took a table in the Grille, away from all the energy and excitement in the tavern where Kayla would be singing. Lou set a bunch of equipment on his table including his fingerprint powder, an ultraviolet light, an expensive camera with an attachment to his computer, and his laptop with connectivity to the internet.

Matt Royster was the next to arrive, and he headed straight to the Tavern and sat on a stool at the far end of the bar. Maggie was busy and paid him no attention even though she knew he was the one who persuaded Kayla to return.

Zander and his wife, Lydia, arrived right on time at 8:00 just as Lyle was announcing Kayla as his guest singer. They took a table in the dining area in a corner of the Grille and settled in for dinner.

Clay picked up Becca, and they arrived just a few minutes later and took a seat at a table alongside the bar. When Sherman and Agnes arrived, Sherman sat, much to the dismay of Becca, right in front of her view of the entertainment. Clay ordered a Coke for himself and a cocktail for Becca. He relaxed at his table as Kayla finished Shania Twain's "Whose Bed Have Your Boots Been Under?" which was ironically about a woman who's had trouble with the man in her life who has a penchant for cheating with woman after woman. She tells him he'd better fess up or she's gonna send him packin'. As she finished the song, Clay noticed Bosley materialize. He was sitting in a chair at the table, unable to take his eyes off Kayla as she sang.

Her voice was terrific and she exuded personality. Clay could see why Bosley was attracted to her, but he knew that Bosley was just a selfish jerk. He didn't deserve to be murdered, but the murder was a result of his self-centered ways. Clay was hoping, with a little bit of good fortune, that tonight was the night he'd figure out who killed Bosley, and maybe they could both move on with their lives. As he looked around, he could see that all the players were in place, and it was time for Tanner to begin his work.

Jeff LaFerney

Chapter 30

Tanner looked at the clock on his phone and determined it was time to get started. His first stop was at the front desk to talk to Corissa. He made a little bit of small talk, flirted a little, but then said, "Corissa, I need you to go to the kitchen and bring me eleven drinking glasses."

"Really? For what?"

"I'm here with a forensic pathologist. We're gonna study friction ridges. I need the glasses so I can gather some fingerprints."

"Cool," she said. "I'll be right back." She came back carrying a tray with exactly eleven glasses. She followed Tanner to his table and set them down for him. "Is there anything else I can do?" she asked.

"Not right now, but thank you," Tanner replied.

"Okay, step one completed," Lou Kirkus said. "I'll shine these glasses up while you get the bottle of whiskey."

"No problem." Tanner waited for him to shine up one of the glasses. He grabbed the glass, pulled a piece of paper from his pocket, and left the table in search of Lyle Riddick. He found him in the short hallway in front of the kitchen, talking to a customer.

When Lyle noticed Tanner, he turned to him and shook his hand. "How ya doin', Tanner?"

241

"I'm fine, Mr. Riddick, but I need a favor."

"Sure, Tanner, anything. What can I do for ya?"

"I need you to sign this paper that I have, giving me permission to go up into your office and take the bottle of Jack Daniels you have stored on a shelf."

"That's the strangest request I've ever been asked. What in the world for? That bottle's got sentimental value to me. My friend, Bosley Pemberton, drank from that bottle the last night he was living."

Tanner didn't even have to look Lyle in his eyes. His powers were stronger than his father's. "Well, there's no longer any reason to keep it, so you're donating the bottle for my research. The paper says I can have it to do whatever I want with it. Just sign right here," he pointed.

Lyle grabbed the pen in Tanner's hand and signed right where he pointed. "I can't think of any reason to keep it, so there you go. Anything else you need?"

"Yep, I need your fingerprints on this glass." He'd been holding the drinking glass in a cloth napkin which he lifted so Lyle could grab ahold of it. Lyle reached out and pressed his fingers onto the glass. "Thank you, Mr. Riddick."

"You're welcome."

Tanner returned the glass to the table and gave it to Lou. "Lyle Riddick's prints are on the glass. I'll be back with the whiskey bottle in a minute." He tossed the paper that Lyle had signed on the table. "It says right here that Lyle has given me the bottle to do whatever I want with it. Who woulda figured?"

Tanner headed to the back of the Grille, rounded a corner, and climbed the steps to the owner's second floor office while Lou started dusting the glass for prints. Lou used a finely crushed fluorescent powder which he gently applied to the surface of the glass. The powder clung to the friction ridge residue, making the print visible. But Lou's

242

plan was to use the ultraviolet light, making the powder, and therefore the print, glow. He would then photograph the print and load the picture onto his computer. When he had the picture ready, he labeled the image and sent his first print to the Automated Fingerprint Identification System to store the information. He planned to do the same thing to each set of prints that Tanner brought him.

Once Tanner was inside Lyle's office, there was a bookshelf behind the desk, and on it was the bottle of Jack Daniel's whiskey. Tanner carefully slid it off the shelf, touching only the bottom and top with the cloth napkin he had brought in an attempt to not damage any of the prints. He then carried the bottle back to the restaurant and set it carefully on the table.

Lou said, "Okay, I have Bosley's prints and now Lyle's. They should both be on the bottle if Bosley drank from it on the night he died. I'll dust it to see if there're prints from anyone else too."

"Have you heard back about the prints on the paper sack yet?" Tanner asked.

"I'll know tonight if there's a match."

Tanner squeezed his own fingerprints on another clean glass. "These are mine," he said. Then he walked a glass over to Zander. "Hi, Mrs. Frauss." She smiled. "Excuse me, but I need your prints, Doc."

"What in the world for?" Zander asked.

"You know, Dr. Frauss. Earning someone's trust is a lot more difficult than losing it. You haven't been shootin' straight to a lot of people lately. I'd like to believe you're not involved in any of this simply because you say so, but today's another day in the process of you earnin' back my trust. More'n likely, havin' the prints will just eliminate you as a suspect. What d'ya say?"

Lydia said, "Give him your prints, Zander."

He did it just as she said.

"Hmmm. You seem to have mind powers too, Mrs. Frauss." Tanner smiled at her.

Lydia smiled back. "You've got more work to do. You'd better get to it."

Tanner carried Zander's glass to the table. "Zander Frauss," he said. "I pray he's not who we're lookin' for."

He grabbed the tray with the remaining eight glasses and headed for the Tavern to get his remaining specimens. Feeling a bit impatient, Tanner decided to take care of everything all at once. As he entered the Tavern, Kayla was finishing up one of her biggest hit songs:

> "Slammed a wrench on the hood of his sports car
> Used a bat and I wrecked his man-cave bar
> Threw the remote through his plasma TV
> Told'm better think twice before messin' with me.
>
> Next time better think before ya cheat
> Next time don't jump b'tween the sheets
> Ohh…better not cheat…
> Ya, ya…better not cheat."

There seemed to be a running theme to her songs. There was applause as she finished up, and then Tanner walked right up to her. He said, "I need to borrow the microphone." He manipulated her mind, so she simply handed him the mike. "Um, excuse me everyone, I need your attention…Excuse me." He waited. "You there," he said to Butch Casserly. "Yes, you…I need your attention." With everyone's eyes upon him, he proceeded to control the whole room. "Dad, you don't have to do this, but everyone else, I need you to close your eyes." The room was totally silent as everyone obeyed Tanner—everyone except Clay.

"You're all very, very relaxed. You're just letting your mind go." Then out of pure impatience he said, "Everyone, you're all hypnotized." He paused a few seconds. "I need you all to reach out your right hand...Yes, just like that. Now hold your hand out in front of you until I tell you that you can stop. It'll be just a minute."

He motioned for his dad to help him. Together they procured prints from Kayla and Butch Casserly, Sherman and Agnes Tankersley, Becca Fonteneau, Maggie and Matt Royster, and also Clay's own prints. They were careful to not leave any of their own prints on the suspects' glasses, and Tanner labeled them with a piece of paper that he dropped inside of each. When he was done, he said, "You can put your hands down now. Thank you. On the count of three, you'll all wake up refreshed, and you'll cheer for the great Kayla Casserly! Thanks for your cooperation. One, two, three."

Everyone opened their eyes and began loud clapping and cheering for Kayla as Tanner slipped away with his tray of glasses. If it all worked out, when Lou was done working his magic, they would have a murderer.

***

Clay had slipped back into his seat before Tanner released everyone from their hypnosis. Everyone and everything seemed perfectly normal except Bosley was still seated in his chair where he was during the whole hypnosis episode. A waitress came and took a food order for Clay and Becca. Bosley seemed mesmerized with Kayla again, but Clay decided that he needed to get away from Becca for a few minutes so he could talk to the ghost.

"You seem preoccupied, Clay. You're not giving me the attention I crave," Becca flirted.

"I'm sorry. It's true. I partly came here to talk to a couple of people, I have to admit. Will you give me a few minutes so I can take care of that before our food arrives?"

"Okay. I need to visit the ladies' room anyway. Excuse me," she said as she rose from the table.

As soon as she was gone, Clay slid a little closer to Bosley and said. "Tonight might be the night that we find your killer."

"Do you see her, Clay?" he said as he nodded in Kayla's direction. "She's amazing."

"Even in death, you haven't changed, Bosley."

"What do you mean?"

"I just got done telling you that your murder might be solved tonight. Your purpose for being a ghost might be solved tonight, and yet, you're only concerned about a woman. Do you want to know what I found out about you?"

"You know who I am?"

"Sure do." Clay was feeling irritated with him. "Seems you lived here in the hotel all of your adult life. Loved the place. Even left your inheritance to Lyle, so he could do all the improvements he's done over the years. You were the right hand man to many a Fenton Hotel owner over the years. But you had an injury to your neck. It caused a partial connection of your medulla oblongata to the fourth ventricle in your brain. It allowed you to have some ability to manipulate people's minds and occasionally have visions. Do you want to know what you did with that ability you were given?"

"If I had that kind of ability, I'd make *that* woman right there fall in love with me," Bosley said as he continued to watch Kayla.

"That's exactly what you did. And you did it to dozens of other women too. Apparently you were nothing more than a womanizer, leaving lots of damage in your wake. One woman committed suicide, she was so distraught, and on the night of your murder, one Kayla Casserly found out that you were cheating on her too. Lots of people had reason to harm you, Bosley."

"So you're saying I deserved to die?"

"No, someone killed you and should be punished, but I wanted you to know that you're not guilt-free. I hope you find peace when this is over, but you're not innocent, Bosley. You hurt a lot of people yourself."

Bosley faded away, leaving Clay to wonder if he really cared.

He stood and walked over to Matt Royster.

"Hey, Coach!" Royster nearly shouted. "You here to make an offer? Lots of other schools are makin' 'em. How d'you think I'm gettin' all this money I throw around? Schools are tossin' more money my way than I can spend." He reeked of alcohol. Clay didn't like him. All of a sudden, he knew that he wanted to stay away from Matt, no matter how good Ace was.

"Matt, I might've been willing to make a scholarship offer to your son, but I'm certainly not willing to cheat and give money to you. I don't give money to recruits or their parents. Royster, I've decided that havin' your son on my team isn't worth the baggage of havin' you around. I'll find me another 'ace' pitcher, and you can go prostitute yourself to someone else." With that, he turned and walked away.

"You'll regret this, Thomas!" Matt shouted to Clay's back. "I'll take him to Ohio State where he'll kick your butt the next four years! Don't walk away from me, Thomas!" he yelled, but Clay never turned back.

Mickey Kidder arrived at the suspect's house with a warrant in his hand. Jasper had made a call to Monica Grey, the assistant district attorney, who actually seemed to like the little guy. She pulled some strings and convinced a judge to issue a search warrant. Mickey had also procured a warrant for the suspect's bank records, and there was an enormous amount of activity in the form of cash deposits. According to Clay, he would find that the suspect drove a red sports car, and sure enough, there was one parked in the driveway—a fiery red Mustang.

He rang the doorbell, but there was no answer. He tried the front door, but it was locked, so he tried a side door, again with no luck. There was a doormat on the ground at the door, so he lifted it in hopes of finding a spare key. Again, there was no luck. Next to the door was a potted plant, but no key was under it either. Then Mickey saw a rock in a landscaped area next to the door. The rock was tucked behind a shrub, and it looked somewhat oddly shaped. He reached for it and discovered it was plastic and could be pulled apart into halves. He pried it apart, and there was a key to the house. Mickey inserted it into the door and helped himself inside.

He was looking for clothing—specifically University of Michigan gear. He checked coat closets, hooks in the mud room, and bedroom closets. Eventually he found what he was looking for, and they matched pictures he'd made from the video Casserly had taken from the Speedway Gas Station. He's found a knit hat, a U of M jacket, and a couple of different pairs of tennis shoes. He took his own luminol chemiluminescence solution, just like what Tanner had used, and sprayed both pairs. The second glowed blue in spots as it reacted to the iron in the hemoglobin. There were traces of blood on the shoes, blood that would match Carlton Thomas's from the crime scene.

Mickey also drove with a crime scene analyst to Shirley Maxwell's house in Fenton and persuaded her to let him search for fingerprints on her Toyota Camry. He printed Shirley and her husband, who claimed he never drove her car, and then his associate dusted for prints on the door handle, the lever for moving the seat back, the buttons for the side-view mirror and window, the inside door handle, the rear-view mirror, the steering wheel, and seatbelt buckle. Most prints were smudged or only partials, but quite a few good prints were pulled and recorded for testing.

Mickey looked at his watch. It was nearly 9:00 by the time he had finished his investigating, and it was time to head for the Fenton Hotel to make an arrest—maybe two if Clay was right about solving an eleven-year-old murder case as well. He made a call to Tanner to let him know what evidence he'd found, and to let him know that he would be at the Hotel in ten or fifteen minutes.

***

Becca navigated her way to the women's restroom. She entered and chose the third stall, the one farthest from the door. The room was cold, and she felt a deep chill as she sat upon the toilet, the cold making her desperate to pee. She listened to the dull, muffled bass sound from the Tavern as her mind wandered to the plans she had for Clay later in the evening. She was imagining his fingertips gently caressing her head and lost herself temporarily in distant memories of her sister gently running her fingers through her hair. Rachel had loved to run her fingertips over the back of Becca's scalp and then lift her hair as she pulled her fingers through before she started over again. It was a feeling—a simple gesture from her sister—that she missed, but it was like it was actually happening as she fantasized about Clay.

Suddenly, she snapped out of the fantasy and realized she was actually feeling the caresses, and her hair was actually being lightly pulled away from her head. She was certain that someone was actually massaging her head and sliding invisible fingers away from her scalp. In a moment of anxiety she looked all around the stall as if she might see the ghostly hands that were running through her stylish locks, but clearly no one was in the stall with her, and fear began to arise within her. What was it—a ghost? She stifled the desire to scream as she quickly jumped from the toilet and began pulling up her underwear and jeans. The toilet paper started unrolling *up* toward the ceiling, and the cold became noticeably colder. She screamed, panicking, and rushed from the restroom, stumbling and blasting into the door as she fell.

She landed in a heap, half in and half out of the door. As she sprawled there in fear, her pants unzipped and unbuttoned, Clay looked down on her. He could see the terror in her eyes as he knelt to see if she was all right. "What is it?" he asked. "You look terrified."

"There's a ghost in there! It was playing with my hair! It was unraveling the toilet paper!"

As Clay was kneeling down to help her, a body materialized. "*She's my sister,*" the voice said. "*She's a horrible person who's done horrible things. When she's punished for what she's done, I can finally be set free.*"

Chapter 31

Clay walked Becca back to her seat at the table. "Are you okay? Can I get you anything? Some water?"

"Maybe a drink to calm my nerves. Look at my hands...how they're shaking."

Clay stood to go ask Maggie for something from the bar, but Sherman grabbed his arm as he started to walk by. "What is it?" Clay asked.

"'Member when I said there was some hot Amazon woman at that New Year's Eve party?"

"Yeah."

"That's her...the babe you're with. Agnes agrees."

"You're kidding! *She* was here that night too?" He hesitated as he thought about the significance of what he'd just heard and what Rachel Fonteneau's ghost had just said. "Thanks, Tank. That's good to know." Clay headed for the bar and told Maggie to mix up something for Becca, and then he went into the Grille section of the hotel.

"Have you matched any of the prints to the sack or the bottle yet?" he asked Lou.

"All the information's been sent to AFIS. It's just a matter of time. I'm surprised I don't have a match yet."

"Let me know as soon as you know something."

"Mickey called, Dad. He has evidence that we can use against our thief. He's on his way now."

That was good news, but Clay was still stuck. He knew who robbed the Speedway and the other venues, but he didn't know how to stop the person in the future, and he was pretty sure if the person's mind control was as strong as Zander suggested, the person would never be convicted—even with the evidence that Mickey had gathered. But possibly he could use his knowledge in some way. What he did *not* know was who committed the murder. Was it Lyle? He seemed unlikely, but with Bosley out of the way, he received a lot of money, and he had total control of the hotel. Was it Maggie? The only thing she seemed likely to gain by a murder would be a better chance at a relationship with Kayla, but that didn't work out at all, so Clay felt she was unlikely. Could it have been Agnes or Sherman? Sherman had a terrible temper and hated Bosley, but his recent behavior made Clay think that neither person was likely. Matt Royster was a jerk, and he might've done something impetuous to help his sister out. He seemed a good possibility. Kayla Casserly seemed a logical possibility also. It would have been easy for her to gain close access, and she would have clearly been angry to find out Bosley had cheated on her. Butch Casserly was a long shot, even though Clay wished it was him. He was home on military leave, but as an officer and a cop, he didn't seem like the best person to consider. Becca Fonteneau now seemed like the best possibility. She was a "horrible person" who had done "horrible things." A murder is pretty horrible. Her sister had committed suicide. Maybe Becca blamed Bosley. And Becca was a pharmacist, so maybe she used her knowledge to drug him. But maybe it was someone else completely—someone he hadn't even met yet.

He decided to make his way back toward the bathrooms in hopes that Rachel Fonteneau's ghost might appear. He looked around, and as busy as the Hotel was that evening, no one was near the restrooms. He knocked on the women's bathroom door. There was no answer, so he tried again. Again it was silent. So he opened the door a crack and peeked in. "Is there anyone in here?" he asked the empty space. "I'm looking for Rachel Fonteneau," he said. "I think you know that I can hear you if you talk. I may be able to help you find your justice."

Clay slipped inside the restroom, but just as the door was about to close behind him, it flew open, and there was Chief Casserly. "What're you doin' here?"

"Um…going to the bathroom?"

"I don't mean *here* in the bathroom—it don't matter to me how weird you are—I mean here at the Hotel. What're you doin' here tonight?" the former chief asked again.

"I'm solving a murder. Isn't that obvious?" he said, even though it clearly wasn't. "You know, I've already solved the robbery cases, so I figured I'd move up to something even more impressive, like murder."

"You solved the case? So you're turnin' yourself in?"

"No, I told you all along it wasn't me. But now I know who really *is* doing it. I'm just waiting for Chief Kidder to show up, so he can arrest both the thief *and* the murderer."

Casserly's face grew a dark shade of red. He advanced toward Clay with obvious intentions of harm. Clay stood his ground and was ready to defend himself if necessary. But instead of a fight, there was a voice. "Get out!" The voice came out in an angry whisper but had the volume of a shout. Casserly didn't even hesitate. He opened the door as fast as he could and fearfully escaped the ghost.

"Thank you," Clay said. "I might have hurt him." There was no response, so Clay decided to ask a question. "You're Rachel Fonteneau?"

"Yes."

"Do you know how you died?" Clay was getting right to the point. He was getting impatient.

"Yes."

"Why doesn't Bosley know?"

"It's part of his punishment, I presume."

"Why do you think your sister needs to be punished?"

"I went to her for consolation when I learned that Bosley was cheating on me, and what she did for me was give me drugs. She turned me into an addict, and then slept with my fiancée. She was having an affair with Bosley while we were engaged, and she continued it after Bosley broke it off. She slept with him on the afternoon of New Year's Eve."

"And Kayla found out? Did she murder him?"

"She found out somehow, but I don't know if she killed him. After my death, I sometimes would sit with Bosley at night. When I came into the room that night, someone was there in the dark, and I said to get out. It was so quiet that night. He usually snored, but that night there were no sounds. He wasn't breathing; he was dead too."

"The murderer suffocated him."

"I didn't know that. And Bosley didn't know either. He's been wandering around ever since wondering who he is and what happened to him."

"Why didn't you tell him?"

"It's not my purpose." That's all the reasoning that she gave, and she didn't say another word.

Clay stood there in silence for another moment, and then turned to leave.

***

Lou's computer beeped, indicating that an e-mail had arrived. He clicked on the icon on his computer's bottom tool bar, displaying his e-mail page. The message was from AFIS and the subject line simply said, "Urgent."

"It's here, Tanner."

Tanner, who had impatiently made a list of each of his father's prime suspects, picked up his pen. He leaned in to read what the message said. Bosley, who was invisibly standing beside the table, leaned in as well. The e-mail was brief.

"Live Scan Device has analyzed friction ridge patterns, comparing suspects' samples to evidentiary prints while eliminating prints from Clay Thomas and Tanner Thomas. Matched minutiae points has determined most-likely match to one suspect..."

As soon as Tanner saw the name, he circled it on his list and rushed from the restaurant into the bar. His father needed to be warned. With flashbacks of his recent vision where his father was getting shot at, he raced from the bar with such urgency that Zander followed at his heels.

**

Tanner saw his dad as he was exiting the restroom. Clay saw the urgency on his face. "What is it? You have the results, don't you?"

"Is Kidder here yet? We have the evidence to make an arrest," said Tanner.

"I'll call him right now," he said as he hit the speed dial for Mickey Kidder.

Tanner had just handed his dad the note with the name on it when Zander arrived. It wasn't a question—it was a statement—when Zander said, "You know who the murderer is, don't you."

"Yes, and we have physical evidence—prints, clothing, blood evidence—against our thief. It's time for you to do your thing."

Just as Mickey answered his phone, Clay glanced down at the name that was circled on the paper. Several pieces of the puzzle tumbled into place. "Mickey, it's Clay. You need to get here immediately."

"I'm just down the road. It'll be just a minute. What's happening?"

"We know the murderer. Get here as soon as you can."

Chapter 32

In the Tavern, Kayla had finished another song, a rockin' song by Kelly Clarkson called "Whyyawannabringmedown." Obviously, the venue at which she was singing was having an impact on her song choices. She had strayed from her mostly country music selections while blasting her emotional song choice out to the audience. Mild clapping ensued. Kayla backed away to get a drink from a water bottle. Then there was a loud squawking sound through the speakers as Bosley picked up the microphone which appeared to be floating in the air. Somehow a folder with all of her songs and notes flew across the stage and the papers scattered in several directions. There were a couple of mild gasps as a handful of people witnessed the act that was perpetrated by an invisible Bosley Pemberton. A startled Kayla bent over to pick up her papers. Then Bosley materialized just to Butch Casserly, who stared at the phantom in front of the microphone.

"Nearly eleven years ago, I died on the second floor of the Fenton Hotel. Ever since, I've been stranded here in this building, left to wonder about the method and the perpetrator of my murder, for yes, I was murdered. My murderer stands before me today."

A lady at one of the tables started laughing at a joke from a friend. Another lady was talking to her date as if nothing was happening. Clay could not see Bosley, but he could clearly hear the voice and see the floating microphone. Otherwise, the place was gradually becoming nearly silent. Clay made his way back to his table with Tanner glued to his side. He noticed that Maggie had stopped working away at the bar and Matt had set his mug of beer on the counter and was curiously looking around. Lyle had been walking down between the bar stools and the customers' tables, but he stopped, curious about the strange happenings in his establishment. Agnes stopped eating the food that had just been delivered, and Sherman stopped mid-shake with the table salt in his hand. Becca swallowed her drink and stared blankly at Zander Frauss who was not more than five feet away. Kayla, mouth gaping open, crouched not eight feet from Bosley's invisible apparition as the microphone appeared to be floating in air. Butch choked back his own fear as he watched Bosley continue his speech. Heads of other diners were beginning to turn as the lengthy quiet became more and more noticeable.

"I was drugged and suffocated in my sleep," Bosley was saying from the stage. "The murder was accomplished by a person in this bar tonight—a person who drugged my drink and then slid a paper bag over my head as I was sleeping, sealing it so that I would eventually suffocate in my own exhaled gasses. The murderer's prints are on the bottle of whiskey I was drinking from that night as well as on the murder weapon of choice, a simple paper sack." Butch Casserly stood, unaware that he was actually the only person besides Clay Thomas who could hear Bosley.

***

Zander sat down next to Becca. "I have some news for you, Becca."

Becca said, "Go away, Zander. I told you to stay out of my life."

"Becca, I'm gonna come clean to the police. Funny...my wife was concerned that I'd had an affair, but what I did was so much worse than that. I've lost my Division of Perceptual Studies, and I may lose my license to practice medicine, but I won't be party anymore to you misusing the abilities I gave you. I happen to know that you're the mysterious Fenton thief, and I'm prepared to go to court to testify. We have evidence," Zander said to a speechless Becca, who happened to be staring at the appearance of the ghost of her sister, Rachel.

Rachel said, "I'm trapped here in this hotel until the day you suffer for all the horrible wrongs that you've done."

Becca's prolonged moment of speechlessness continued as she raised her arm to point at her sister.

***

"I stand before you, Butch," Bosley continued, "with one single objective: to name you as my killer, the killer that Clay Thomas tracked down for me."

Clay continued to look up at the stage where Kayla looked terrified, but Bosley was invisible to him. "You're dead!" Butch screamed. Diners' heads turned toward Casserly.

"My killer," Bosley yelled into the microphone, "is Butch Casserly!"

As Bosley yelled, patrons covered their ears from the squawking sound that screeched through the speakers. "No!!" roared Casserly as Bosley made his accusation. He dove toward the stage and did a flying leap in an attempt to tackle the man, but Bosley was just a phantom, and Casserly crashed on the stage in an embarrassingly futile effort. The ghost had vanished.

***

"You have to pay for what you did to me," Rachel Fonteneau said to her sister as Lyle and Kayla hurried toward Butch and the destruction he had caused.

"There's a ghost! I see a ghost!" screamed Becca. "You're dead! You hanged yourself!"

Heads turned from Casserly's embarrassing display to Becca and her outrageous outburst. As heads were turned, Casserly pulled himself away from Lyle and his sister and marched toward Clay Thomas while pulling his gun from his shoulder holster. Clay and Tanner, like everyone else, had turned toward Becca and didn't see Casserly coming. "You're a dead man, Thomas!" yelled Casserly as he released the safety and pulled the trigger three times—three loud blasts from his police revolver.

***

When Clay heard his name and the loud gun blasts, he ducked, attempting to pull his gun from his back pocket. Screams rose from several of the female diners as people ducked under tables or ran for the emergency exits. All three bullets entered the right shoulder and chest of Sherman Tankersley, who had stepped in front of Clay to protect him from Casserly. Sherman, all six foot nine and a half, and nearly five hundred pounds, fell back onto Becca, whose chair fell backward. With the entire weight of the massive giant driving her into the floor, Becca fell on her neck with a crack.

As Clay fumbled with his gun, time seemed to stand still. Focusing all the mental strength and energy he could muster, he directed his mind telepathy on Butch Casserly's gun as Butch fired three more shots Clay's way. Through all the confusion, a distinct "clank, clank, clank" was heard. Casserly looked down and saw the three bullets that he'd just shot at Clay Thomas bounce on the dark brown, hardwood floor.

Bulletproof

He looked at Clay in utter confusion. "What *are* you…*bulletproof?*"

It was then, finally, that Mickey Kidder burst into the room with his gun drawn. "Put your gun down, Chief."

Tanner got into Casserly's head. *"Freeze! Don't move a muscle!"* Casserly continued to point his gun, but he stood perfectly still as Tanner manipulated his mind. Tanner moved to Casserly, grabbed his gun out of his hand, and gave him a jarring elbow right in his teeth, knocking Casserly to his knees. He looked his dad in the eyes and communicated telepathically. *"I enjoyed that."*

Clay smiled. *"I'm definitely jealous."*

Mickey rushed to Casserly's side and snapped a pair of handcuffs on his former boss. Tanner handed him the gun and then walked straight to his dad. "I told you you were bulletproof." He hugged his dad. Clay was grateful that Tanner's head was temporarily buried in his shoulder because he didn't want Tanner to see the tears in his eyes.

Jeff LaFerney

Chapter 33

Sirens blared and confusion reigned. Zander had slowed the bleeding of Sherman and had moved on to Becca. Sherman was in pain, but somehow appeared to not be seriously injured—maybe that's how it is when you're the size of a pole barn. Agnes was crying, but Sherman had a look of peace on his face—the look of a man whose heart was tested and he passed with flying colors. Clay knelt by his side. "Thank you, Tank. You saved my life."

"Heck, Clay, you know how many friends I got? I can't afford to lose one. Besides, it was the right thing to do. No big deal, buddy."

Clay glanced at the paramedics who were standing next to a stretcher and conversing silently. He said, "Hey, Tank. Those paramedics over there are havin' nightmares about the discs they're gonna slip tryin' to get you on the stretcher. Do ya think you can walk to the ambulance?"

"Sure, Clay. Wouldn't wanna put anyone in traction while I'm over here bleedin' to death. No sweat."

Clay laughed at his new friend, and then worked his way over to Becca. She was in much worse shape. She was being attended to by Zander and another set of paramedics. Becca caught Clay's eyes. "I can't feel anything, Clay. I can't move my arms and legs."

"Luckily, Zander's here, Becca. He'll do whatever he can to help you."

"Clay?"

"Yes."

"I'm sorry about your dad. Zander just told me. I didn't know."

"Sometimes, Becca, we're blessed with a gift. If we're good people, we learn to use it for the benefit of others. I know you didn't hurt my dad intentionally, but you set out to hurt others by stealing from them, and my dad paid for your selfishness with his life. He's in a better place now, so I forgive you, and I hope you'll be all right; I really do. Maybe someday you'll find peace and happiness, but I won't be a part of it. I have the perfect woman already."

He turned to see Rachel Fonteneau with tears in her eyes. She was looking at her sister, but she didn't say a word before she simply faded away to wherever she was meant to be.

As Rachel faded from sight, Bosley seemed to materialize one last time. "You did it, Clay. I've been released. Thank you."

"Bosley, you need to know that you're not without guilt in this. Your selfishness led to all of this trouble. I don't know what or where your future is, but the world, sadly, is a better place without you. I'd be embarrassed if anyone ever said that about me."

Clay's next encounter was with Kayla Casserly and Maggie Royster. Maggie was holding Kayla's right hand, and was consoling her as Clay stepped up. "I don't know what just happened here," Kayla said, "but Maggie just filled me in on some of it. When Bosley died, I never suspected it was murder."

"Why did you come back today?" Clay asked.

"Matt convinced me. But mostly I came to say my final goodbyes. I didn't do that the first time I left. I'm going to this time. I'm getting married, Maggie. I'm cutting way back on my singing career, and I'm finally gonna get married."

Maggie had a look of disappointment as she released Kayla's right hand and picked up her left to reveal an engagement ring. "Congratulations," she said without much enthusiasm. "Goodbye for real this time, Kayla. Best wishes to you." She left Kayla there and found Lyle, giving him a genuinely affectionate hug.

Matt had stumbled out of the bar without a word to Clay. Agnes followed Sherman's ambulance to the hospital. Zander rode in a different ambulance with Becca, and Lydia left for home. Maggie stayed at Lyle's side, and Kayla slipped away. Mickey hauled his former police chief off to prison. That left Lou Kirkus and Tanner as the only remaining holdovers. Lou packed away his evidence and equipment. "It was sure interesting working with you guys. If you ever start your own detective agency, Clay," he said with a smile. "I'll be here to help. You guys are quite a team."

That just left father and son. "Well, Dad, how're you feelin'?"

"I'm pretty much sick of this place, to be honest. I think it's time I took a little vacation and headed for Florida. There's someone there I'm missin' a whole lot right now."

"I understand, and I'm pretty sure she'll be really glad to see you too. Lou was right, ya know. We *are* a pretty good detective team." Tanner reached out and handed his dad three bullets—the ones from the floor. "We've done some pretty unusual things over the last couple of years, Dad, but stopping speeding bullets with your mind pretty much takes the cake."

Clay smiled. "You're the one who said I was bulletproof. I guess I took you literally. Besides, there's been enough death in this family. It's time to live life and live it abundantly. For me, that can only truly happen with Erika in my life. I need to go see her."

"I knew you'd say that, and so did Zander. This is a gift from your best friend." Tanner handed his dad some plane tickets: one round trip ticket to Tampa, Florida and back, and one one-way ticket for Erika to come home. Tanner hugged his dad and said, "Love you, Dad."

"I love you too, Tanner. Thank you."

Epilogue

She was lying out on a lawn chair in a bikini. Her sunglasses made it impossible for Clay to know for sure if she could see him or not. She was so stunningly beautiful to Clay that he simply stopped and stared. She had a beautiful tan and her nearly white-blond hair was bleached even lighter than normal. Her fingernails and toenails were painted a North Carolina powder blue—her favorite color. Every curve was perfect to Clay. Even the small birthmark on her left thigh was perfect. It was a beautifully sunny day in Tampa, and Clay was sweating in his khaki shorts and t-shirt. Clay had met Erika Payne's parents for the first time when he arrived at their door just moments before. They were happy to meet him, but quickly directed him to the patio outside the back door where Erika could be found.

Clay continued to stare as he fought back his nervousness and excitement. Finally, he said exactly what he was thinking. "You are the most beautiful woman in the world."

Erika turned her head slightly and giggled. "I've been watching you since you came out that door, and I was thinking you're the most handsome *man* in the world."

She stood, and Clay went to her and hugged her with the most warm, sincere, loving hug he'd ever given. "I've missed you so much," he whispered. "I love you."

"I love you too. I was worried about this moment."

"I'm sorry. But you were right. I needed to solve my mystery and figure out what exactly I wanted in my life. How I truly felt about you."

"So tell me what happened."

"Well, we found out who killed Bosley, the ghost. Believe it or not, it was Chief Casserly."

"The idiot with the butch cut?"

"Yep. What we discovered was that Bosley was a womanizer and among other horrible things, he cheated on Casserly's sister, who Bosley was engaged to. Casserly had big plans for his sister's singing career, and wasn't fond of Bosley to boot, so he put some sleeping pills in his whiskey and got him ridiculously drunk. Then he suffocated him in his sleep. We located the bag he used to kill Bosley and found prints, plus there were prints on the whiskey bottle which Lyle had saved all those years. The whiskey had evidence of sleeping pills, and the sack had a receipt that was traced to Casserly as well. He was sloppy because a ghost scared him out of the room."

"I have sources," Erika said, "that tell me you got shot at again."

"It's no big deal. Happens all the time," Clay said with a smile. "My new friend, Sherman Tankersley took the bullets for me."

"Who's that?"

"Remember the friendly giant at the shooting range?"

"Friendly?"

"I think we caught him on a bad day. Anyway, he's doing fine. The bullets didn't do any serious damage, and I'm pretty sure he's not gonna hold it against me."

"Speaking of friends…what about Zander?"

"Well, apparently Zander's very first parapsychology patient years and years ago was a man named Bosley Pemberton. Bosley had some mind-control powers and some clairvoyant ability. But Bosley died suddenly, and after that Zander's next prized patients were me and Tanner. I guess he was feeling pressure to produce evidence that his Department of Perceptual Studies was cost-effective, but because Tanner and I refused to cooperate, he was losing his funding. Then a lady by the name of Becca Fonteneau came along."

"Becca Fonteneau? She's the lady who was calling you."

"Yes. She had cancer, and Zander performed the surgery, but he opened the closed part of her medulla and created a monster. Becca also refused to cooperate, plus she was running amok, committing crimes and manipulating people. I'm pretty sure she even got into my head, Erika, which would explain a lot—at least to me, it would. Zander was embarrassed to come to me, and then when Becca critically injured my father, he withdrew even more. He basically blamed himself. Once we got together, we started putting the pieces together, and we solved the crime."

"So Becca's in jail?"

"Not exactly. There are charges pending, but when Sherman took my bullets, he fell on Becca, and she broke her neck. Zander went with her to the hospital, and he, as her doctor, performed emergency surgery. She has a long road to rehabilitate herself because she was paralyzed before the operation, but she can live a normal life if she commits to it. The thing is, while in surgery, Zander reversed what he'd done. The closed part of her medulla oblongata is forever closed once again. She'll no longer have mind-control abilities."

"So she won't be coming after you anymore?"

"Well, I'm still the same hunk I used to be, but I'll have the ability to resist her now—if she tries again."

"I see." She smiled.

There was a lull in the conversation. Erika was still smiling, but she had kept her sunglasses on, probably so Clay couldn't read her mind. He couldn't tell what she was thinking, but Clay had already given himself his pep talk—dozens of times, actually. So he took a breath and started in.

"Erika, after Jessie died, I was lost for quite a while. I didn't know what to do with my life, and I didn't know how to deal with my abilities. Having Tanner and Zander helped a lot, but it wasn't until I met you that I began to really figure things out. I loved you almost from the beginning. But there were still issues, and my dad's injury brought them back to the surface again. People who I love seem to die. It hurts. And I'm really not ashamed to say that being with you scared me too. I loved Jessie with my whole heart, and I didn't know for sure if I could love you like that. And I lost Jessie. And then when I lost my dad, I worried about how it would feel to lose you too. I truly think that Becca had influenced my feelings, but that's just an excuse. I was afraid. I've always done things one hundred percent, and I didn't want to just give you ninety or ninety-five.

"But since you've been gone, and since you told me I needed to sort out my feelings, I've been doing that. You said I needed to love you completely, and I needed to determine if I was capable of doing that."

There was another long pause, and Erika's pulse quickened. "*What if he can't do it?*" she thought. She felt as if she was going to cry even before he said it. He'd come all the way out to Florida, like Clay Thomas would do, to face her like a man and tell her that he couldn't love her the way she wanted and needed.

"Erika?"

"Yes?"

"I've never loved someone or wanted someone more in my life than I love and want you. But to do that, I know I'll have to commit to you one hundred percent." There was another pause as Erika choked back the tears of rejection.

Clay reached into the right pocket of his shorts and got down on one knee. "Erika Payne, I cannot nor do I ever want to live without you, so I'm asking...will you marry me?"

Before he could even open the box and show her the ring, she screamed, "Yes!!! Yes, yes, yes, I'll marry you! Of course I'll marry you!"

Clay stood and she jumped in his arms. She threw off her sunglasses and looked him in the eyes. *"Clay Thomas, I love you. You've made me the happiest woman alive."*

Clay couldn't help but laugh, probably more from relief than from the fact that she let him read her mind. A lot had happened to him in the last two years, but all the pain, all the trials, all the lessons had been placed in his life so that God could show him what wonderful things he had in store for him. There was nothing that God had put in his life that was more than he could handle, and like Tanner said, all things had worked out for the good. "Maybe I really am bulletproof," Clay said. "Maybe I really am."

Jeff LaFerney

Catch the other two books in
The Clay and Tanner Thomas Series:

Jeff LaFerney

About the Author

Jeff LaFerney has been a long-time language arts teacher and coach. He and his wife, Jennifer, as well as both of their kids, Torey and Teryn, live in Michigan. Jeff loves sports and exercise as well as reading and writing (his blog is called "The Red Pen"). *Loving the Rain* and *Skeleton Key* are suspense mysteries which also include Clay and Tanner Thomas. Each novel stands alone and can be read in any order. *Jumper* is a science fiction adventure and is the first in his Time Traveler series.

Made in the USA
Middletown, DE
27 September 2016